Legal Privilege

Margaret Barnes

First Edition

ISBN 978-1-9164471-7-2

The cover design is by Berni Stevens @bernistevensdesign.com.

The photograph is of Grays Inn London.

Reviews for Crucial Evidence.

This is an excellent novel from a writer that really has painted a very true picture of the Courtroom. I am looking forward to the author's next book. I recommend this book for all who like this subject

This is a good well written story with some interesting twists. It shows the workings of the legal system in a different light especially the subsidiary theme of sexism in the profession!

Very absorbing, exciting and realistic story of an attractive barrister character. A must read. Highly recommended to all legal thriller followers

Reviews for Reluctant Consent.

Reluctant Consent is a superb follow up to Crucial Evidence and I can't wait for the trilogy. The characters are real and you are kept guessing right to the very end. As well as this, the books give a fascinating insight (educational, in my case) to the workings of the British legal system.

Really enjoyed this book. Found it very hard to put down. Lots of twists and turns. Can't wait to read the next book.

Thoroughly enjoyable sequel. Fascinated by the world of criminal defence barristers and this book serves up two compelling cases intertwined into an absorbing story.

Acknowledgements

The coronavirus pandemic has taken its toll on all of us and it has certainly delayed the completion of this, the third Cassie Hardman. I have again drawn on my experiences as a barrister working in the criminal courts of England, but the case described is entirely fictitious

I would like to thank the following who read the first and subsequent drafts, Teresa Hunter, Maggie Noon, Sandy Kennedy, Kate McCormick who continued as my writing buddy, and my husband, Alan Taylor. Their comments and suggestions have been both pertinent and helpful.

Lesley Jones of 'perfecttheword' did the final edit of my novel with her usual precision and I am grateful for her making this as good as it is. Any mistakes are mine alone.

Chapter 1

The thin morning sun of winter seeped through the curtains of the bedroom at number 38 Fulham Road. Henry Bolt came to with a start. He could hear banging. He wasn't sure if the noise was in his head or not. He and his partner, Vincent Setchell, had drunk a bottle, or was it three, of wine the night before. Perhaps, there was someone at the front door?

Bolt swung his legs to the floor, hitched his liberty-print pyjama bottoms up, and leant over to pick up his dressing gown. He was still half asleep. 'You'd think they'd use the bell,' he said, more to himself than to Vincent. He was struggling to put one arm into the sleeve of his dressing gown when someone flung open the bedroom door. Light from the sitting room silhouetted a man who, by now, was standing at the foot of the bed.

'What the hell?' said Bolt. Vincent Setchell simply grunted and burrowed his head under the pillow.

'They're here,' said the intruder. At that moment Bolt realised he was looking into the barrel of a handgun pointing towards him. He wasn't sure if it was real, but he wasn't prepared to take the chance of finding out. He shrank back towards Setchell, pulling the dressing gown with him, and reached out towards his partner, who gripped the proffered hand. The man pointed the gun at Setchell and said, 'Don't move, either of you, or I'll blow your head off.'

'What do you … you want …?' Bolt said.

'Shut up,' the man said.

Bolt's head was thumping. It could have been a hangover or the effect of fear. He was definitely afraid. He wanted to keep his attention on the gun, but his eyes strayed to the face of the man holding it. His mouth and nose were partially covered by a navy scarf; only the eyes were visible.

Bolt saw some movement behind the gunman and heard books and ornaments falling onto the carpet in the sitting room. He thought about his antique wine glasses and hoped not too many had been broken. Then he heard the sound of pans dropping onto tiles followed by pottery. There must be somebody in the kitchen. The gunman turned towards the living room and spoke to whoever else was in the flat. 'Found anything?' The reply was muffled.

'There's the drawers in here,' the gunman said. He thrust the gun forwards towards Bolt, who pulled his dressing gown to his chin as if it could protect him.

Another man appeared in the doorway and pushed past towards one of the two chests of drawers on either side of the double bed. Bolt was distracted by this second intruder, worried he too may have a weapon. The man was wearing a black polo-necked sweater, which covered his mouth, and a black baseball cap pulled low hiding his eyes. This second man opened the drawers of the chest starting with the lowest and spilling the contents on the floor. The first male remained at the foot of the bed; Bolt was still conscious of the gun aimed at him. Then the second man flung open their wardrobe door, pulled out his cashmere sweaters and polo T-shirts and scattered them across the velvet comforter. He thought he could still hear crockery being broken in the kitchen. He became aware Setchell was now awake, sitting up, open-mouthed and spluttering.

'Is it in there?' the man with the gun shouted at his colleagues.

'Nope,' someone replied.

Bolt thought about asking them what they were looking for, but decided against it.

'It must be here somewhere,' a voice from the living room said.

'You'd better tell us where you've hidden it. The guvnor wants his property back,' the gunman said.

'I don't know what you're talking about,' said Bolt. Setchell shook his head. The gunman moved to let the second man get to the chest of drawers to the right of the bed and Bolt could see into the living room. There was a man standing near the door of the kitchen. He was wearing jeans and a light-coloured bomber jacket. His face was partially covered by a woollen beanie, the brim pulled down, shading his eyes. He wore a red scarf over his nose and mouth.

The man with the gun took a step forward and brandished the weapon. He was near enough for Bolt to think about lunging forwards and grabbing the gun. He was concentrating on that when someone in the living room shouted, 'I can hear sirens.'

The two men in the bedroom stiffened and turned in the direction of the bedroom door. The man with the baseball cap ran into the sitting room and looked out of the window. 'Police,' he said. The gunman waved his weapon around as he backed out of the bedroom and pulled the door shut behind him.

Bolt heard the front door of the flat crash against the wall and then the clatter of footsteps as the men raced down the stairs to the street. He grabbed his dressing gown, which had slipped onto the floor, struggled to get his arms through the sleeves and wrapped it tightly round himself. After the door to the street banged shut, he went to the window of the living room and looked down. He could hear the shopkeeper downstairs shouting. On the pavement running in the direction of the Tube station was a man with a red scarf. Bolt saw the scarf fall to the ground. The man didn't stop to pick it up. Bolt heard the police sirens getting closer and then a large white Volvo pulled over in front of their house; two officers got out and ran to the street door.

The doorbell rang and Bolt made his way downstairs, still in his pyjamas and dressing gown. A female police officer was hovering outside the shop.

'We had a telephone call about a disturbance here,' she said.

'We've been burgled,' Bolt said. He turned round expecting her to follow him.

He went into the living room, sank into their large chintz-covered sofa and covered his eyes. When he looked up, two male officers were standing in the doorway.

'Bit of a mess,' the older of the two men said as he looked around the living room.

Bolt pointed towards the door leading to the kitchen.

The younger one crossed the living room and peered in. 'Same here.'

Bolt got up from the sofa and went to stand by the policeman. Now he could see the extent of the damage. He stared at the shards of pottery lying amongst brown sugar and pasta shapes. There was a strong smell of vinegar. He couldn't say anything.

Setchell came from the bedroom. He was dressed in blue jeans and a dark red sweater. 'He had a gun.'

The younger policeman said, 'A gun,' and spoke into the radio clipped to his coat collar.

'I don't think it was real,' Bolt said.

'Can't take the risk,' said the older officer.

'No, I see that.' Bolt sat down on the green leather sofa.

Setchell went into the kitchen. 'I'll make some tea.'

'We'll get forensics here. They'll want to take some photos so don't move anything. CID will be here soon as well. Do you know what's been stolen?'

Bolt shrugged his shoulders. 'We've not had time to look, but … I don't think they took anything. They heard the sirens and ran for it.' He walked towards the bedroom door. 'If we're having visitors, I'd better get dressed.' As he pulled on a T-shirt he wondered what he was going to tell the detectives.

Chapter 2

Cassie Hardman climbed the forty-two steps to her flat on the top floor of a white stuccoed building in Notting Hill. Once inside she dropped the bag containing her wig and gown on the floor, walked over to her desk, and put her computer and mobile phone onto the large mouse mat. She stood for a moment to look out of the window into the branches of the sycamore tree growing in the garden below her. There was just a hint of green, signifying spring was on its way. As she removed the black jacket of her suit, the uniform of her profession, she wandered into her bedroom. The bed was still unmade; there was never time for breakfast in the mornings before she left to travel to whichever court she was appearing in that day, never mind anything else. She pulled the duvet up and plumped the pillows, then made her way to the kitchen and poured a glass of wine. Back in the bedroom she placed the wine on the bedside table and lay down. She went back over her day's work. She was defending in a trial but a plea in mitigation had been listed before the same judge that morning. Her client was a young mother who had been persuaded to bring drugs into the country in order to pay for her child's education. She thought the sentence was harsh for a woman who was as much a victim as any ultimate drug user. For a moment she considered appealing against the long period of imprisonment, but although her heart was in favour, her head told her it was useless. She didn't want to be chewed up by the judges in the Court of Appeal for a case she knew was unwinnable.

Much as she wanted to rest, she had work to do for court the next day and she needed to eat. She enjoyed cooking; standing in the kitchen preparing a meal and sipping on a glass of wine was one of the few periods in her life when she was able to relax. She decided to make spiced carrots with lentils and was peeling the vegetables when her mobile rang. The caller was Lee Shaw. Cassie liked the rather eccentric female solicitor, who maintained her integrity while nibbling at some of the stuffy conventions of her profession. 'Hi, Lee. What can I do for you?'

'Hopefully take on another case for me. It's a multi-hander, and they each need separate representation. Your mate Tim Durrant is the solicitor for the main defendant. You've not had instructions from him, have you?'

'Not that I know of. He may have spoken to the clerks. I'll check but he does usually call me before he talks to my clerk. Doesn't trust him.'

'Do you?' Lee said.

Cassie laughed. 'Some of the time.'

'Right. The client's name is Theo Clements.'

'What's he charged with?'

'Aggravated burglary and possession of a firearm. They're alleged to have burst into a flat when the occupants, two men, were still in bed, ransacked the place, threatened them with a gun and then ran off when the police arrived.'

'You said a multi-hander. How many defendants?'

'Four. The main defendant is a guy called Lucas Radpole. He's Tim's client. Then Thom Cravitz and Dean Morris. Clements is tail-end Charlie. He's on bail – and that's the other thing. His dad is a good client of ours.'

'He's a villain as well, is he?'

'Definitely not. Not now anyway. We do some work other than crime, you know. But … he's been sniffing around his son's case. Wants to know who the two complainants are and what they're saying.'

'Not unnatural. Just concerned for his son.'

'I think there's more to it than that. Jeff Clements has a shop on Lower Richmond Road selling – well, he describes it as antiques, but I'd say bric-a-brac. Does house clearances and hopes to pick up something worth selling. Theo helps him out on the removals and looks after the shop. The flat that was burgled had what looks like antique furniture and paintings from the photos. I showed the photos to Theo and his father. Jeff took them and had a good hard look at them.'

'Maybe he thinks he knows the occupants of the flat. Recognises something, one of the paintings or a piece of furniture.'

'I'm more concerned he wants to interfere with the witnesses.'

'Have you told him their names?'

'No. But he'll find out when I send Theo the papers. I can't exactly say don't talk to your dad about it, can I? Theo was identified by the victim as one of the burglars.'

'So, what's the son say?'

'He knows nothing about it. Never been to this flat on Fulham Road. Can't explain why this guy has picked him out.'

'Was there an ID parade?'

'For one of the two witnesses.'

'Alibi?' Cassie said.

'At home with girlfriend Anne. Anne Ellis. They live together over the shop.'

'No one more independent?'

‘Fraid not. I’ll send the brief to you this evening. If you want hard copies of anything let me know.’

‘Thanks. I’ll sort out anything I need.’

Lee Shaw had been sending work to Cassie regularly after she had successfully defended a man called Paul Sadler on a charge of rape. To begin with, all the cases involved clients who were charged with sexual assaults of one kind or another, but now, because Lee and her firm were listed in the lawyers’ directories as being in the top hundred criminal defence firms, they had a wider range of work. Cassie was benefiting from that and had been instructed by them in a couple of fraud cases, a large drug conspiracy and now an aggravated burglary. She needed to ring Jack Heely, her senior clerk, to tell him about this new piece of work and ensure it was in her diary.

Lee had asked her if she trusted him. It was a question she asked herself frequently. He controlled her life and sometimes she found that very uncomfortable. What was more he was fickle. Although he’d been supportive ever since she’d got her place in chambers, she was only too aware she was replaceable. There were plenty of young men itching to knock her from her pedestal, but if she got Silk?

She picked up her mobile and rang her chambers at 3 Burke Court. 'Is Jack there?'

'Yes, Miss Hardman. I'll tell him you're on the phone.'

A moment later Jack said, 'Have you finished at Southwark? We need someone to cover a couple of pleas at the Bailey.'

'No. I'll be there for another day or so, I think. The judge is very slow and is hinting at not summing-up until Monday. Jack, has Tim Durrant offered a brief in a four-hander at the Bailey? An aggravated burglary. Possession of a firearm.'

'He did call me, but he's instructed Silk for his client Lucas Radpole. Is that the one?'

'Yes. Instructing Silk. Expensive. I'm surprised – I assumed his client would have got Legal Aid.'

'He hasn't. Father's put up the money. I asked about the junior brief but he says the defendant wants a man. I suggested Mr Davenport and he went along with that.'

'That's great. I've been offered one of the other defendants. Lee Shaw is sending me the brief tonight. The client's called Theo Clements.'

'I'll book it in.'

Cassie finished the call. It was going to be an interesting case. What was so important that one man's father was prepared to pay for his son's representation and another one appeared to be a little too interested?

Chapter 3

A few months ago, Cassie had moved into a smaller office on the second floor of her chambers at 3 Burke Court but still had to share it; instead of four barristers sharing there was just one other desk. It belonged to Courtney Harris, one of only three ethnic minority members of chambers – a rugby-playing African. She had chosen to share the room with him because he didn't come into chambers very often, preferring to pursue his career in politics. She didn't share his views – he was too right wing for her – but she admired his tenacity. They often argued, but always amicably. More importantly, as far as she was concerned, he was reasonably tidy; he didn't leave half-full cups of coffee or uneaten sandwiches on his desk. Nor were there papers strewn everywhere, although that might have been because they were using their computers more and more, rather than his personal habits.

She had chosen the desk facing the window, which gave her the same view of the rather dismal paved square at the rear of their building. The room was darker than the one on the top floor, and now the London plane was in full leaf it threw its shade on to her desk. Courtney had wanted to paint the room dark green but when he was away at some conference or other she had arranged for the decorator to use a pale cream. The black spines of the *All England Law Reports* and the red of the *Criminal Law Reports* stood proudly, if unused, in the bookcases either side of the cast-iron fireplace. Below them were the remains of abandoned papers from long-finished cases still tied with pink tape. On the mantelpiece was a photograph of Courtney taken for his campaign leaflets and one of Cassie's sister Amanda with her two children, and above was an etching of the medieval hall in Gray's Inn. If she worried the room was still rather dark, at least she didn't have to lug her bags up three flights of stairs.

She glanced at her watch. If Lee Shaw and her client were on time, they would be arriving any minute. Perhaps there was time to remind herself of some of the details of the case against him. She opened her computer and found the file labelled 'Clements/character'. It contained two letters that had been scanned into the file. The first one was typed and was from a Norman Thomas.

> *Dear Miss Shaw,*
>
> *I was surprised to receive your request for a reference for Theo Clements in respect of a charge of burglary. He was one of*

my students from 2007 to 20012 – I was his personal tutor during that time and he was not one of those I had anticipated would be involved in any criminal behaviour. As you are no doubt aware, he was raised single-handed by his father. I later discovered his mother had died when he was four years of age. He had little or no recollection of her and, I felt, struggled when other children spoke of holidays or birthday parties. Despite that he was a cheerful, well-mannered boy.

He wasn't academic but showed an aptitude for woodwork. He joined the school drama society – a non-acting member – and used his skills building scenery for school productions.

I never had any cause to doubt his honesty nor was he ever aggressive to members of staff or other pupils.

I would be prepared to attend court and speak on his behalf.

Yours sincerely

Norman Thomas.

Before she could read the second reference, the internal phone rang. Hamish, one of her clerks, said, 'Miss Shaw and your client are here.'

'Can you show them up, please?'

A few minutes later she heard the outer entrance to the set of rooms open and then a tap. She stood up as her door opened. Lee Shaw pushed her way in carrying a large rug holdall. Cassie noted, with some amusement, Lee's clothes: a pair of jeans and a grey double-breasted jacket – always unconventional. Following her was her client, Theo Clements.

Cassie held out her hand and smiled. 'Mr Clements, thank you for coming to see me in chambers. Take a seat, will you.' She waved a hand in the direction of one of the two upright chairs in front of her desk. Lee took the other one and pulled her laptop from the bag.

'Give me a minute to open the damn thing,' Lee said. 'It was easier when we used paper, whatever anyone says.'

'I know, but it does save dusty piles of documents.'

Lee looked at the bookshelves behind Cassie and rolled her eyes. 'Really?'

'Well, I do print bits out.'

Cassie took a moment to observe her client. She wanted to see how he might appear to others during his trial. She also wondered how she might appear to him. This was probably the only time they would meet before the hearing at the Old Bailey. Like someone on a blind date, she wanted to make a good impression on him and hoped he would trust her. During the course of the trial she would be making decisions on his behalf, and she needed that trust. Theo Clements met her gaze; his dark brown eyes were steady if a little wary. He looked younger than his twenty-four years. His light blond hair curled round his ears and flopped across his forehead. To Cassie's relief he didn't have any facial scars or any sign of a broken nose that might suggest to a jury he was a fighter. He plucked at his shirt collar as she introduced herself. 'You don't look too comfortable in that,' she said. 'If you want to take it off, I don't mind.' He nodded at her and removed the tie he was wearing, putting it into the pocket of the blue tweed sports jacket.

'Right, Theo. Do you mind if I call you that?' Cassie said.

'No, miss.'

'Right, tell me a bit about yourself. You live on Lower Richmond Road, Putney?' She already knew the answer, but these questions about his personal life rather than the trial were to give him time to settle and relieve, or at least reduce, any anxiety he might have.

‘Above my dad’s shop. I work there as well. That’s when I’m not out with him in the van.’

‘What exactly do you do?’

‘It’s antiques in the shop. Not posh stuff, but good stuff we’ve got from house clearances. Or picked up from skips. I help Dad with that. Then I look after the shop. I do some repairs, polishing stuff up. Try to make it look good.’

‘Is the shop busy?’

‘We get customers in mainly at the weekend. People browsing. But there’s eBay, Gumtree, like. Dad’s not that good on the computer so I do it. We sort everything out. What’s to go in the shop, what’s to go on eBay, and then any really good stuff, Dad takes up west.’

‘So, you’re kept pretty busy. How much do you earn?’ Cassie said.

‘’Pends. In a good week, Dad’ll give me a couple of hundred. But I don’t pay for the flat or my mobile.’

‘Do you drive? Have a car?’

‘I drive the van and then Annie’s got a little car. Parking’s too expensive. We’re not that far from the Tube.’

‘Annie’s your girlfriend?’

'She lives with me. We've been together since school. She works on the High Street. Putney High Street.'

'Her full name?'

'Anne Davina Ellis.'

'Ok. On the morning of the burglary, let's say between eight and ten, where were you?'

'Annie has to be at work by nine, she's a hairdresser. So I, I'd be at home between eight and nine. It doesn't take her long to get to the shop. Ten minutes at the most. Then I wait for Dad to turn up …'

'We have his dad's diary for the fifteenth of January. He had an appointment to look at a house in Chelsea, Worlds End,' Lee said.

'What time was the appointment?'

'Ten.' Lee handed Cassie an A4-size diary and pointed to some writing on the left-hand page. Cassie looked at the entry; it said 'St Luke's Road SW3 10 a.m. Mr Green'.

Cassie turned the book round so Theo could see. 'Do you remember going to that address?'

'It's the only one in Chelsea I've been to in quite a while. They usually go to more flashy set-ups than my dad's.'

'Tell me about it. What did you do when you got there?'

'This Green guy met us and showed us round the place. It wasn't his house – a distant relative. An old woman's place. Smelt funny, musty like. She'd died. Lots of brown furniture. We had a good look round and then Dad gave him a price. A few hundred, he said, then Dad asked when he wanted the house cleared. The man wasn't sure, said he needed to talk to … I think he said his sister. We left it at that. Haven't been back so I guess he changed his mind, or perhaps decided to wait until the property was sold.'

'How long were you there?'

'I'd say an hour.'

'Dad says the same,' Lee said. 'He got to the shop about nine twenty. Theo got the van and they drove straight to St Luke's Road. Traffic was slow across Putney Bridge and they arrived a few minutes before ten.'

'How long would it take to get to the shop from 38 Fulham Road? It looks like it's fairly close to the Broadway.'

Theo shrugged his shoulders. 'Fifteen, twenty minutes, I guess.'

'By car. I'd say the same,' said Lee, 'but on foot forty to fifty minutes.'

'And by Tube – Fulham Broadway to Putney Bridge, or bus?' Cassie said. 'We need to check those out. The defence notice will need to include details of the alibi. Lee, do you want me to draft it? And Theo, you'll need to see it and make sure it's right. Basically, we're saying you were at home at the time of the burglary, and Annie can confirm you were there at eight fifty and your dad at nine twenty.'

'That's about it,' Theo said.

'Now, your co-defendants. Do you know them? Any of them?'

Theo didn't reply. Cassie repeated the question.

'I've never seen them before we were in court … but …' Theo said.

'But?'

'Lucas. When I was a kid we lived on the Atlee Estate, Fulham. He lived there too.'

Cassie underlined the name Lucas Radpole on the indictment. 'So you knew him from there. Were you friends?

'Too young, but his dad …'

Cassie flicked through the file and found Lucas's custody record. 'He's six years older than you?'

'About that.'

'You were about to say something about his father,' Lee said.

‘His father was sent to prison. I don’t know what for, but Dad might know. They knew each other from the market.’

‘North End Road Market?’ Cassie said.

‘No, Portobello. Antiques or, well, second-hand stuff.’

Cassie wrote a reminder in her blue counsels’ notebook and then said, ‘Theo, the real crux of this case is this – one of the two men whose flat was broken into named you as one of his assailants. Henry Bolt says he recognised you and he gave the police your name. Have you met Bolt before?’

Theo slowly shook his head. ‘No, not that I know of.’

‘He describes meeting you in a pub in Parsons Green. The White Horse.’

‘It’s possible but … We moved to Putney five, six years ago. I don’t remember meeting anyone called Henry but …’ Theo’s raised his voice. ‘I wasn’t involved. I don’t know these men. I can’t explain it.’ There was nothing more to say.

After Lee and Theo had left, Cassie leant back in her chair and flicked her computer awake. *Was he telling the truth? Certainly his teacher, Norman Thomas, believed him to be honest.* Cassie opened the character file again and read the second testimonial.

I am a retired nurse and I have known Theo since he was born. I was a friend of his mother's and when she became ill I would look after Theo when she had hospital appointments. Jeff was in prison at the time.

After she died, I continued to visit the family home, at first to ensure Jeff was looking after Theo properly. But then, because I had become very fond of the child, I invited him to visit my home. He came quite frequently to play with my children and often stayed for tea.

As he got older he still came to see us. Sometimes alone but also with his girlfriend Annie. That continues to be the case.

Jeff has done a great job bringing Theo up to be an engaging young man. I have always found him to be honest and non-aggressive.

Yours, Helen McIntyre

PS I would be prepared to come to court and give evidence on Theo's behalf.

A second character witness who believed her client was an unlikely burglar. She hoped they were right.

Chapter 4

DC Alexis Seymour stared at the copies of two defence statements on her computer screen. The notices were headed *R v Radpole, Cravitz, Morris and Clements*. Sections highlighted in red gave details of alibi witnesses. Her job was to interview them, check their criminal record, if they had one, and try to identify any weaknesses in their account. Both defendants had provided details of their whereabouts at the time of the offence, an aggravated burglary at an address in Fulham, and given the names and contact details of their witnesses. There was no further information.

The first notice was for a man called Theo Clements; it named a woman called Anne Ellis and someone Alex assumed was a relative of the defendant, Jeff Clements. The signature on it was Cassie Hardman. She reached for the cup of coffee on her desk; her previous dealings with the barrister had been problematic, and that was an understatement. She hoped there would be no similar misadventures this time.

The other notice was for the first defendant on the indictment, Lucas Radpole. The notice claimed he had been in Ledbury Grove, Notting Hill at the time of the offence, where he had an appointment with the owner of an art gallery. This one was signed with a name that gave her heart a jolt, Oscar Davenport. Alex closed her eyes and took a deep breath. She remembered his touch, the feeling of dancing through those few days in her life when he had been its centre. Although he was a barrister, at the time he had been suspected of involvement in the supply of drugs and she had decided not to answer his calls. He had been persistent in trying to contact her – phone calls, notes written in sepia-coloured ink, and even large posies of flowers from the Turquoise Island in Westbourne Grove. After a while he had stopped and she thought she would never see him again. She opened her eyes. Just because she was investigating an alibi witness did not mean she would have any contact with the defendant's barristers. *Ignore it*, she told herself. *It's just a job.*

Attached to Radpole's defence statement was an appointment card showing the recipient had been expected at the gallery, Paint and Print, at nine thirty in the morning. Alex printed both the card and the details of the alibi. She decided to go there before investigating the other witnesses. It wouldn't take her long to get from Notting Hill Police Station to the gallery. It was a bright spring morning. She would walk.

Ledbury Grove was a smart street of shops and restaurants. Her father took her to one of them frequently; he was on first-name terms with the manager. He was good at turning mere acquaintances into lifelong friends. He always got the best tables in the busiest restaurants, theatre tickets for sold-out shows and invitations to private views where champagne flowed. Since he had separated from her mother he asked her to accompany him, and when she wasn't working she took up his invitations. They added some glamour to her life. Police work was, in the main, tedious.

She approached the door of the gallery. It was painted a bright blue and there was a notice in copperplate writing asking customers to press a bell to be admitted. She did so and immediately heard the sound of a buzzer. She pushed open the door. Her feet sank into a sand-coloured carpet and she could smell beeswax polish. She didn't have time to look around her; a man in his early fifties with a shock of white hair came towards her.

'Can I help you?' His thin lips were curved in the smile of a professional salesman.

Alex pulled her warrant card out of her pocket. 'I'm not here to buy anything, unfortunately. I'm looking for a Mr Poynton.'

'I hope I haven't done anything wrong.' He laughed as if to emphasise that he was joking.

'You're Mr Poynton?'

'I am. What is it you want? I'm very careful about who I buy my lovely things from. Usually just friends and on recommendations.'

'I'm not looking for stolen property. I want to ask you some questions about a man called Lucas Radpole.'

'Do I know him?'

'I don't know, but he was in possession of a card with your name on it.' Alex produced the copy of the card and handed it to the shopkeeper.

Poynton studied it. 'That is my card. What's this about?'

'Radpole has been charged with a serious offence and he says he was here with you at the time. I'd like to take a statement from you. Could we sit down somewhere? I'm sure you'd rather that than come to the station.'

'Of course.' He held out his arm and directed her towards the back of the shop where there was an open door. Alex walked through the doorway into an office. Two desks were piled high with papers and framed pictures were stacked along the walls. Behind the smaller of the two desks sat a young woman aged somewhere in her mid-twenties. 'This is my assistant, Miss Wilcox. Harriet, my dear, could you rustle up a couple of cups of your wonderful coffee.'

Alex didn't like to refuse and hoped it would be better than the coffee supplied at the station canteen.

Harriet got to her feet and mumbled something Alex couldn't quite hear, but she was sure the word 'dogsbody' figured. Poynton walked behind the other desk and sat down. He pointed at a chair to one side of the room. Alex moved it forward, looking for a flat surface on which she could write.

Poynton was shuffling through the papers on his desk. 'I'm just looking for my diary. I know all you young things keep your dates on your phones but I like …' He pulled a large leather-bound book from the bottom of the documents and opened it. 'What date did you say?'

'January fifteenth.'

'Right.'

Alex watched him as he turned over the pages. His thin face gave nothing away. She thought his hand was trembling slightly but she wasn't certain. She could see the right-hand page of the diary showed the date – a page for each day – and the left-hand page was blank.

'Here we are, fourteenth, fifteenth. I was in the shop that day …' Poynton said.

Alex leant forward. She could see there was writing on both pages but couldn't read any of it from where she was sitting.

Poynton ran his finger down the right-hand page. 'I don't seem to have an appointment with anyone of that name or at nine thirty.' He turned the diary towards Alex. Four names were listed at different times of the day but nothing as early as nine thirty. None of them was Radpole. On the left-hand side were notes about paintings and other objects, with what appeared to be prices. Alex didn't have time to read them, but something more important caught her eye. There was an uneven strip of paper on the right-hand side. A page had been torn from the diary – the blank page facing 15 January.

'Do you know anyone called Lucas Radpole?' Alex said.

Poynton didn't answer immediately. 'I'm not sure … it's familiar.'

Harriet reappeared carrying a tray with two cups of coffee and a plate of chocolate biscuits on it, which she set down on the desk.

'Harriet, can you get my address book.'

'Please …' Harriet said as she turned to a large cabinet.

Alex pursed her lips to prevent a smile crossing her face. Poynton didn't appear to notice his assistant's comment and waited while she rifled through the drawers and produced a black book stuffed with papers. She put it down on the desk and a number of business cards fells onto the floor. Alex picked up one or two. One was either a firm of accountants or solicitors in the City. Alex was able to read the words 'London Wall', and there was something written on it as well, but she didn't have time to read it.

'Radpole, you say.' Poynton flicked through the book. 'I'm not the most organised … Harriet does the filing and I tend to just stick cards in here.' He shuffled a collection of cards and then looked at the entries in the book. 'I do have the name Radpole here. Bernie Radpole, and I appear to have written something. What date did you say?'

'January fifteenth.'

'I think I've written "one one five" by his name.'

'Is there an address there?'

'A mobile number, that's all. I must have forgotten to put the appointment in the book after I took his name and number.'

Alex reached out and he pulled the book towards him, but then turned it round so she could see it. She made a note on her mobile of the phone number. 'You have the name Bernie? Can you remember what he looked like?'

'Not really. Late fifties, rather nondescript.' Poynton shook his head. 'I really can't remember. Harriet, do you remember this man?'

Harriet didn't reply.

'Was the man alone?'

'He came by car and parked it outside. Actually, I warned him the traffic wardens were quite hot round here and he said his son was in the car.'

'What did he want?'

'I assume he was interested in buying a painting. Why else would he come here?'

Chapter 5

'Cassie, can you meet me for a drink in Daley's in half an hour?' Marcus Pike said.

'Sure. Any hint what it's about?'

'No, I'll see you there.'

Cassie heard the click of the call being terminated. Half an hour, she thought, just time to speak to Lee about Clements' alibi notice. She called the solicitor's office but Lee had already left.

She went down into the clerks' office and found Eleanor Hesketh in a heated conversation with their clerk Jack. They immediately dropped their voices, but she heard Eleanor say, 'Are you sure?' and then Jack handed Eleanor a letter. Eleanor read the note and Cassie saw her eyes widen. Then Eleanor looked up and their eyes met. Cassie wasn't surprised to hear Eleanor arguing with Jack. Chambers' only female Silk and their senior clerk rarely saw eye to eye about the way he ran her practice. Eleanor spent weeks working away from London, staying in hotels during the week, while she worked on very heavyweight cases. Even with a junior barrister sharing the workload, as Queen's Counsel she was responsible for every decision. It made for a hard life. Cassie had applied for Silk and, for a moment, asked herself if she was ready for the changes to her work and possibly her lifestyle.

'I'm going to meet Marcus Pike,' Cassie said. 'I'll be in Daly's if anyone wants me.'

She walked quickly to the wine bar on the Strand opposite the Royal Courts of Justice. It was already full of lawyers and she had to push her way through to find Marcus, who was sitting at a small table. He was dressed as usual in a well-cut black jacket with a bright blue cravat round his neck disguising, she assumed, a collarless shirt. In front of him was an open bottle of Bordeaux and a wine glass containing some of the dark purple liquid. Next to it was an empty glass. As she approached, he poured some of the wine.

'Here,' he said, 'what do you think of this?'

Cassie swirled the liquid round and sniffed at the contents. 'Fruity, blackcurrants.' She laughed. 'You've not asked me here to get my opinion on the wine?'

'I was thinking about your application for Silk. It's such a complicated system now. Selecting your best twelve cases and for each one listing the judge, one of the other advocates and the solicitor. Thirty-odd people, and then the panel chooses which of those to ask for an assessment. It's almost as bad as the old system.

Your pupil mistress fell foul of that.' He shook his head.

'I know she was very upset about it. She asked for feedback and was told she didn't have quite the right style for Silk. She thought it was a second glass ceiling, one based on class.'

'She was probably right. I thought she was a very good advocate. She taught you well. Now, this little case we're co-defending, an aggravated burglary.'

'Why are you … I know – it's privately paid.'

'I represented young Radpole's father several times, usually successfully, and now he wants me to get his pride and joy off this charge.'

'What was Radpole Senior up to then?'

'Country house burglaries mainly, although there were a couple of thefts from hotels in London. He had a speciality of taking from the rich, although the only poor who got anything was himself. The hotel jobs were all jewellery from quite famous actresses. He read *The Stage*, *Who's Who* and the gossip columns, following their whereabouts.'

'Was he always acquitted?'

'No, but often enough. He made quite a packet out of crime. Reckoned it was better than working. He was always careful, never left fingerprints. I thought he planned the burglaries, drove the getaway car, let others do the dirty work. He took the property and disposed of it. Of course, forensics weren't as sophisticated as they are now. DNA in its infancy and no mobile phones. But I didn't want to talk about Bernie. I'm leading one of your fellow tenants, Oscar Davenport.'

'I don't know him that well. His father-'

'I know, Henry Davenport. We were at Bar School together. I was rather surprised when he went on the bench. What's the son like? He didn't go into his father's set. Chose crime over life at the commercial bar.'

'I've never spoken to him about it. We don't have much in common. I gather female solicitors like him. He doesn't seem short of work.'

'A ladies' man then?'

'Not my type. We don't exactly belong in the same class.'

Marcus reached across and flicked her left shoulder. 'Is that a chip I see?'

Cassie chuckled. 'I'm quite happy where I am … look, Oscar works hard and—'

'You're representing tail-end Charlie?'

'He may be last on the indictment but he's the only defendant identified by one of the victims.'

'A faulty ID is easier to deal with than DNA on an abandoned scarf. Jurors find scientific evidence compelling.'

'There's no DNA evidence against your client either.'

'There's a baseball cap, which Bolt says is similar, and the telephone calls to his co-defendants. Fortunately, his fingerprints aren't the only ones on the gun. He's living in an empty pub – one of those guardian things – with about six others. Could be any of the squatters.'

'What's his defence?'

'Same as yours – alibi. The real problem is Morris.'

'Do you know who's defending?'

'Simon Wade. Australian. Qualified there about twenty years ago and then came here. He's been in chambers about three years.'

'Morris has admitted being in the flat and named your man,' Cassie said.

'That's what makes it difficult. Radpole says Morris has got it all wrong. But it's a cut-throat defence, Hopeless, they'll all go down. Perhaps not your lad. I assume you'll stay out of the fray.'

'What about the bits of glass and pottery in Radpole's clothes?' Cassie said.

'Contamination. I've asked Oscar to seek discovery of the various exhibit lists. The prosecution are being a bit cagey about them so perhaps there's a crack in the case there. How does your lad explain the ID?'

'He hasn't any explanation. He says he doesn't know either Bolt or Setchell.'

'Strange they seem to know him. Or at least Bolt does.' Marcus poured another glass for them both and took a sip from his. 'I've heard a rumour, nothing more, that Richard's leaving you.'

Cassie's was shocked. 'Our head of chambers?'

'You've obviously heard nothing.'

Cassie shook her head as questions whirled round. What was Richard up to? Was he going on the bench? Who would be the next head of chambers? Would Jack leave as well? What would it mean for her practice?

Chapter 6

Cassie took the Central Line Tube to St Pauls station where she emerged into the daylight of a June morning. She walked west along Newgate Street to the Old Bailey – the street that gave its name to the Central Criminal Court. She passed the large metal gates where the prison vans drove into the building. There had been many occasions when she along with others had been held at the junction with Warwick Square by armed officers wearing body armour as a van hurtled east along Holborn Viaduct and swerved at speed through the entrance. Sometimes she worried she and other pedestrians waiting for a high-security defendant being brought for trial could be caught in the crossfire between the police and any gunman wanting to free the prisoner. Mostly she thought it was just a display of macho behaviour by the police force. Today there was no such delay and she turned left along the bulk of the old Edwardian court to the low, rather intimate entrance to the new building. She waited patiently for her turn to enter, waving to the staff she knew scrutinising visitors from behind protective screens. She stepped into the tubes, which acted like modern-day sniffer dogs, and queued while her bags went through the scanner.

The security guard welcomed her by name. 'Here again, Miss Hardman.'

She grinned at him. 'Not so busy, this morning?'

'Few courts not sitting, miss.' She nodded; this was one of the signs of austerity, a cutback in the number of courts working, the delay to trials causing distress to defendants and victims alike as memories dimmed, partially erased by time.

Upstairs in the robing room she fastened the lace collarette round her neck, put on her gown, but tucked her wig under her arm before climbing the stairs to the Bar Mess. Most of the rows of long tables were still empty. She was early; there was time for some toast with her coffee. She picked up a copy of *The Times* from a nearby table and sat down. She had been checking the appointments columns every day since her conversation with Marcus about her head of chambers. She soon found the civil lists but there were no judicial appointments. She turned back to the front page as someone said, 'I had you for a *Guardian* reader.' She looked up into the round bespectacled face of David Jennings. His wig was a little askew and stained with cigarette smoke.

'Hi, what are you doing here?' she said, pulling a chair back so he could sit next to her.

The smell of bacon from the plate he placed on the table wafted across her nostrils. She wasn't a great breakfast eater, but sometimes …

'Same as you. We're co-defending.'

'Are we? Which one of these miscreants?' She was pleased to see him; they had been in a number of cases together and trials ran more smoothly if counsel knew and trusted each other.

'Cravitz. I got the brief last night when his counsel went part heard. I've been up half the night working on the papers. I thought Oscar might be here. We've both got these forensics and I was hoping he'd got some of the exhibit lists from the police.'

'I know Marcus asked him to get them. He's looking at contamination. I think they've instructed their own expert as well.'

'I'm not sure about contamination. Cravitz talks about the two of them working on a house clearance and getting the shards of pottery there.' He paused to take another mouthful of bacon and egg. 'Do you know who's got Morris? Or what he's going to say? His interview rather puts Radpole in it.'

'Simon Wade. I don't know him, do you? He's in Marcus's set.'

'I was hoping he'd be pleading, but … And to add to my woes, Jane Rostron-Smith is the judge.'

'You don't sound too happy …'

'I'm not. She really doesn't like me. I was in front of her a while back, not long after she was appointed, and she was in such a bad temper. One of the jurors passed a note across to me – I guess I must have been the closest to him.' He took another mouthful.

'And?'

'She insisted I hand the note to her. This guy had written "*How would you like her as a mother-in-law?*"'

Cassie laughed. 'Oh dear. She thought you'd written it?'

'No. She knew where it had come from. She's a—'

Before David could finish his sentence, Cassie heard her name being called over the loudspeaker. 'See you in court, David.'

She dashed into the robing room and picked up her papers and her computer. She couldn't get used to using it rather than a book, so took her copy of Archbold, the criminal lawyers' bible, as well. She had to descend a spiral staircase to get to the long spacious waiting area leading to courts nine to twelve on the floor below the robing rooms. She loved the moment she took the last step out into the concourse where the theatre of a criminal trial began.

Lee Winters and her client Theo Clements were hovering outside Court 9. Cassie had advised Clements to wear something comfortable but fairly smart. 'Don't wear a tie if you don't normally. I don't want you squirming in the dock.' He'd done as she had asked and was wearing a dark bomber jacket, clean jeans and a pale blue shirt. For once Lee had abandoned her jeans for a pair of black trousers and a dark denim jacket.

'I don't know how far we'll get today,' Cassie said. 'You'll have to surrender to the custody officer. I assume you've no mobile with you. The judge may order you to stay in custody over the short adjournment. You'll be taken downstairs. I'm afraid the food isn't very good in the cells.' She saw his face drop. 'Don't worry, I don't think she'll detain you overnight. The first thing that will happen is the jury will be sworn in. Forget what you've heard about objecting to any of them. You can only do so if you have a good reason – something like you know the person. So, if you do know anyone or think you do, you need to let us know straight away. Take a good look at them. The dock is enclosed with glass walls, so any conversations are difficult. Lee will keep an eye on you in case you do recognise anyone. After that the prosecuting counsel will make his opening speech. He'll tell the jury what the trial is about, give an outline of it and briefly explain the evidence against each of you. It always sounds like it's an open-and-shut case at that point. But that's what we have to challenge. Then Bolt will be called to give evidence. Have you got that, you understand?'

Theo Clements nodded.

'Good. Lee, have the police interviewed Anne and Mr Clements?'

Before Lee could answer, an usher emerged from the courtroom and asked Cassie if Theo would surrender to the custody officer. As he disappeared through the door, Cassie went to follow him but Lee took hold of her arm.

'Haven't you got copies of their statements?' Lee sucked her upper lip.

'What is it? Is something wrong?'

'Our alibi might not be as tight as it should be. The police went to see Green, the man who wanted a quote for a house clearance.'

'And?'

'He says they were late. Here, read it.'

Cassie took the document Lee held out.

My name is Archibald Green and I am the executor of my

mother's estate. She owned a house in St Luke's Road, Chelsea. In anticipation of selling it I decided to have the property cleared of the furniture and unwanted personal effects. I contacted a number of possible companies including Clements and Son. I spoke to a man who said his name was Jeff Clements and I made an appointment for him to see the contents of the property on 15 January at 10 a.m. I arrived at the address promptly but had to wait for Mr Clements to arrive. I'm not sure how late he was but I was about to leave when he turned up with his son. The father explained his son was late picking him up. The son, I don't remember his name, said the traffic was very bad that morning.

They looked around the house and Clements Senior gave me a quote of £800. I told them I needed to consult my sister and would contact them if we decided to go ahead. In the end we waited until we had sold the property and used another company for the house clearance.

'I'll need to speak to prosecuting counsel about this. You know Peter Maynard – he's from my chambers. He's prosecuting. If he decides it contradicts our alibi he should call the evidence as part of the prosecution case. But if it's just reliability …'

'I've got copies of the defence statements for Radpole and Cravitz and the police interviews with their alibi witnesses. Actually, it's just Radpole's witness. Cravitz isn't calling any witnesses, just saying he wasn't present. And the police officer who interviewed him, and Anne and Theo's dad, was your friend Alex Seymour. It doesn't make any difference to you representing Theo, does it?'

Cassie considered for a moment. 'I don't think so. She's not a witness or anything, nor likely to be. No, I'm not embarrassed. Does Anne have any previous? Have you got Clements senior's criminal record?'

'Anne hasn't. Dad has a couple for handling, all over twenty-five years ago. And a serious robbery.'

Cassie was concerned. Witnesses with previous convictions, particularly for offences of dishonesty, were not good news, but Jeff Clements was essential to his son's case. 'That's fine,' she said. 'You'll need to tell him I'll ask him about those when he gives evidence. Better we put them before the jury than the prosecution does.'

'Aren't they spent?'

'Not for the purposes of criminal trials, so better not to try and hide them.'

Court 9 wasn't one of the more traditional courtrooms. The walls were wooden like a ski chalet and beginning to show the effect of the fifty years since their installation. The leather chairs on the judge's bench were green and had the City of London's insignia embossed in gold on them. The coat of arms on the wall behind the judge's bench looked as if it had been drawn for a children's book. The court smelled of dust, books, ink and screen cleaner and the overhead lights flickered subliminally. There was no view of the outside, not even the clouds; it was a self-contained world, where justice might or might not be done.

Cassie walked round counsels' benches towards the jury box. Defence advocates traditionally sat closest to the jury and as Theo was the last defendant on the indictment, she took a seat on the front bench, nearest to their box. She put her computer to one side and opened it up, placed her notebooks in front of her, then arranged her pens in a neat row together with a packet of mints, a ritual she repeated at the beginning of every trial.

While she waited for the other counsel to arrive, she looked at the photographs of the flat. The floor was strewn with shards of pottery, but the furniture looked valuable to her eyes. On her screen she was able to zoom in and look more closely. A Windsor chair with a patina that revealed it was an antique stood next to a small table, and on the wall behind were two paintings of yachts in a harbour. The other photographs revealed works of art hung on the walls. Pictures that didn't look like prints. Was Mr Bolt something of an art lover?

Chapter 7

Cassie's perusal of the photographs was interrupted by the court usher coming towards her with the news that Judge Rostron-Smith had a sentence to deal with before the trial started and Cassie would have time for a coffee. Cassie decided it would give her time to speak to prosecuting counsel, Peter Maynard, if she could find him. She needed to catch him before the court sat. She poked her head round the men's robing room door but he wasn't there, then she went up to the Bar Mess hoping she would find him having a coffee. She scanned the long refectory tables, checked the green leather sofas at the library end of the room, but couldn't see him. Then she spotted Oscar in the queue at the cafeteria-style counter. She walked over to him.

'Can I get you a coffee?' Oscar said.

'Thank you. Have you seen Peter?'

'I think he's in the library.'

'I'll be back for that coffee in a minute.'

She found Peter leafing through a set of papers. 'Peter, I've just been given the statement of Archibald Green. Are you intending to call him?'

'I think so. He contradicts your client's evidence about the time he arrived in Chelsea. If he got there at ten thirty he has plenty of time to go to Bolt's flat before he meets his father.'

'Isn't it arguable it only goes to the reliability of their evidence?'

'You could try that with the judge. I'll not use it in my opening speech if you intend to do that.'

'Thanks, if you could.' At least that would give her time to take instructions from Theo and for Lee to interview Jeff Clements again.

Soon after eleven, all those involved in the trial of Radpole and others were called to Court 9. Once the court had assembled there was a sharp rap on the door leading from the judges' corridor; the usher shouted, 'Be upstanding in court.' A tall man in breeches carrying a mace over his shoulder walked onto the judge's dais and stood to one side, followed by the short fussy figure of Judge Jane Rostron-Smith. She made her way to her chair in the centre of the bench, sat down, put a notebook on the desk and opened the lid of a laptop.

Cassie felt a chill run round the room as Judge Rostron-Smith glared down at counsels' row.

'Mr Maynard, you're prosecuting?' the judge said.

'Yes, My Lady, and Mr Pike—'

'I know who's defending. Mr Pike, how long is this trial likely to last? I would like to finish by Friday week. Is that possible?'

Marcus took his time standing up. 'My Lady, we were originally fixed to begin two days ago—'

'I know, but my previous trial overran. This jury panel are due to finish their service next week. We really should get it completed by then.'

'Quite, My Lady. It's quite difficult to predict but we, that is Mr Davenport and I think about eight to ten working days depending …'

The judge's face relaxed a little when she saw Oscar Davenport. *Even a judge can fall for his charms,* Cassie thought, *or was she influenced by his father's position?*

'Does everyone agree on two weeks?' Judge Rostron-Smith said although she didn't look at any of the other counsel. There were murmurs of agreement. 'Right, let's have the jury panel in.'

While they waited for the would-be jurors to arrive, Cassie turned to look at the other defendants. It was the first time she had seen them. She knew their ages from the custody records, but she was curious to know what they looked like. The four men were seated as far apart as they could get in the confines of the dock. They were looking straight ahead, avoiding unnecessary eye contact. Lucas Radpole was thirty years old and looked it. It was difficult to tell what colour his hair was as it was cut so short. His skin had the appearance of being unwashed and he had a tattoo on the left side of his neck. Thom Cravitz was twenty-nine, tall and heavily built; his body bulged out of the leather jacket he was wearing. He had an American-style crew cut. Cassie shuddered when he caught her looking at him; his eyes were pale and piercing. Dean Morris was ten years younger, the youngest of the four men. On his custody record he was identified as being IC3, Afro-Caribbean, but Cassie though he was probably mixed race. If his nose hadn't shown signs of being broken, she would have said he was handsome, but even so he was a good-looking young man. She assumed he had got the injury from his time spent in the boxing club. It was his bad luck that a police officer stationed at Fulham was also a member and identified him from CCTV footage.

She looked at her own client, whose fair tousled hair and small stature made him stand out from the other defendants. She caught his eye and nodded in an attempt to reassure him. The courtroom began to fill up with the potential jurors; because there were four defendants, over twenty ordinary members of the public were led in by the usher. They spread out around the room; some remained standing under the public gallery and the rest crowded round the back of counsels' benches. The clerk to the court stood up and began calling out names from the cards she was holding and the usher directed them towards the jury box. Cassie observed each one, hoping to glean something about the prejudices and the experiences they would use as they listened to the evidence and considered the verdicts. There was so little to go on. Some carried a newspaper, which helped; *The Daily Telegraph* or *The Mail* indicated a tough approach to law and order. Clothes, too, gave some indication of background, but that was more difficult in these relaxed times, when dress-down Friday appeared to refer to the whole week and hardly anyone wore a suit and tie.

Cassie was reasonably happy with the twelve jurors – a mix of ages, gender and ethnicity. Clements hadn't wanted to challenge any of them and neither had any of the other defendants. Once they were all sworn in, Judge Rostron-Smith told them the trial was likely to last between two to three weeks and asked if that caused any of them any difficulty. One woman said she had a holiday booked; she was excused and was replaced by an elderly man in a shabby tweed suit.

'Now, before the trial starts, I want to impress on you that you are trying the case on the evidence you hear in this court,' Judge Rostron-Smith said. 'I must ask you not to start doing your own research on the internet. The reason is that defendants and their counsel and indeed the prosecution won't know what you've found and are not in a position to confirm or rebut whatever it is. Do you understand?'

The members of the jury murmured they did.

'Right, Mr Maynard.'

Because Peter Maynard and Cassie were in the same chambers and shared the clerking arrangements, she knew him fairly well. They weren't great friends but still after twenty years she had some idea of his strengths and weaknesses. He was some years senior to her and was always dropping the names of judges as if they were bosom buddies. He was a good lawyer with an incisive mind, but he looked a little like an overgrown choirboy. At his best he was a formidable opponent, but as Cassie knew, could get sidetracked.

'Members of the jury, you are about to try the four men who are in the dock,' Peter Maynard said and turned to indicate the defendants. 'Lucas Radpole sits furthest from you and he is represented by my learned friends Mr Pike and Mr Davenport, sitting next to me here.' He waved his hand towards Marcus who nodded at the jury. Peter continued. 'Next to Radpole is Thom Cravitz, and he is represented by Mr Jennings.' Again, he pointed in the direction of David. 'Second in from the left is Dean Morris and his counsel is Mr Wade.' Simon half rose in his seat. 'And nearest to you is Theo Clements, and Miss Hardman appears on his behalf.' When he said her name, Cassie looked along the two rows of jurors hoping to get a response from at least one of them. A young woman, probably in her early twenties, with dark hair scraped back from her face, looked directly at her. Cassie thought she looked like a ballerina. The rest continued to watch Peter.

Cassie listened to him outlining the prosecution case but continued to observe the members of the jury. In addition to the man in the tweed suit and the dancer with whom she had already exchanged glances, there was a woman of about thirty with auburn hair cut in a neat pageboy bob and a twenty-something man whose blond hair fell in curls around his face; he wore an earring in his right ear.

Once Peter had told them about the incident at the flat where Henry Bolt and Vincent Setchell lived, he turned to the evidence, which he said identified the four men in the dock as the burglars. 'Dean Morris was the first to be identified,' he said. 'Police officers who attended the scene had searched the area for the men unsuccessfully, but they did find a red scarf in a dustbin. As Mr Bolt had described one of the assailants as wearing a red scarf, it was taken back to the police station.

'The scarf was not treated at first as an exhibit, although it was sent for forensic examination eventually, but events overtook the investigation. Videos taken from a number of shops along the Fulham Road were viewed and on one of them a man could be seen throwing a scarf onto the pavement. Another officer believed the person on the video to be Dean Morris. I should say at this point that Mr Morris does not have any previous convictions. The officer thought he knew him from a local boxing club.

'Dean Morris was arrested and, as is usual today, his mobile phone was taken and the calls made in the days preceding the burglary and around the time of the offence have been analysed. What they reveal is that the day before, and indeed on the morning of January fifteenth, Morris had spoken to both Thom Cravitz and Lucas Radpole.

'Morris was interviewed by Detective Sergeant Adam Moore and Detective Constable Jason Crawford. At first he denied being there, then he said he had gone with Cravitz and Radpole. Radpole had told him the occupant had property belonging to him and he wanted it back. Morris denied knowing anything about a gun.

'When Lucas Radpole was arrested and his home searched, a gun was found at his address. I use that phrase advisedly because he was living in a kind of legal squat along with a number of other young men. His fingerprints, amongst others, however, were found on the gun. His trainers had small shards of glass and pottery embedded in the soles. These fragments match the items broken at the flat. As I have already said, some of the plates and glasses broken during the burglary were antiques and therefore quite rare. It is unlikely the small pieces found in Radpole's trainers could have come from somewhere else. Radpole in interview said he was at an art gallery in Ledbury Grove and denied he knew Henry Bolt or Vincent Setchell.

‘Thom Cravitz’s clothes were also examined and similar pieces of glass and china found on his jacket and in the soles of his trainers. He refused to answer questions, as he was entitled to do, when he was asked about the burglary.

‘A few weeks after, Henry Bolt contacted the police and told them he had identified one of the men. He said a few weeks before the burglary he’d been in the White Horse pub on Parson’s Green when a young man had been introduced to him as the owner of an antique shop in Lower Richmond Road, which he had visited to look at a few pieces of furniture some months before, possibly longer. He’d been thinking about the burglary and he became convinced that one of the intruders was the man from that shop. He decided to return to the premises to confirm he was right and to ascertain the address. He was then able to identify Theo Clements as one of the burglars. Clements was arrested and there was an identification parade, but Mr Setchell didn’t pick anyone out.’

Cassie opened her packet of mints and slipped one into her mouth. Simon Wade, who was sitting next to her, leant over and took one without asking. Simon was a couple of years older than her with a shock of brown hair streaked with gold. His face was lopsided, which made him look a bit like a cartoon. 'Bit of a curious case against your bloke. First there were three men and now there are four.'

Chapter 8

Henry Bolt was the first witness to be called for the prosecution. He was a tall slender man in his early fifties. His hair was dark with no hint of grey. Cassie thought Bolt dyed it. He gave his full name to the court and confirmed his occupation as a solicitor.

'Do you live with Vincent Setchell in a flat at 38 Fulham Road?' Peter said.

'I do. Vince and I have been together for some years and we've lived at that address for the last three years.'

'Can you tell us what happened on January fifteenth this year?'

'We'd been out the night before and gone to bed late. Normally we'd be out of the house by eight, but we'd both overslept and were still in bed. I was woken up by the most almighty crash. I was about to get up – to see what had happened – but before I could a man came into the bedroom waving a gun around.'

'Can you describe the man?'

'The curtains were still closed so it was dark in the bedroom. I saw—'

Peter cut in. 'Was there any light at all?'

'From the living room. The curtains there were open.'

'You were about to give the court a description of the man who came into your bedroom.'

'It was dark and he was silhouetted against the light. I'd say he was over six feet and of slight build. He was dressed in a short black jacket, a kind of blouson, black trousers. A blue scarf – it covered his mouth and nose.'

Cassie noticed several of the jury look at the men in the dock, no doubt comparing the description, such as it was, with the occupants.

'Can you describe the gun?'

'It didn't have a long barrel – some kind of handgun.'

'Can I have Exhibit 2 please?' The usher handed Peter a clear plastic bag with blue printing on it. 'Is this the gun?'

'It's the right sort of shape and size, but I can't say it is the same one.'

'Did you see anyone else in your flat?'

'I saw two other men in the living room. One of them went into the kitchen. I could hear the sound of pans being dropped on the floor followed by crockery smashing. But I didn't pay a lot of attention to them.'

'Why was that?'

'The man in the bedroom was shouting at me. He was saying something like "Where is it?" I didn't know what he was going on about. I reached for my dressing gown. He then screamed, “Don’t move or I’ll blow your head off.” I wasn’t sure about the gun – whether it was real or not, but I wasn’t going to risk it. You wouldn’t, would you?’

‘Quite. Did you say anything to him?’

‘I asked him what he wanted.’

‘Did he tell you?’

‘The noise from the living room had stopped and he turned towards one of the other men and said, “There’s the drawers in here.” A second man came into the bedroom and began searching through one of the chests and our wardrobe. Everything was thrown across the bed. All our clothes just strewn across the quilt.’

‘Can you describe the second man?’

‘Similar height to the man with the gun. He had a red scarf across the lower half of his face and a black baseball cap pulled down over his forehead. I couldn’t see the colour of his hair. His eyes were black … I think.’

Peter handed a brown folder of photographs and asked the usher to give them to the jury. ‘Members of the jury, this bundle contains photographs of the flat taken on January fifteenth. There’s one bundle between two. Exhibit 3, My Lady.’

Cassie pulled her own set of photographs out from her file and turned the pages. The first photograph showed the bed with a large number of sweaters and shirts thrown across it. Others of the lounge and kitchen revealed how destructive the invasion had been; shards of pottery and glass were scattered all over the floor. The floor in the lounge had a pale beige carpet whilst the kitchen had white tiles. She reached for her packet of sweets.

Henry Bolt browsed through the bundle. 'We lost a lot of fine things.'

'Can you tell us about any of the porcelain or glass that got broken?'

'There were some Chelsea and some Georgian wine glasses that I was particularly fond of. I'd collected them over a number of years. Usually I didn't pay a lot for the pieces.'

'Did you know any of the men?'

'When they were in the flat their faces were disguised but …' He looked towards the dock. 'After they left the flat I looked out of the window. I can see the street from there and one of the men took— dropped his scarf. He looked familiar but to begin with I couldn't place him. A few days later I realised I had seen him in a second-hand shop on the Lower Richmond Road. I went to the shop and the man was there. That's when I told the police. They came and arrested him.'

'Was he the only one you recognised?'

'Yes. They … the two men who came into the bedroom had their faces covered. I never saw the man in the living room or the one who was in the kitchen.'

Peter Maynard told the witness he had no further questions but he would be cross-examined by other counsel.

'I am familiar with courtroom procedures,' Bolt said.

Smug, thought Cassie.

Marcus Pike got to his feet. 'Mr Bolt, I'm representing Lucas Radpole and I have a few questions for you about your collection of antiques.'

Cassie thought Bolt was startled by the question. Observing the reaction of witnesses was part of her job, even if those reactions were fleeting. If Bolt was surprised by the line of questions he quickly recovered his composure.

'Antiques is rather a grandiose description. Baubles really. I'm more interested in their decorative quality than their age or value.'

'So, the pieces in your flat were not unique in any way?'

'Sometimes I was lucky and I spotted something in a charity shop or in a market that was a bit special. Not unique but rare.'

'Have you been shown these?' Marcus held up a bag of tiny pieces of porcelain.

'I think so. They are too small to identify as being mine.'

'Have you any idea what the men were looking for?'

'No, I haven't.'

'They didn't ask for money?'

'No. They didn't. They didn't have time.'

The next defendant on the indictment was Thom Cravitz. His counsel, David Jennings, told the judge he had no questions for Bolt.

'Mr Wade, have you any questions for this witness?'

'Yes, ma'am, I do. Mr Bolt, I represent Mr Morris. He's the second man on the left.' Henry Bolt looked at the dock and then back at Simon Wade.

'You don't know him, do you?'

'No. I don't recognise him and to my recollection I've never seen him before today.'

'What about Lucas Radpole? Do you know him?'

Cassie thought Bolt stiffened; it was momentary and she could have been wrong, but still … Then he replied, 'I've never met him before. Or if I have, I don't remember him.'

‘From what you’ve said you are interested in antiques, the decorative arts. Does that include paintings?’

‘I do go to art galleries quite a lot, but my budget is limited so—’

‘You can’t afford to buy the works you might like?’

‘That’s about it. I like looking at pictures.’

Cassie listened carefully. She wasn’t sure where these questions were going. Did Simon Wade know something about Bolt she didn’t?’

‘Do you trade antiques from time to time?’

‘I’m not sure what you mean.’

‘You have an eye for paintings, glass, pottery – do you buy things to sell rather than for your own collection?

‘I have bought things and then sold them on. Usually they’re things I change my mind about or I want room for something new, but I have bought items to sell.’

‘What about coins?’

‘I’m not interested in coins or medals.’

‘You did have some in a desk in your sitting room?’

'I did. I don't remember when I bought them. One of the medals had some interesting decoration. They were inexpensive.'

'Do you remember who you bought them from?'

Bolt didn't reply immediately.

'Is this relevant, Mr Wade?' said Judge Rostron-Smith.

'I believe so, ma'am.'

The judge nodded to him to continue.

'Can you help us, Mr Bolt?'

'No, I can't.'

'If I suggested the name Poynton, would that mean anything to you?'

'I don't know … I really can't remember who I bought the medals from.'

Cassie watched Bolt – he'd licked his lips. He was lying. This time she was sure.

'What about jewellery?' Simon waved his hand in the air. 'Do you buy rings, necklaces, the odd tiara?'

There was a titter from the jury. Judge Rostron-Smith frowned at them.

'Of course not,' Bolt said.

Although Simon and David Jennings were between her and Marcus Pike, she could see Marcus turn to whisper to Oscar. Simon Wade looked down towards Marcus and then said, 'You've described the men making a fairly thorough search of your flat. Can you think what they were looking for?'

'I assume money.'

'In your kitchen cupboards. Doesn't it suggest they were looking for something they thought was hidden?'

'I don't know. You'll have to ask your client and his associates what they were looking for. I believed they wanted money.'

'Can you look at photograph four in the bundle, Exhibit 3.' There was a pause while Henry Bolt found the picture. 'That's your living room, isn't it?' Simon said.

'It is.'

'Is that your wallet on the coffee table?'

Henry Bolt took a moment or two. 'It looks like it.'

'Was any money taken from it?'

'No, no, I didn't count it, but I don't think anything was missing.'

'So, if it wasn't money, it must have been some other item you had? Possibly some antique or work of art?'

'Possibly.'

'Doesn't that suggest the burglars knew you owned some valuable property?'

'I don't know. How can anyone know what I have unless—' Bolt stopped.

'You were about to say, unless he knew you or had been told by somebody about the pottery and paintings in your flat.'

'Must be somebody like that. Somebody who'd been to the flat. A workman, loose talk in the pub.'

'Can you think of anybody who might have done that? Have you had any work done in your flat recently?'

'No, no I can't.'

'Or somebody who sold you some of the artefacts you own? Do you have receipts for them?'

'Are you suggesting I have stolen property?'

'Have you?'

'I'm a solicitor. I don't handle stolen property.'

'Do you always pay for all your – baubles?

'Of course.'

'Thank you, Mr Bolt.'

Judge Smith rapped on the bench. 'I think we'll stop there. Miss Hardman, we'll hear any questions you may have after the weekend. I assume you will have questions. Mr Bolt, don't talk to anyone about the evidence you've given in court today. Ten thirty on Monday, gentlemen.' She got up and bustled out of the court.

As soon as she vanished, Cassie heard Marcus ask Simon, 'What's this about Poynton?'

'I noticed that invoice with his name on it. Morris thinks there's some connection between Poynton and Bolt, something to do with stolen property. Bit odd – he's your alibi, isn't he?'

Chapter 9

As Cassie collected her papers and closed her computer down, Simon Wade put his hand on her arm. 'Any chance of meeting – having a drink this evening?'

'I'm … I have a …' She didn't want to say *date*. She didn't discuss her private life with her colleagues and she hardly knew Simon.

'Surely you can keep him – I assume it's a him, waiting for half an hour or so?'

'I have to go back to chambers first, but, ok. Six thirty at Daley's?'

Simon picked up his papers from the desk. 'That's fine. See you then.'

Cassie walked back to the Temple, turning over her reaction to Bolt's answers to cross-examination from her co-defending counsel. She'd been sure he was lying, and she'd noticed the juror with auburn hair had shaken her head at some of his responses. He was a difficult man to assess; for a commercial lawyer he appeared to be very much at ease in a criminal court.

She turned into Inner Temple deep in thought and passed the Round Chapel built in the twelfth century. The ancient buildings, courts and gardens were the home of the legal profession of which she was proud to be a member. She loved it – the calm of the lanes and squares after the frantic pace of twenty-first-century Fleet Street. When she had started in practice, she and her colleagues came in most days to collect their briefs and other paperwork. Now most of her work arrived by email so coming here wasn't so necessary, but she continued to do so. She liked to see her clerk rather than just talk to him on the phone – she still believed in that personal touch. Watching how he reacted when they were discussing her practice was more informative than trying to read his sincerity, or lack of it, as they talked on the telephone. She used the same skills when she cross-examined witnesses, looking for the shuffling feet, the pursing of lips, the flicker of the eyes that betrayed the lie.

As she climbed the stone stairs to the first floor towards the clerks' room, she heard her name being called. She stopped and Eleanor Hesketh QC came level with her.

'Cassie, can we have a word before you go in?' Eleanor walked ahead and up the next flight of steps. Cassie followed into Eleanor's room, which was immediately below her own and identical in size. Eleanor didn't have to share, so it was a reflection of her personality and designed to impress her instructing solicitors and set at ease the lay clients. Cassie glanced at the mantelpiece but there were no family photographs there, although above it was an etching by Eric Gill. Cassie thought it was a strange choice for someone who did more than her fair share of sexual abuse cases. The senior woman sat down in one of the two pale beige armchairs in front of her desk and motioned to Cassie to take the other one. 'Have you heard anything about Richard leaving chambers?'

'Marcus Pike told me he understood he was going on the bench.'

'I wish. Then he'd take that … beastly man with him. I know Jack's looked after you in the past but the only person he's interested in is himself. He thinks you're a good bet at the moment but if he thinks there's someone, anyone he can make more money out of he'll change horses. Anyway, Richard isn't going on the bench. He's giving up.'

'Retiring?'

'He met someone the last time he was on a cruise, a shipboard romance.' Eleanor raised her eyebrows. 'Anyway, she lives in France. He's been going there most weekends. She's quite wealthy so he doesn't need to work and if he sells his house, he'll have a few million to keep him going.'

'He's got it all worked out.'

'Appears so, but that leaves us without a head of chambers and still with Jack. I'm not sure I want to spend what little free time I have negotiating with him.' Eleanor leant back in her chair and pressed her lips together. 'I've been thinking about trying to find another Silk to come to chambers or possibly a merger with another set. I'm thinking out loud, Cassie. Have you any ideas?'

'I don't know what to think. Why are you asking me?'

'You've applied for Silk this year. So has Peter and, I guess, there's a good chance one or other of you will get it. Perhaps both. If Peter does he'll probably want to be head of chambers and he is senior in call to me. I'm not sure how good he'll be but …'

'But you've been in Silk for what five, six years. Shouldn't you be head?'

'Would you want it?'

Cassie hesitated. She was flattered Eleanor thought she was capable enough, but she thought it was too early in her career. Another year or so and she would be proud to take it on; she wasn't going to admit to that. 'You know I wouldn't,' she said.

'Quite. There is an alternative. You know Marcus Pike quite well?'

'We get on. What are you thinking?'

'A merger. Sets are getting bigger every year. We're nearly fifty so why not a lot more. It spreads the expenses, rent, IT systems, all the administration costs over more people. Most members come into chambers less and less. Makes space less of a problem. A few rooms for conferences and somewhere for the clerks to work. It makes a lot of sense.'

'And Jack?'

'He'd have to compete for his job with Marcus's clerk.' Eleanor paused. 'I understand he's on a salary and a small percentage.' Eleanor tapped her hand on her knee and held Cassie's gaze. 'Would you sound Marcus out?'

'I … I don't know. I'll have to think about it.'

'Don't take too long.' Eleanor stood up and held the door open for Cassie to leave.

Cassie checked her watch. She had ten minutes to .to get Daley's. She found it hard to think about the Clements case when Eleanor's request was whirling round her head. She didn't know Marcus's clerk, not even his name. Was it a good idea to replace the clerk she knew with one she didn't know? Better the devil and all that, and she had a successful relationship with Jack. Meeting Simon Wade might be the opportunity to talk about his chambers. What he thought of their senior clerk and how the rest of the office was run.

Daley's was crowded, lawyers shrugging off the week's work with alcohol before going home to their other halves. She hadn't contacted Ben. She pulled her mobile from her bag and pushed the speed dial. 'Ben,' she said, 'something's come up and I'm going to be a bit late.'

'Again. Cassie, where are you?'

'I won't be long. Promise. Meet me at the flat. There's a bottle of white in the fridge or take a red from the rack. Whatever you want. We'll order a takeaway when I get back.' She tapped the red icon. A few seconds later her phone rang. She pushed it to the bottom of her bag.

At the bar she ordered a bottle of Chablis and picked up two glasses before looking for a table. The bag containing her papers and her computer was a hindrance and she was relieved when Simon Wade elbowed his way towards her and took the bottle and glasses out of her hands. He pushed his way through the crush of lawyers braying about the week's work and sat down at a small round table over which he had draped his coat.

'That was good thinking,' Cassie said.

'Will you be mother,' Simon said, 'or shall I?' Without waiting for an answer, he poured out the wine.

'Now what's this about?' Cassie said.

'Morris thinks Bolt has something Radpole wanted. Something he was entitled to. At one point, he thought it was payment for drugs – Bolt had welched on a deal. He still thinks it might be that. He says there was a lot of talk about what sort of things would be at the flat, paintings, silver, antiques, but he hadn't picked up Radpole was looking for anything specific. But we know they didn't pick up Bolt's wallet. I think it's fair to assume Radpole wasn't interested in taking cash, was he? We know Bolt collects antiques, baubles he calls them. Poynton knows Radpole—'

'How well? And what's the connection to Bolt? I know there's that receipt but it's years old. Just proves he bought something,' Cassie said.

'Poynton's the alibi witness…'

'I know that.' She frowned. 'Clearly there's a connection between Poynton and Radpole but you're suggesting Bolt is part of – what?'

'Some antiques fraud? Stolen property? Fake paintings?' Simon said.

'And Poynton will be giving evidence?'

'I guess so.'

'We can't prove anything. Anyway, Clements' case is the ID is wrong and we have an alibi. How can Radpole's connection to Poynton help me? I prefer to take the line I don't know either of them.'

'Is that true? Wasn't your boy at the same school as Radpole? And your guy's father is in the antique trade like Radpole's. The Crown may well suggest they do know each other and their denials are lies.'

Cassie took a sip of her wine; she knew that was a possibility, but she wasn't sure how much weight it would carry with the jury. 'You may be right. I'll think about it.'

'Cassie, we're on the same side. Whatever is going on it's not a straightforward burglary and, one way or another, our clients have been dragged into it.'

Cassie pursed her lips and smiled. 'I prefer to keep out of any spat between your client and Radpole. The case against me is on a different basis to the rest. I want to keep it that way.'

'It's a matter for you. Do you think your client's guilty?' Simon said.

'That's not my concern. I think the evidence is weak and he should be acquitted, but juries …'

'You never can tell.' Simon leant forward and picked up his glass.

Cassie changed the subject. 'Tell me,' she said, 'what made you choose to go to Marcus's set?'

'A mate of mine from home, a solicitor, suggested them. His firm use them a lot – that helped. Paul didn't want to risk losing their business.'

'Paul's your senior clerk?'

'Paul Scanlon. I understand he's one of Jack's protégés.'

'Didn't do very well with him if he's on a salary plus.'

'Marcus is much too tough to agree a percentage.' He took another sip from his wine. 'I'm not interested in talking about chambers. Tell me about yourself.' He grinned at her. 'I've been told you have three settings – refrigerator, freezer and permafrost, is that right?'

'Really. Who said that? I don't think …' Simon was looking towards the door of the wine bar. Cassie half turned to follow his gaze and saw the back of a man leaving. She was sure it was Ben.

Chapter 10

Usually, on a Friday night as she climbed the three flights of stairs to her flat, Cassie felt the cares of the week slip away. The one-bedroomed flat she had bought several years ago in this prestigious part of London was her refuge. She had chosen the furniture with care; a grey leather chesterfield and a mimosa yellow armchair faced the television she hardly watched. The bookshelves were packed and not just with law books; sets of Dickens, Shakespeare and the Brontës fought for space with thrillers by John Le Carré and Ian Rankin. There were books on art, catalogues from exhibitions she had been to and on one shelf a selection of cookery books. By the window, which looked over a triangle of gardens, was the desk her grandfather has made for her – a treasure she had fought her ex-husband for and for which she had been prepared to relinquish everything else she owned.

Tonight she was tense, knowing Ben would be furious with her. She had been stung by the comment Simon had made that implied she was unemotional. Was she really that cold? Part of the job was to control one's reactions to clients' behaviour, not to reveal one's emotions. She had noticed that some of her fellow barristers controlled their own feelings so well that they ceased to have any at all. Was she the same?

She certainly had feelings now. She was as angry with him as he was with her. She didn't blame him for being vexed, but following her was not something she could condone. She opened the door, dropped her bags in the small hall from where she could see Ben sitting on the sofa. On the coffee table in front of him was a half-full glass of red wine and an empty bottle of white. She picked it up, went into the kitchen and dropped it into the recycling bin.

'I'm surprised you've had the time to get through the whole bottle.'

'What'd you mean?'

'You came to Daley's spying on me.'

'I … I wanted to … it's Friday evening. I wanted to see you. You're always working. Do you need to be? You seem unable to walk away from it. I thought I'd see what it was all about, but you were with some bloke, enjoying his company, leaving me to hang around waiting for you. Sometimes I don't get you – don't understand what you want from me. What kind of relationship you're after.'

'He's—'

Ben got to his feet. 'Don't try and explain. I'm going.'

The door of her flat banged as he left. She heard his footsteps as he headed down the stairs and then the sound of the front door closing. She wasn't going after him. She had nothing to apologise for. He had to live with her career as she lived with his. All thoughts of food vanished. She grabbed the already opened bottle of Cabernet and took some cheese out of the fridge; there would be no takeaway this evening.

Cassie expected Ben to call on Saturday morning when he had sobered up, but then she remembered he had arranged to play golf. He would probably call later. She went to do some shopping in Portobello Market. She didn't know whether to buy food for two or not. The variety of foodstuffs on the market was unlimited; she had plenty to choose from. She just had to make a decision: meat, fish or vegetarian. She'd see what looked good.

She wasn't in any rush and wandered through the crowds at the southern end of the street where the antique shops and stalls attracted tourists from all over the world. The sun was shining and the crowds moved slowly. The smell of coffee mingled with the scent of beeswax polish. A steel band had attracted a large crowd. The noise of their playing crushed the unintelligible chatter in so many different languages. She had to push her way through, holding her shoulder bag close to her; the market was well known for pickpockets.

When she finally got away from the antique stalls, she continued walking north checking the food stalls for aubergines and tomatoes. The fish shop had some red mullet; she could cook that with orange. She bought two fillets. If she didn't hear from Ben, she would put one in the freezer. She saw sourdough bread and made a note to buy some on her way back towards home. As she wandered north she reached a stall she knew well. Sammy who stood the pitch had helped her find an alibi witness in a murder case she'd defended a couple of years previously. She stopped and admired the boxes of fruit and vegetables arranged on the barrow with herbs between them. Sammy had a flair for displaying the produce he had bought earlier that day. She often purchased fruit and vegetables from him and today she was looking for some aubergines and a pot of basil.

Sammy grinned at her. He was a big man and despite the sunny weather he was wearing the same battered Barbour jacket he had worn when she first met him.

'Cassie, what you up to these days?'

She looked at his hands; they were twisted by arthritis and she knew he was often in pain, but he was such a cheerful man. 'How are you?'

A woman dressed in a dark denim jacket approached the stall and asked for a cauliflower, mushrooms, basil and rosemary. Cassie waited.

Sammy held up a cauliflower. 'This one?' The woman nodded. He weighed out some mushrooms and held up a pot of basil and a bunch of rosemary. After she paid and moved away, Cassie asked Sammy again how he was keeping.

'I'm not so bad these days,' said Sammy, 'better now the weather's not so cold and damp.'

Cassie selected a couple of aubergines and some basil and asked him to weigh her half a dozen apples.

'New Zealand, now, this time of year.' He picked six from one of the pyramids of fruit and tucked a sprig of rosemary in the bag 'That ok?'

'A couple of oranges as well.'

'Ok, my lovely.'

Cassie pulled her purse out and searched for some coins. 'Sammy, how long have you worked on the market?'

'Over forty years. I were a kid when I started. I did all sorts of things until I got the veg stall.'

'Did you ever work on the antiques?'

'Antiques.' He chuckled. 'Most of it's rubbish, just polished up a bit. I helped move stuff around for some of the guys.'

Cassie bit her lip; it was a long shot but … 'Does the name Radpole mean anything to you?'

Sammy nodded. 'Bernie Radpole. Nasty bit of work. Why do you ask?'

'His son is a defendant in a case I'm doing.'

'You defending young Radpole?'

'No. My client is Theo Clements.'

Sammy took a deep breath. 'Keep out of those Radpoles' way. I don't know anything about the son, but the father. Served time for burglaries.'

'So I've been told.'

'Big country houses. Stole antiques, paintings, silver, small things. Anything he could carry. Took them to Bermondsey Market. Some law about selling stuff there makes it legal.'

'Market ouvert. It's been abolished now. I've only read about it. Quite clever. If stolen property was sold in daylight hours the buyer got a good title, superseding the original ownership. Did he do that a lot?'

'He was always a bit dodgy. He had a partner who bought the stolen goods from him and then brought them here to sell as legit. Radpole took his share.'

'Neat.'

'That's until his mate shafted him. I'm not saying it's true. A rumour round the market, like. He'd stolen a painting, I think it were, and this guy bought it but instead of selling on Portobello he found a private buyer. He told Radpole it weren't worth much but he got over a hundred grand for it. Or something like that. Enough to buy a shop in Ledbury. Mind you, it wasn't that posh then.'

'A painting? Wouldn't the police know a painting was stolen?'

'Nobody seemed bothered. I heard there was a bit of a dispute as to whether it was genuine.'

'Do you know the name of the Radpole's partner? Does he still have the shop in Ledbury Grove'

'Don't know. It was a long time ago. Not seen them for years.'

'Thanks, Sammy. See you soon.'

'Next week?'

She nodded and waved as she turned to walk back south through the market. She bought bread from the Magpie Bakery and turned into

Westbourne Grove. The flowers from the florists that shared the Turquoise Island with the public toilets spilled out onto the pavement. She stopped and decided to treat herself to a small posy – no one else would.

When she was at the junction with Chepstow Villas, she turned left walking east towards her home. Her route took her to one end of Ledbury Grove and, on a whim, she turned into the tree-lined street. She wasn't sure why she wanted to, but she strolled south looking at the expensive shops and restaurants. Her home wasn't far away and she had walked along it many times to Westbourne Grove, but she hadn't taken much interest in the properties on Ledbury Grove. They sold expensive art and antiques outside her price range. Today she looked more closely at them, hoping to identify the one where Lucas Radpole had been, or said he had been, at the time of the robbery. Close to the junction with Westbourne Grove she saw the name she was looking for, 'The Paint and Print Gallery'. She crossed the road towards it. The window was empty and it appeared to be closed. There was a notice on the door. She went to read it. It was written in an erratic hand and informed any callers that the shop was open by appointment only.

As Cassie climbed the stairs to her front door her mobile rang. She pulled it out and saw the call was from Lee Shaw.

'Hi Lee, can you hang on a minute, I'm just opening the door to my flat.' Once inside and the bags in the kitchen she retrieved her phone from her pocket. 'Right, how can I help?'

'I've had a strange conversation with Theo's dad. He's very worried about his son. Absolutely adamant Theo wouldn't get involved with young Radpole. He believes the Radpoles, father and son, have implicated Theo to extricate Lucas from this offence.'

'And how is he suggesting they've done that? How have they got Bolt to identify Theo?'

'He gets a bit cagey at that point but said he'd send me some photographs that he wants you to show Bolt and ask him about them.'

'Have you got them?'

'No, I'll forward them as soon as I do.'

Chapter 11

Cassie spent the weekend alone. Ben didn't contact her. She considered asking one of her friends to have lunch with her on the Sunday, but she was behind with paperwork and there was a VAT return to prepare as well. She went for a walk in Holland Park where the large white canopy was in place for the opera season, and then went back to the oak desk and her computer.

She called her parents, something she did every Sunday evening, and after a few words with her father she gossiped with her mother. When her mother asked her about Ben, she said he was fine but didn't tell her she hadn't seen him over the weekend. Lee hadn't been in contact with her since the enigmatic call the day before so the cross-examination she had prepared didn't need any alterations to it. She closed her computer and was about to put her mobile on charge when an email from Lee arrived. Attached to it were three photographs. She opened them. They showed different views of a ring. One was from the front, a large red stone set in yellow metal, with two smaller white stones either side. A second had been taken at an angle so she could see the ring as from above, and finally one of the inside of the band revealing the hallmarks. *What has this ring to do with the trial*?

Returning to the Old Bailey on Monday morning, Cassie ruminated about her cross-examination of Henry Bolt. The photographs Lee had sent seemed irrelevant to Theo's case. She needed to speak to Lee and ask her what she was expected to do with the pictures. She found her instructing solicitor and asked her if she had any idea why Clements Senior had sent them to her.

'Jeff wants you to ask Bolt if he's seen this ring before,' Lee said.

'Why? Can he explain why?'

'If he can he's not saying.'

'And what does Theo say? He's the client.'

Lee shrugged her shoulders. 'Whatever his dad says. Can't help you any further.'

Cassie was bewildered, unsure of what she was should do. She took her seat in court and reread the statement of Mr Bolt, as well as her notes of Simon Wades's cross-examination. Then she took out the copies of the photographs she had made yesterday evening and added to the series of questions she had prepared. Simon Wade took his place next to her and asked her if she'd had a good weekend. The jury were brought in, so she was saved from replying.

It was a few minutes before everyone was fully assembled: the defendants in the dock, Mr Bolt in the witness box and Judge Rostron-Smith on the bench. 'Yes, Miss Hardman.'

Cassie turned towards the witness. 'When you went to Richmond Road, did you go into the shop?'

'I didn't want to face the man who'd threatened me with a gun,' Bolt said.

'Are you saying the man wearing the red scarf was the first one who came into the bedroom?'

'I believe so.'

'Didn't you describe that man as having a blue scarf?'

'I don't think so. The scarf was red.'

'Mr Bolt. I'm going to ask you to look at a copy of your statement.' Cassie waited whilst the bundle of documents was handed to the witness. 'I think they're open at the right page. Is that your signature on the bottom?'

'Yes.'

'Now look at the third paragraph on the first page. Can you read it out to the jury, please?'

'Miss Hardman,' Judge Rostron-Smith said, 'I'm sure the jury remember Mr Bolt saying on Friday that the man with the gun was wearing a blue scarf. It's just one of those mistakes, isn't it, Mr Bolt?'

'Yes, Your Honour. I must have got the men mixed up. It was very frightening.'

'Perfectly understandable,' said the judge.

Cassie kept a straight face although inwardly she was seething. It wasn't the best point for the defence, but Bolt was clearly trying to make out her client was the ringleader.

'You waited outside the shop in Richmond Road until the man came out and then rang the police?'

'As soon as I was sure it was the same man.'

'When the men were in your flat you have already said their faces were covered so you couldn't see their features?'

'That's right, but I was able to observe their gestures.'

'Emptying your wardrobe, throwing clothes around – not normal gestures, are they?'

'No, but I had an impression of them.'

'You saw two men?'

'Yes. I've said so.'

'You described the two men in your bedroom as being of similar height?'

'Yes, that's right.'

'My Lady, I would like all four men in the dock to stand so that the jury can compare them.'

'Really, Miss Hardman. Do we have to go into theatrics?'

'I think it would help the jury.' Cassie looked at the jurors and saw a number of them nodding, including the ballerina and the man with the white stone earring. The judge must have seen the jurors' reaction too because she asked the defendants to get to their feet. When the four were standing the discrepancy in their heights was obvious. The judge waited for the jury to look at the defendants then she motioned them to sit again

'I'll repeat the question. You only saw two men, not four?'

'I heard noises from the living room and the kitchen. So there must have been others.'

'But you never saw any others?'

'No, I didn't see anyone other than the two men who came in the bedroom, but I heard others.'

'The noise of crockery was from the kitchen?'

'I assume so. The floor is tiled.'

'The living room is carpeted and there is a rug as well?'

'Yes, there is.'

‘Can we look at the photograph of your flat taken on fifteenth January?’ The usher handed the album of photographs to Vincent Bolt.

‘Photograph number three please,’ Cassie said. There was a flurry of albums being opened by both counsel and jury.

‘What number, Miss Hardman?’ Judge Rostron-Smith said.

‘Three, My Lady.’

‘This is a photograph of the living room …’

‘That’s obvious, isn’t it?’ Judge Rostron-Smith said. ‘I’m assuming there is only the one living room, Mr Bolt. Is that right?’

‘Yes, My Lady, it’s a quite small flat. Lawyers’ incomes aren’t what the public imagine.’

‘Quite so. Yes, Miss Hardman.’

‘We can see broken pieces of pottery on the surface of the rug. Some broken glass and quite a number of books. Indeed some of your baubles, as you call them, seem to have survived intact?’ Cassie said.

‘I think only two pieces from that particular shelf were broken,’ Bolt said.

‘The kitchen is a bit different. Photograph five.’ Cassie paused while the jury turned the pages of their albums. ‘Lots of broken crockery on the floor. Most of the shards normal household pieces?'

'Everyday dishes, as you say.'

'The books hitting the floor must have made a lot of noise?'

'I would think so. It was hard to differentiate.'

'Hard to differentiate where the noise was coming from?'

'I suppose so.'

'Perfectly possible it was just one man?'

'I thought two because I could hear them at the same time.'

'When the police first arrived at your flat, you told them there were three men. Isn't that right?'

'That was my immediate reaction, but when I thought about it, I realised it must be four because of the noises from the kitchen and living room.'

'Wasn't your first account of only three men correct?'

'I think there were four. I could be wrong but …'

'You don't think you are,' Judge Rostron-Smith said.

Bolt smiled at the judge. 'I don't think I am, My Lady.'

‘What did you do when they left your flat? Did you try to follow them?’ Cassie said.

‘I wasn’t dressed. I put on my dressing gown and ran to the sitting room window. I can see the street from there. I looked down and saw a man running towards the Broadway. He was pulling a scarf from his face. Once he’d got it off, he dropped it on the pavement.’

‘Can you remember what he was wearing?’

‘A bomber jacket, jeans and the scarf.’

‘What colour was the scarf?’

‘Red. Definitely red.’

‘And the jacket. What colour was the jacket?’

‘Green, I think it was green.’

‘That was the only man whose face you saw?’

Bolt didn’t reply until the judge told him he must answer the question.

‘The only one.’

‘And that was the man you say you recognised?’

‘When I saw his face he looked familiar and I tried to think where I had seen him before. At first …’

‘Mr Bolt. Before you decided you knew who he was, did the police ask you to look at photographs to see if you could identify any of the men?'

'They did. I didn't see anyone I recognised. As I've said, it was their gestures I thought would enable me to identify them. Photographs don't have gestures.'

Someone on the jury laughed.

'Quiet,' Judge Rostron-Smith said, 'this is a court of law, not a comedy club.'

'Your view of the man with the red scarf was from above and he was running in the direction of the Broadway. Let's look at the photographs again. There is one at page two showing the front of the building. Downstairs is a shop and the door to your flat is on the right-hand side of the property? Upstairs on the first floor we can see two windows. Can you help us which one you were standing at when you saw the man?'

'The one on the right in the photo.'

'Was the man coming out of the door or was he already on the pavement?'

'He was on the pavement. I didn't see him leave the flat.'

'At that point the man must have been directly below you?'

'Almost.'

'Then he went off towards the left-hand side of our photograph?'

'That's correct.'

'At that stage he was running away from you?'

'Yes.'

'You could no longer see his face, could you?'

Bolt didn't reply and pursed his lips. 'I guess not.'

'Your view of his face must have been very brief.'

'If you say so.'

'How long did you have him in view?'

'Not very long. But for a few seconds I had a very good view of his face and I knew he was familiar.'

'You knew he was familiar but you didn't know his name?'

'I didn't even know where I had seen him before. I kept thinking about it and then I was talking to a friend about various antique shops and I remembered where I'd seen him.'

'Who was the friend?'

'I don't … do I have to answer that, My Lady?'

'Where is this getting us, Miss Hardman? I can't see how the name of this friend helps your case at all,' Judge Rostron-Smith said.

'As you please. This conversation about antique shops. Did your friend mention the shop on Richmond Road?'

'Miss Hardman, I really don't see where this is going,' the judge said.

'My Lady, I am trying to establish whether the "friend" knew my client or not. If he did then Mr Bolt may have been influenced in his identification of my client by that knowledge.'

'I really don't think …'

'I'll ask a different question. Mr Bolt, is this the picture? Some weeks after the burglary you are talking to a friend about going to various antique shops and you suddenly remember where you had seen the man with the red scarf before?'

'Something like that.'

'Something like that. Can you help us as to when you had been to the shop before?'

'I don't think I can. Possibly … a couple of years ago.'

'Did you have any specific reason to go to this particular shop?'

'I was just browsing. I saw this man sitting in a chair and I believed him to be the shop assistant. I think he asked me if he could help. I told him I was just looking around. I've not been that side of the river very often. I think it may have been the day of the boat race.'

'You've only been once?'

'It's really a second-hand shop, bric-a-brac rather than antiques. There are better places to find the sort of thing I like.'

'The Portobello Road?'

'I do go there.'

'What about the Bermondsey Market?'

'Yes. It's Friday mornings and I work, but I have been.'

'How long have you been collecting antiques?'

'Thirty years or more.'

'Did you go to Bermondsey in the early nineties?'

'Miss Hardman, I am getting a little concerned about your questions, most of which seem to be irrelevant,' Judge Rostron-Smith said.

'Can you answer, Mr Bolt?'

'I would have thought so. I probably had more free time then.'

'The market starts early doesn't it?'

'It does, yes.'

'It's a good place to pick up a bargain?'

'Definitely.'

'And as a lawyer you would know that you could buy stolen property there and you would obtain ownership of it?'

'Market ouvert. It's been abolished.'

'Can you look at these photographs? Cassie handed the pictures of the ring to the usher who passed them to Mr Bolt.

'Have you seen this ring before?'

Henry Bolt blanched.

'Miss Hardman, what is this to do with this trial? I'm not going to allow …'

The intervention by the judge must have given Bolt time to compose himself. 'I am unable to answer that as my reply would be in breach of the rules on legal privilege.'

Chapter 12

The rest of the court day had been taken up with a number of non-contentious witnesses: the two police officers who had been the first to attend the scene, the photographer and the scenes of crime officers, then the policemen who had made door-to-door enquiries and taken possession of the CCTV recordings. After court rose Cassie didn't go back to chambers but made her way home. She was still angry with Judge Rostron-Smith for the unwarranted interventions in her cross-examination. Not that it had prevented her probing Bolt's evidence, but it would have been better without the judge's comments. Had she done enough to weaken the ID? Certainly the height difference between Theo and the others had made an impression on the jury. Upstairs she threw her bags onto the floor next to her desk and checked her mobile. There were no urgent messages and nothing from Ben. She'd have to ring and try and sort it out, but not immediately. For the moment she was engrossed by the Clements case. She pushed the mouse on her laptop and waited as it sprang back into life. She smiled at the screensaver, a photograph of her sister, Amanda, with her two boys, Jeremy and Anthony. Cassie was about to download the papers for a drugs importation when she noticed the email from Lee Shaw sending her the photographs of the ring. Why had her client's father wanted her to ask Bolt about the ring? What was the connection between the ring and this trial? Bolt's claim to legal privilege meant the ring had been the subject of some kind of litigation. Possibly family proceedings of some kind, a contractual issue, or was it the proceeds of crime? Various possibilities crossed her mind and eventually she picked up her mobile and found the contact page for Alex Seymour.

'Alex,' Cassie said, 'how's things?'

'I'm fine. What about you?'

'Ok. I noticed your name on a witness statement in the case I'm doing.'

'I'm not expecting to be in court on anything. What is it?'

'You interviewed my client's father and girlfriend. Jeff Clements and Anne Ellis. They're alibi witnesses. There's a man called Poynton as well. One of the co-defendants says he was in Poynton's shop at the time of an alleged aggravated burglary.'

'Case of Radpole? What are you after this time?'

'Don't be so suspicious.' Cassie paused. Alex didn't respond so Cassie continued. 'I'm not asking you anything about them. I really want some help. Could you pop round and see me this evening?'

There was a pause. 'In about half an hour?'

Cassie felt a sense of relief. 'Great, see you then.'

Alex was prompt and when she arrived Cassie offered her a glass of wine. 'I'm sorry to call you out of the blue like this—'

'But you've got a problem.'

'Always on the button. This trial I'm doing.' Cassie always worried about talking to Alex in case she said anything she shouldn't. She too was aware of client confidentiality, but she wanted to find out more about the ring and she couldn't do that herself. 'I've been sent these photographs.' She handed the copies to Alex. 'And I think the ring was stolen at some time. Can you discover where it came from?'

'That's a big ask. You've no dates or names or are you not telling me?'

'I don't know any more really. It may have a connection to my current trial. It may not. You've interviewed the alibi witnesses so you know the names of the defendants. My client has instructed me to ask the complainant in the case about this ring. I don't like asking questions without some idea of what the answer might be.'

'Who is the victim?'

Cassie may have called the person whose flat had been broken into a complainant, but she knew it was a traumatic event for anyone to have their home invaded. Somehow the word victim didn't fit Henry Bolt. She ignored Alex's question; the less the officer knew the better.

'Can you help me find out who it belongs to?' Cassie said.

'I don't know what I can do,' Alex said.

'Any information would help.'

Alex examined the photographs. 'I see the ring is hallmarked. That may help. Can I take these? Actually, it might be better if you emailed me the files.'

'I'll do that.'

As she walked back to the station, Alex wondered why she had agreed to help Cassie Hardman again. What was it about this softly spoken barrister that led her to assist her? By the time she was sitting at her desk, the photographs had arrived on her mobile. She looked at them again and then rang the antiques squad at Scotland Yard. The officer who answered asked her to send him the pictures and he would ring back. She stressed it was urgent and he reassured her he wouldn't be long. True to his word he rang back almost immediately. 'The ring was assayed ten years ago and the maker was a jeweller in Hatton Garden called Adam Vinny. You'll have to find his address – I think they've moved premises. I'll look and see if there's any reference to it on our files of stolen property.'

Alex thanked him and searched for the goldsmith's name. She found it and made a note of the address on the website. Time to pay Mr Vinny a visit. She printed the photographs of the ring; she would need those.

Alex took the Tube to Chancery Lane and made her way towards Holborn Circus. Hatton Garden runs north from High Holborn and has been the centre of the jewellery industry for over two hundred years. Approaching from the west, the equestrian statue of Prince Albert dominated the confluence of streets, as if supervising the traffic along this important route into the square mile. On Alex's left was the junction with Leather Lane, and just after that an unpretentious street which was Hatton Garden. The shop windows dazzled her eyes with their display of rings, bracelets and necklaces. Alex fingered the diamond studs her father had bought her for her twenty-first birthday. About halfway up she found the shop with the name Adam Vinny above the window and on the glass door was a notice asking all visitors to ring the bell. Alex did so and a woman's voice sounded from the speaker to her left. 'Do you have an appointment?'

'I'm a police officer. I want—'

'We don't allow anyone in without an appointment.'

'I'm a police officer and I'm investigating a burglary.' Alex thought it was a reasonable assumption that the ring was stolen. 'I think you may be able to help.'

'There's a camera on your right. Can you hold your warrant card up and then I can see it clearly.'

Alex did as she was asked and when the door made a buzzing noise she pushed it open and walked into the shop.

She was met by, she assumed, the same young woman who had been speaking to her. She was wearing an artist's smock over jeans and a pair of bright green stiletto heels. Her red hair was piled up on her head and her eyes were a startling blue.

'We can't be too careful,' the woman said, holding out her hand. 'How can I help?'

'I wanted to speak to an Adam Vinny.'

'That's me. The business was my father's. He died – I'd worked with him. Decided to keep the name.'

'So you're …'

'Abigail Vinny.'

'I'm sorry about your father. Was that recent?'

'Two years ago in January.'

Alex's heart sank. If he had made the ring she wouldn't get any answers as to who had brought the stone to the shop. 'Can you look at these photographs?' She handed the prints she'd made to the young woman, who examined them. 'Do you recognise the hallmark?'

'Yes, that's this firm's. It's a lovely stone.'

'It is real then?'

'It's difficult to tell from a photograph. It might be a spinel.'

'A spinel?'

'They are very like rubies to look at. The Black Prince's Ruby is a spinel. The Crown Jewels, you know. I'd need to see the stone to be sure.'

'Did your father make this ring?'

'Someone in the firm did. We do employ a couple of craftsmen so it may have been one of those, but I would think Dad would have done this. The stone, at least from the photos, looks of a high quality and he liked doing those himself. Let me see if I can find the piece in our records. It may take a little while. Do you want to come back or will you wait?'

'I'll wait, thank you.' Alex didn't want to give Abigail Vinny the opportunity to talk to anyone about her inquiry.

About ten minutes later, Abigail came back with a sheet of paper which she handed to Alex. 'As you can see. The ruby, and my father did identify it as a ruby, was already in a ring with two diamonds.' She handed Alex a photograph of a more conventional ring than the one in the photographs she had been sent by Cassie Hardman. 'A Henry Bolt wanted it in a more modern setting. Dad would have done some sketches and provided an estimate for the work. The owner must have agreed to that and when the work was done it was sent to be assayed and hallmarked.'

Alex photographed the receipt, which described the work carried out and the date it was assayed in 2011.

'Do you get these requests frequently? Isn't it a way of disguising stolen property?'

'It can be. Usually it's people wanting rings they've inherited updated. Anyway, for a stone this size we would make sure it was legit.'

'So was this legit?'

'If you look at the bottom of that sheet, there's an invoice for the sale of a ring from the market in Bermondsey Square in 1993. At that time it was a—'

Alex took the invoice. 'A market ouvert.' She gulped but quickly recovered. She didn't want to give anything away. 'The market trader sold it to a Mr Poynton. He would then have acquired a legal right to the ring?'

'That's right,' Abigail Vinny said. 'He got it for a good price.' She pointed to another receipt attached to the invoice Alex was holding. 'Mr Bolt bought it from Poynton. It's a lovely piece. Who has it now?'

'It's not important. It's who sold it to Poynton?'

Alex left the shop and walked back to Holborn Tube station with the name of Poynton buzzing in her brain. Was it just a coincidence he had owned the ring and was an alibi witness in the same case in which Cassie Hardman was representing a co-defendant? There must be some connection between the two, but what was it? Who had owned the ring before Poynton? Who was the man, Henry Bolt, who had had the stone refashioned, and why?

Chapter 13

When the trial of Radpole, Cravitz, Morris and Clements resumed the next day, Vincent Setchell was the first witness to be called. He was a similar height to his partner but a different build. His face was round and pinkish with large blue eyes, and his hair was sandy coloured. He grasped the edge of the witness box and looked around. When his eyes lighted on Cassie he attempted to smile. She thought that meeting him in different circumstances she would have liked him, but today she needed to ensure he stuck to his evidence. There was always a risk that he might have been influenced by Bolt and give a similar version of the events of 15 January.

After he took the oath, promising to tell the truth, he replied to Peter Maynard's questions carefully. He didn't deviate in any significant way from the statement he had made to the police soon after the burglary. He repeated that from his position in the bedroom he couldn't see into the living room. He'd hidden under the duvet so the only one of the intruders he saw was the man with the gun. He assumed there were at least two others because he could hear noises from the kitchen as well as the living room. When Peter asked him to describe the man he did see, he said he really couldn't remember. He had been concentrating on the gun.

None of the other counsel wanted to cross-examine Setchell and Judge Rostron-Smith was turning to thank him when Cassie got to her feet. 'I have a couple of questions for Mr Setchell, My Lady.'

'Go ahead then,' the judge snapped. Cassie glanced at the jury. The man in the tweed suit sitting on the back row frowned at the judge; Cassie hoped he thought she was being unfair.

'Mr Setchell. I'm representing Mr Clements, the young man on the left in the dock. You attended an identification parade, did you not?'

'Yes, but I didn't pick anyone out. As I've said, I didn't really look at the man's face.'

'I take it then that there was no one on the parade who you had seen before.'

'There was no one I recognised at all.'

'How long have you and Mr Bolt been together?'

'Over ten years.'

'Do you share his interest in antiques?'

'Very much. We spend most weekends in, not the expensive antique shops, kind of small second-hand places. Sometimes Portobello or Bermondsey.'

‘Do you remember going to a shop on the Lower Richmond Road at any time?’

‘I don’t, I’m afraid. Should I? I can’t think why we would go there.’

‘You’ve described the man as being all in black. Any recollection of a red scarf?’

‘No. I know Henry, Mr Bolt, says one of them was wearing a red scarf, but I don’t remember that.’

‘Turning to the noise in the flat. Could you tell where it was coming from?’

‘I heard the thud of books, at least I assume it was that from what I saw when I went into the living room. Then there was the sound of crockery landing on the floor. I thought in the kitchen.’

‘They were sequential. First the sound of books, followed by the crack of broken pottery?’

Setchell screwed up his eyes. ‘I would have said so.’

Cassie pulled the photographs of the ring from under her computer and asked Setchell to look at them. He held them in his hand for a moment.

‘Not again, Miss Hardman. I can see no relevance to this case at all,’ the judge said. Her intervention failed to prevent Setchell replying. He said he had never seen it before.

Cassie smiled and, ignoring the judge's comment, she thanked the witness and said she had no more questions for him.

Prosecuting counsel, Peter Maynard, stood up. 'I'll call PC Claire Machin. Page twenty-three, My Lady.' There was a rustle of papers and the clicking of computers as the judge and counsel found the relevant statement in the file.

A woman probably only just twenty came into court wearing her uniform and carrying her hat, which she carefully placed on the edge of the witness box. She picked up the bible and, without looking at the card the usher had given her, took the oath and then gave her name and number.

'Thank you, PC Machin. Now can you tell us where you were on January fifteenth at about 9 a.m?'

'May I refer to my notes?'

'When were they made?' Peter Maynard said.

'As soon as I got back to the station at about 11 a.m. I went straight to the canteen and …'

Marcus got to his feet. 'I've no objection, My Lady.'

'Thank you, Mr Pike. Anyone …'

The remaining defence counsel nodded their agreement.

Peter Maynard repeated the question and the police officer told the court she had been on foot on the south side of Fulham Road close to a row of shops about a hundred metres from the junction with Parson's Green Lane.

'Which way were you walking?'

'I was walking west.'

'What did you see or hear?'

'At first I heard someone shout at me and I looked in the direction the cry had come from and saw a woman in the doorway of a shop. I went towards her and she beckoned me inside.'

'Did you go inside?'

'Not at first. I radioed for assistance. She was very agitated and I thought she was saying she had been attacked. She pointed into the premises. I wanted to be sure other officers would be available before I went in. I heard the sound of a siren and by that time, she had calmed down. I was able to ascertain that the attacker was in the upstairs flat. She told me she'd heard steps going upstairs followed by the sound of a fight. Crashing and banging. Someone had screamed and she was afraid somebody was injured. I asked her who lived upstairs and she told me two men.'

‘And then?’

‘I asked her if she’d seen who’d entered the upstairs flat. Before she answered the outside door burst open and a man came running out. I yelled for him to stop and ran towards him. I chased him along the street.’

‘Did anyone else leave the flat?’

‘I can’t say. I only saw the one.’

‘Did you catch up with the man you had seen?’

‘No. He vanished and then two other officers arrived. They spoke to the woman at the door of her shop and then went upstairs. I followed. There were two men only partly dressed. They gave their names as Henry Bolt and Vincent Setchell.’

‘Did you then ask them what had happened?’

‘I did.’

‘And if you’re asked what they said you can tell the court?’

‘I made a note of what they told me and asked them to sign it.’

‘As a result of what they told you did you make a search of the area outside the flat?’

‘I did and I found a red scarf in a litter bin a short distance from the entrance.’

‘Thank you. Stay there, you’ll be asked some more questions.’

The young officer looked along counsels' row, her eyes wide and her mouth set in a grimace.

'What did you do with the red scarf?' Marcus Pike said.

'I took it back to the station and asked my sergeant what I should do. He told me to find an exhibit bag and label it.'

'Exhibit number 5 please. Is that the exhibit bag and the scarf?'

'That's my handwriting and signature. It looks like the scarf.'

'Are there other signatures?'

'There's one of Sergeant Moore and one I can't read. There's a stamp as well.' She twisted the bag around. 'City and County Forensic Services.'

'Please can you take the scarf out of the bag.' Marcus waited as the officer tore the bag open and pulled out a red scarf with black lines on it. 'Now, please will you hold the scarf up.' The officer held the cloth at arm's length so that it draped over the side of the witness box. Towards the end of the scarf was what looked like the imprint of a shoe.

'Miss Machin, the mark on it, is that a shoe print?'

'Yes. I dropped the scarf and trod on it. I did make a note of it.'

‘Yes, yes. I know. But only moments before you had been in the flat where there was broken pottery and glass all over the floor.’

‘I did try to avoid standing in it but …’

‘Thank you, officer.’

Neither David Jennings on behalf of Cravitz nor Simon Wade who represented Morris had any questions for the police officer.

Cassie got to her feet. ‘Just one question, PC Machin. From your notes, can you tell us how many men Mr Bolt said had entered the flat?’

‘He told me three.’

‘Just three. Thank you.’ Cassie resumed her seat.

Peter Maynard had no re-examination of the officer, who marched out of the courtroom.

While they waited for the next witness to be called Simon Wade pulled the photographs of the ring from Cassie’s papers. He looked at them and asked her if the stones were real. She told him she didn’t know.

Chapter 14

Cassie wasn't very interested in the evidence of the forensic scientist. She knew Oscar Davenport had advised a second examination of the clothes should be carried out, but she didn't know what that had revealed.

'Did you examine the clothing taken from the defendants?' Peter Maynard said when the scientist was in the witness box and had taken the oath.

'I did a visual examination of the clothing of three of the defendants,' Terry Nevin, the scientist from the forensic services company said. He was a small pale man with the smattering of freckles that often accompanies that kind of colouring. He blinked frequently and fiddled with his notes. He had placed them on the edge of the witness stand, and now looked down and ran a finger along the first page. 'Radpole, Cravitz and Morris.' He read out the three names. 'I saw nothing that warranted any further testing. The shoes taken from Morris were new and had only been worn on a few occasions.'

'Did you make any further examination of…'

'I did examine the trainers of Radpole and Cravitz in more detail. I was able to extract small pieces of glass and porcelain from the soles of both men's shoes.'

'What did you do with the pieces?'

'I compared them with the sweepings taken from the floor of the flat. There were … there were similarities between them.'

Peter Maynard looked down at his file, trying to control his impatience with the witness.

'Can you help us with the sort of tests you carried out?'

'I used spectroscopy to—'

'Mr Maynard, do we need the details? Isn't it enough for the jury to know that the shards of glass and pottery were similar?' the judge said. 'I suspect the pieces were so small one couldn't tell if any particular piece was Crown Derby or Meissen. Is that right –' she stopped and looked towards her computer screen – 'Mr Nevin?'

'Yes, My Lady.' His jaw relaxed. 'There was nothing so distinctive about the pieces, except I could say that most of them, particularly the glass, were probably pre-nineteen hundred.'

'Just a couple of other things, Mr Nevin,' Peter said. 'Did you examine the red scarf, Exhibit 5, for samples to enable you to do a comparison of DNA?'

'I did, but I was unable to get any satisfactory samples.'

'What about Exhibit 2, the gun?'

Nevin looked puzzled. 'I didn't examine the gun for DNA samples.'

'Fingerprints?' Peter said.

'There were a number of different fingerprints on the gun. It had been handled by quite a lot of people, but only those of Radpole were present. None of the other defendants.'

Peter Maynard thanked the witness and sank into his seat. Marcus stood and smiled at Judge Rostron-Smith.

'I don't think the scientific evidence adds much to the prosecution case, Mr Pike. Do you want to take the matter any further?'

'With your leave, My Lady. Mr Nevin, a few days after you'd completed your examination of the clothing the police submitted to you, did you attend a second inspection conducted by Duncan Stanning?'

'I did. Mr Stanning is well known to me.'

'I think you and he worked together before forensic services were privatised?'

'That's correct.'

'On this occasion the examination was conducted by Mr Stanning, but you saw everything he did?'

'I watched the inspection of the clothing and it complied with normal forensic services standards.'

'The items included three pairs of jeans and two denim jackets, all belonging to Mr Radpole?'

'They did.'

'Who had produced them?' Judge Rostron-Smith said.

'My Lady, they were items the police had seized from Mr Radpole's home. My learned junior found a list of clothes amongst the unused material and asked for them to be inspected. As you are aware, Mr Radpole works in the antiques business and he believes all his work clothes would have similar shards of pottery and glass—' Marcus said.

The judge interrupted him. 'Was that the finding of this further examination?'

'Yes. On two pairs of jeans and one of the jackets,' Mr Nevin said.

Marcus thanked the witness and sat down.

Cassie pressed her lips together as she suppressed a smile. She could hear Marcus whispering to Oscar that her ladyship had done his job for him and he was leaving to go to another case in Court 6.

Judge Rostron-Smith was determined to get through this case as quickly as possible. 'Now, who are you calling next, Mr Maynard?'

'Before I call my next witness, there is a matter of law I wish to raise in the absence of the jury.' The judge looked at David Jennings who shook his head and then at Simon Wade who indicated he had nothing to say.

When her gaze fell on Cassie, Cassie got to her feet. 'The application is in respect of my client and I would also ask that it is discussed in the absence of the jury.'

'Very well,' the judge said. 'Members of the jury, can I ask you to go with the usher. There's probably time for a cup of tea or coffee.' She waited until the jury had left. 'Now, Mr Maynard, what is this about?'

'My Lady, as you will have seen in Clements' defence statement he provides details of an alibi. That alibi relies on the evidence of his girlfriend, Anne Ellis, and his father, Jeff Clements. The conclusion the defence wish to draw is that between Ellis leaving their home and his father meeting him to keep an appointment in Chelsea, there was insufficient time for Clements Junior to have gone from his home address in Lower Richmond Road to Bolt's flat and back again in order to meet his father and then get to that appointment. They say they arrived at the address in Chelsea on time at ten a.m. We have obtained evidence that they did not arrive until ten thirty and that they provided different explanations as to their late arrival. The Crown takes the view that this is evidence in rebuttal of the alibi and accordingly we propose to prove that part of the defence statement and then call the witness, a Mr Archibald Green.'

'Miss Hardman, what do you have to say?'

'I would submit that this evidence only goes to the reliability of the defendant and his father. It relies on an estimate of time. The Crown are not calling evidence of the time it takes to get between the various addresses.'

'Can I see the statement of this witness?' the judge said.

The document was passed up to her and both Peter and Cassie waited whilst she read it.

'Miss Hardman, I'm against you. I think this is evidence that should be called as part of the prosecution case. I assume you and Mr Maynard can deal with the defence statement by way of admissions?'

'Yes, My Lady,' Peter said, 'we have already agreed some admissions about the telephone evidence. If we could have a few minutes we can add to that.' Peter handed a sheet of paper to the usher who walked up to the judge's bench and handed it to her. Judge Rostron-Smith took a few minutes to read it. 'Mr Davenport, are these agreed?'

'They are, My Lady.'

The judge's eyes swept along the row of barristers almost daring them to disagree. No one said anything. 'I'll rise while you do that,' she said.

It didn't take long for Peter Maynard and Cassie to agree a form of words outlining the details of Theo Clements' alibi. Peter asked the usher to tell the judge they were ready to proceed and shortly after the court reassembled.

Judge Rostron-Smith began by speaking to the jury. 'Thank you for your patience. I know it is annoying when matters are dealt with in your absence. Mr Maynard is going to read some admissions. That means all counsel in the case agree that these facts are correct and you can accept them as if they had been given in the witness box.' She then addressed Peter Maynard. 'It may help if before the jury retire they have copies of these.'

'As you please, My Lady,' Peter Maynard said. 'The admissions, members of the jury, relate to records of various mobile telephone numbers.' He then read them to the jury. Cassie didn't really listen because they had no bearing on the case against Theo. She knew that examination of the calls made on the mobiles belonging to Radpole, Cravitz and Morris showed that they had been in touch with each other about half an hour before the invasion of Henry Bolt's flat and that they had been in the vicinity of Fulham Road close to the flat. There was no call to or from Theo's mobile on that day, or in the days preceding the burglary or, indeed, in the period immediately after but before Morris, Radpole or Cravitz were arrested.

Peter then read out the admission they had agreed. 'Theodore Clements was at home at 9 a.m. on the morning of January fifteenth. His girlfriend Anne Ellis was with him until about 8.50 a.m. and his father, Jeffery Clements, arrived about 9.20 a.m. From the premises on Lower Richmond Road, father and son went to an address in St Luke's Road, Chelsea, arriving there at about 10 a.m.'

After reading the admissions, Peter said he would move on to the evidence of the police interviews. 'Detective Sergeant Adam Moore, please.'

A tall well-built man came into the courtroom, dressed in an expensive-looking dark blue suit. He took a pocketbook from the left-hand pocket of his jacket and placed it on the side of the witness box; he waited for the usher to hand him the bible then took the oath to tell the truth without needing to read the card. 'DS Adam Moore stationed at Fulham, ma'am.'

'Sergeant Moore, you were the officer investigating the burglary of Mr Bolt's flat.'

'I was under the supervision of DCI Saltburn.'

'Did you begin by asking to see the CCTV recordings made by property owners in the vicinity of the flat?'

'I did. There were about five cameras in the area, and we looked at them for about ten minutes before the call from PC Machin and five minutes after. One of them failed to operate and three of the others were incorrectly set, so the only view was the tops of heads. One of them showed a man throwing or dropping a scarf on the ground. The man's face was quite clear. As is normal, we showed local officers a still from the video and one officer recognised the man.'

Simon Wade rose to his feet. 'There is no objection to this officer telling us what the officer said. Mr Morris accepts that the officer knew him.'

'Thank you. Can you tell us what you were told?'

‘I was told that the man’s name was Dean Morris and he was a member of the same boxing club as the officer.’

‘I take it that’s accepted?’ Judge Rostron-Smith said.

‘It is, My Lady,’ Simon said.

‘Was Morris arrested that same day?’

‘He was. We, that is myself and DC Crawford, went to the club in Putney and arrested Dean Morris for the aggravated burglary at 38 Fulham Road. He was cautioned—’

‘Can you give us the words of the caution?’

‘I told him he didn’t have to say anything but anything he did say would be recorded and may be given in evidence, and if he failed to mention something he later relied on in court that could be used against him.’

‘Did he say anything?’

DS Moore pulled out his pocketbook and flipped through it. Cassie thought he was making a show of it – she could see coloured markers identifying various pages.

‘He said, “I don’t know what you’re talking about.”’

‘What was Mr Morris wearing at the time of his arrest?’

'Boxing shorts. Just boxing shorts. Oh, and he had a pair of gloves on.'

'Gloves?' the judge said.

'Yes, ma'am. Boxing gloves.'

Cassie looked at the jury. One or two of them had put their hands over their mouths and others pursed their lips in an attempt to suppress their giggles.

'Did you take him back to the station dressed like that?' Peter said.

'We did. We also took items from his locker, which included a light green bomber jacket and black trainers. There were other clothes and a mobile phone. We seized that as well.'

'What happened to the phone?'

'It was examined by forensics and then the records of all calls made on that phone were obtained from the network provider.'

'We've heard that examination revealed phone calls between these defendants around the time of the burglary. And that Morris or at least his phone was close to 38 Fulham Road. As a result of that information did you interview Mr Morris?'

'In company with DC Crawford. Morris had requested a solicitor and he was present.'

'Can you tell us what was said?'

‘After cautioning, Morris refused to answer any questions. He was released on bail to begin with.’

‘Released on bail. For such a serious offence?’ Judge Rostron-Smith said.

‘The presiding judge at this court ordered it, ma’am.’

‘Really.’ The judge shook her head in apparent disbelief. ‘Carry on, Mr Maynard, carry on.’

‘When we had the telephone records he was rearrested and interviewed a second time.’

‘By the same people?’

‘Yes, and his solicitor was present throughout.’

‘Are there copies for the jury?’ the judge said.

‘There are.’ On the bench behind Peter Maynard was a pile of bundles; a CPS clerk handed them to the court usher who took them to the jury box.

‘One between two, members of the jury,’ Peter said.

When the jurors had the statements in front of them, Peter Maynard asked them to mark the first page as Exhibit 6. ‘This is the transcript of the interview of Dean Morris. Have you all got that?’ He turned to the sergeant. ‘Can you tell us what Morris said?’

Cassie pulled up the file of Dean Morris's interview onto her screen. She hadn't bothered to print it off because it didn't affect her client. As DS Moore and Peter Maynard acted out the interview for the jury, she skipped the introductions and the caution and read the transcript.

DS Moore: I think you have been told that the records from your mobile show that you were in the vicinity of Fulham Road on 15 January. Can you explain why you were there?

Morris: I went with Thom and Lucas.

DS Moore: Can you give us their full names?

Morris: Thom Cravitz and Lucas Radpole.

DS Moore: Where did you go?

Morris: We went to a flat in Fulham.

DS Moore: Why did you go there?

Morris: It was Lucas. He said the man had something that belonged to him and he was going to collect it. He said he wanted some help in case the bloke got nasty.

DS Moore: Right. What happened when you got there?

Morris: Lucas pushed the door open.

DS Moore: Pushed the door open; was it locked?

Morris: I don't know. He pushed hard – it opened.

DS Moore: You went inside and then what happened?

Morris: Lucas ran into the bedroom and began shouting at the guy. Thom began searching all the drawers and I went into the kitchen and did the same.

DS Moore: What were you looking for?

Morris: I ... I thought we were looking for money. Lucas was owed money.

DS Moore: Was that what he told you?

Morris: I just ... must have been money.

DS Moore: You were looking for money in the kitchen?

Pause

DS Moore: Was it money? Or?

Morris: Drugs.

DS Moore: Who had the gun? Lucas or Thom?

Morris: Gun – no gun.

DS Moore: You said Lucas went into the bedroom, did he have a gun?

Morris: I can't ... don't ... I didn't see it. Didn't go into the bedroom.

DS Moore: Didn't you know he had a gun?

Morris: No, I didn't. Wouldn't go if I'd known.

DS Moore: So why did you go?

Morris: Lucas wanted to have some backup. Knew I boxed. Thom knew. Thought I could ... guess throw a punch or so.

DS Moore: Did you see the two men in the flat?

Morris: Only as I went past the bedroom door. No problem, I thought.

DS Moore: What made you leave?

Morris: Didn't find anything. Thom yelled 'police'. Just scarpered.

DS Moore: Right, I think that's it. You'll be charged with aggravated burglary shortly.

'DS Moore, can we turn now to the interview with Lucas Radpole. You interviewed him in the presence of his solicitor, Mr Durrant.'

'Yes. We did.'

'Did he answer any of the questions you put to him?'

'He had prepared a statement which Mr Durrant handed to us and we were told he would answer each and every question by referring to that.'

Just as Peter Maynard began his next question, Marcus got to his feet. 'My Lady, there is a matter of law I'd like to raise at this point.'

'Do you want the jury to withdraw?' the judge said.

Marcus confirmed he did, and the judge asked the jury to go to their room with the usher. When the door had closed behind them, Judge Rostron-Smith said, 'I assume you are going to ask for the next portion of the interview to be deleted?'

'I am, My Lady. Mr Radpole did answer some questions relating to knowing his two co-defendants. There would be no problem with the answers relating to Morris. He was introduced to him by Cravitz, but he met Cravitz while the two of them were serving a sentence of imprisonment. It is our submission that any references to my client's or indeed Mr Cravitz's previous convictions should not be placed before the jury. On behalf of Mr Radpole we will make an admission that the two men knew each other. I believe Mr Jennings is agreeable to that course.'

'Mr Jennings?' Judge Rostron-Smith said.

'I am in agreement with my learned friend.'

'Mr Maynard. What is the Crown's position?'

'At this stage, My Lady, I accept the proposed amendments to the transcript. Indeed, we have already prepared new copies of the interview for yourself and the jury.'

'I'm pleased to hear that. We can have the jury back immediately then?'

'We can,' Peter Maynard said.

The jury shuffled back into their places in the jury box. The young woman who had made eye contact with Cassie at the beginning of the trial raised her eyebrows at Cassie as she sank into her seat.

The copy transcripts were handed out and when everyone had settled down again, Peter said, 'DS Moore, can you read out the statement?'

'I Lucas Radpole have never been to Flat 38 Fulham Road. I do not know either Mr Bolt or Mr Setchell. I will provide details of my alibi at the appropriate time.'

'Was he asked if he knew Thom Cravitz and Dean Morris?'

'He said he did know Cravitz, but declined to say when they had last met.'

'Turning now to the interview with Thom Cravitz. How did that begin? Did he have a solicitor present?'

'His solicitor was present. There was some discussion as to whether an interpreter was necessary.'

'Was an interpreter requested?'

'His solicitor said one wasn't needed. His client understood English well and was able to answer any questions. The solicitor added he had advised his client to make no-comment answers to all questions.'

'And, as he was entitled to, did he say no comment to each and every question you asked?'

'He did.'

'Did you charge Radpole, Cravitz and Morris with aggravated burglary? Were they cautioned again and did they make any reply to the caution?

'I charged all three of them in the presence of Mr Durrant, Radpole's solicitor. They all made no comment after being cautioned.'

Chapter 15

'Before you move on to the next part of DS Moore's evidence, I think we'll have a break,' Judge Rostron-Smith said. Cassie saw some of the jurors nod and others immediately got to their feet. 'I'll say thirty minutes, give you time for a coffee.'

Cassie drifted out of the courtroom followed closely by Oscar. 'Cassie, what is this about a ring? You're running alibi. It might suit Simon's clients to stir things up, but …'

Simon Wade was heading in their direction. 'Coming upstairs?' he said.

Cassie declined the invitation. 'Chambers stuff,' she said.

'I'd watch it,' said Oscar, 'he's quite keen on you. Talking of chambers, I've heard some gossip about Richard …'

The two of them ambled along the concourse outside the courtrooms as they discussed Richard Jago's plans and the future of their chambers.

'Mm, I don't know much.' Cassie lifted one eyebrow. 'Richard has told Eleanor he intends to retire. Moving to France to live with a woman he met on one of the cruises he likes so much.'

'Won't make much difference, will it?' Oscar said. 'He's not exactly hands on, is he? I suppose we do need a head of chambers. Is Eleanor going to take it on? Jack … he'd be unbearable if—'

'You don't have to tell me. I'm not happy about it. Actually, Eleanor is well aware there would be fireworks all the time. She'd only do it if Jack goes as well.'

'I'm not sure about that. He's a good clerk. He looks after you pretty well.'

'I know. There are other possibilities.'

'Peter, if he gets Silk. Or you? You seem to be able to handle Jack, make sure he toes the line.'

'You think so. Maybe. We rub along alright but I don't for one minute think I'm the one in control. Anyway, I'm not senior enough. We might have to look at alternatives.'

'Such as?

'Finding a Silk from outside who might want a move. A merger with another set. They're all possibilities,'

'It could split chambers. Those who want to stay with Jack and those who are happy moving on.'

'I know. What would you do if there was a split?'

David Jennings wandered over to them. 'Serious conversation?'

'No. Just teasing Cassie about Simon,' Oscar said.

'The problems of conducting one's love life at the bar,' David said.

'Talking of keeping secrets, I saw one of your old squeezes yesterday, Oscar,' Cassie said, leaving Oscar open-mouthed as the usher called them back into court.

Once everyone was in their place, the judge told DS Moore he was still under oath and nodded to Peter Maynard to continue with his examination in chief.

'On the twelfth of February did you receive a telephone call from Mr Bolt? Don't tell us what he said.'

'I did, and as I result, myself and DC Crawford went to an address on the Lower Richmond Road.'

'What sort of premises was it?'

'An antique shop with a flat on the first floor.'

'Was Mr Bolt there?'

'He was standing on the opposite pavement. I spoke to him and then went inside the shop. It was open.'

'Who did you see there?'

'I saw Theodore Clements. He was in the back of the shop mending a chair leg.'

'Was there anyone else?'

'Not as far as I am aware.'

'Did you say anything to Mr Clements?'

'I told him he had been identified as being at the scene of a burglary at 38 Fulham Road on the fifteenth January and I was arresting him for aggravated burglary. I cautioned him.'

'Did he say anything?'

'He said, "What? Where? I've never done anything." I allowed him to lock up the shop and escorted him back to the station.'

'Was he too interviewed in the presence of his solicitor, Miss Winter?'

'Yes, he was.'

'There are copies of the transcripts of the interview available for yourself and the jury,' Peter said to the judge.

'Now, can we read the interview to the court?'

They began to play-act the transcript with Peter playing the role of the officer and DS Moore reading out the answers Clements had given. Cassie followed the dialogue from her copy.

DS Moore: Your full name is Theodore Hugh Clements and

you live at 108 Lower Richmond Road?

Clements: That's right. I live there with my girlfriend Annie, Anne Ellis.

DS Moore: Where were you on the morning of 15 January at 9 a.m?

Clements: I was probably at home. The shop opens at 10 a.m. and I usually spend the time between Annie leaving and opening up sorting things out.

DS Moore: What time does Annie leave for work?

Clements: Around quarter to, ten to nine. She works in Putney High Street. It's not far.

DS Moore: We'll speak to Annie in due course.

Ms Winter: I think you should follow the usual procedure and interview any potential alibi witnesses after the defence statement has been served.

DS Moore: Are you sure you were in the shop that morning?

Clements: That's what I usually do. I can't remember that day exactly.

DS Moore: What else might you have done?

Clements: Sometimes I go with my dad to pick up stuff. House clearances like.

DS Moore: Did you do that on the morning of 15 January?

Clements: I don't know. Lee, my dad would.

Ms Winter: Ok, Theo, we'll contact him and see if he can tell us whether you were with him that day.

DS Moore: Do you know Lucas Radpole, Thom Cravitz and Dean Morris?

Clements: Lucas was at the same school, but not in my year. He's older. Don't know the other two.

DS Moore: We've got your mobile; it won't show calls to them or them as contacts of yours?

Clements: No, no way.

DS Moore: What about Henry Bolt or Vincent Setchell?

Clements: Haven't any idea who they are. Why are you asking?

DS Moore: It was their drum that was burgled. Do you know them?

Clements: I haven't burgled anywhere.

DS Moore: Why would Mr Bolt identify you as one of his assailants?

Clements: Don't know. Don't know him.

DS Moore: Did you know Radpole had a gun?

Clements: I don't know anything about this. I don't want to answer any more questions. Lee, can we go?

DS Moore: You're refusing to answer questions?

Ms Winter: He's told you he wasn't there and he doesn't know the others. What is the point of questioning him about what happened at the flat when he said he wasn't there?

DS Moore: It might jog his memory.

Ms Winter: Really. You've got his mobile. Now I'd suggest you grant my client bail and if and when you have further evidence implicating him in the offence he may be prepared to answer further questions. If there is nothing more, you'll have to decide whether to charge him or not.

'At that point, did Clements and Miss Winter leave the room?' Peter Maynard said.

'They did.'

'And was Clements later charged with the offence of aggravated burglary?'

Simon Wade leaned towards Cassie. 'Feisty lady, your solicitor.' Cassie offered him one of her mints.

Chapter 16

'Do you have any cross-examination, Mr Pike?' said Judge Rostron-Smith.

'Just a few, My Lady. Sergeant Moore, when you arrested my client, Lucas Radpole, you took a number of items of clothing from him.'

'We did. He was living in a squat. The property owner allowed him and a few others to live there to prevent the house being vandalised. He didn't have a lot of clothes but we took what he had.'

'I think it was three pairs of jeans and two jackets?'

'That's correct.'

'You've said he lived in a squat with others. Do you know how many others?'

'It was a big house. Probably eight bedrooms, three or four receptions rooms, a number of bathrooms and a kitchen. I didn't count the number of mattresses – they were mostly sleeping on the floor. I would guess about twelve. There may have been more.'

'Did you interview any of the other occupants?'

DS Moore grinned. 'It was a mobile population, you might say. We'd make arrangements to speak to one of the other squatters, but when we arrived they'd just left and there was no forwarding address.'

Even the judge smiled at the officer's answer and the light it shed on the transient population of London's underclass.

'Where did you find the gun?'

'In an outhouse.'

'Not in Lucas Radpole's room?'

'No. It was in an unlocked outhouse and anyone living in the house would have had access to it. There was a key hanging by the back door that unlocked it.'

'Thank you, Sergeant Moore. Can we return to the clothes? Why did you take all of them?'

'We didn't know which items he was wearing at the time of the burglary, so we took them to ask the witnesses if they recognised any of them.'

'Did they?'

'Mr Bolt picked out the dark denim jacket with the fur collar and a pair of jeans.'

'Those were the items you sent for forensic testing?'

'Yes.'

'Did you think about sending the other jeans and jacket?'

'Mr Bolt was very sure so there didn't seem much point.'

'In interview, Radpole had told you he worked with his father in the antiques trade, so I would suggest you might have considered if he had tiny pieces of pottery and glass embedded in those other items of clothing?'

'I didn't consider that possibility.'

'You only wanted to find evidence that supported your case?'

'I just didn't think other items might have similar bits of china. I wasn't trying to find evidence to suit the prosecution case. I didn't think anyone would damage property they wanted to sell.'

'Accidents do happen. Do you now accept that his clothes, clothes he couldn't have been wearing at the time, unless he had two pairs of jeans on …'

Some of the jury laughed but stopped when the judge frowned at them.

'Thank you, sergeant, I've no further questions.'

Cassie turned and caught Oscar grinning. They'd done a good job of neutralising that piece of evidence against their client. She was less sure Marcus had undermined the strength of evidence about the gun.

'Mr Jennings?' the judge said.

'I don't …'

'Very well.' Judge Rostron-Smith wrote something in her book. 'Mr Wade.'

'Sergeant Moore, can you confirm that Dean Morris has no previous convictions?' Simon said.

'Yes, I can.'

'You viewed a number of videos taken at several premises along Fulham Road. Can you help us with how many and over what period of time?'

'I think about five or six nearby shops had security cameras that showed passers-by. Most of them take pictures only of people entering and leaving the shop. We looked at the videos from about eight thirty to five past nine – the time we knew the police had arrived. Because the angle of them is quite limited it's difficult to identify anyone on them. I don't think there were any shots of anyone other than your client. We were just lucky that there was a good section of the video to enable a local officer to identify your client.'

'Were the cameras on shops on either side of number 38?'

'Yes, they were.'

'Were there any other people on those that might have come from the scene of the crime? Anyone running away?'

‘Not that we could identify. If they kept to the outside of the pavement they would not have been caught on these cameras.’

‘Because the videos show Mr Morris walking along the pavement, don’t they? Not running?’

‘Walking quite fast.’

‘The red scarf was found in a litter bin. Can you see that on the video?’

‘No. I don’t think there is a litter bin near the flat. We assumed someone had picked it up from where Mr Bolt saw it being dropped and put it in the bin.’

‘Quite an assumption,’ Simon said as he sat down.

‘I’m sure you’ve got questions, Miss Hardman. You’d better get on with it,’ the judge said.

‘Thank you, My Lady. Sergeant Moore, Theo Clements has no previous convictions, does he?’

‘That’s correct. There is no record of any previous convictions or indeed other contact with the police.’

‘There is no one on the videos you seized that resembles Mr Clements?’

‘That’s right.’

'Nor are there any mobile phone records that show any contact between Mr Clements or the three other defendants?'

'There are no calls on the fifteenth of January to any of the other three defendants.'

'Mr Radpole, Mr Cravitz and Mr Morris do not appear in any contact list on Mr Clements' phone?'

'I believe that's correct.'

'We know Mr Bolt initially said there were three men, not four?'

'He did say that to begin with, but after we took a full statement from him, he said he thought there must have been four.'

'Did you ask him to look at a number of photo albums of possible suspects?'

'I did.'

'Wasn't it clear from what he said that he only saw the two men who came into the bedroom and they had their faces covered?'

'He said he hadn't seen the other men who caused the damage in the sitting room or the kitchen. And, yes, their faces were partly concealed.'

'So what was the point of showing him the photo album? You had arrested three men by then – Morris had described going with Radpole and Cravitz. You'd asked him if there was anyone else and he'd said no.'

'This isn't an appropriate time for making a speech, Miss Hardman,' Judge Rostron-Smith said.

'I'm just trying to establish the context in which DS Moore decided to embark on a search for a fourth man. Sergeant Moore, is that the correct position?'

'Mr Bolt had decided there were four men, so I thought it only right we should pursue that.'

'The three men were charged with the aggravated burglary. Just the three of them – the charge didn't read with other or others unknown, did it?'

'No, it didn't.'

'Had you thought there was another involved that would have been the correct charge?'

'So I've been told. But the CPS decide on the actual wording of the charge.'

'Miss Hardman, you know that quite well. Members of the jury, I want you to ignore those last questions and answers. They are not relevant,' the judge said.

Simon Wade pushed a note towards Cassie. *'Nice try, got in front of the jury that the police didn't think there was a fourth man.'*

‘Sergeant Moore, you must have been surprised when Mr Bolt telephoned and said he had identified the fourth man?’

‘He said he had seen this man who he believed was one of the burglars. I wasn’t troubled by whether there was a fourth man or not. Although Morris had admitted going into the flat, Radpole had denied any involvement and Cravitz was refusing to answer any questions.’

‘What you’re saying is as the investigating officer you don’t care if there were three or four men. That’s for this jury to decide, as is the identity of those men?’

‘That’s correct.’

‘If there were only three men then one of these four in the dock is innocent?’

‘That’s the obvious conclusion,’ the sergeant said.

‘An identification parade was held, and Mr Setchell was asked if he believed that anyone on the parade had entered into his flat on January fifteenth?’

‘We did hold a parade and Mr Setchell was unable to identify anyone. He made it clear that his view was so limited he wouldn’t be able to recognise anyone.’

'Thank you, Sergeant Moore.' Cassie sat down and made a note of the officer's answers to her questions.

'Mr Maynard, have you any re-examination?' Judge Rostron-Smith said.

'Just one question, My Lady. Sergeant Moore. On the film you recovered Morris was walking away from the scene – walking quite fast, I think you said.'

'As if trying to get away without drawing attention to himself.'

'My Lady, Sergeant Moore can't give evidence as to my client's intentions,' Simon said.

'Quite right, Mr Wade,' the judge said. 'You believed Morris was trying to distance himself from the vicinity of the flat? Is that right?'

'Yes, that's correct,' the officer said.

Chapter 17

Once DS Moore had left the courtroom, Peter Maynard looked at his watch and then at the judge.

'Have you any more witnesses to call?' the judge said.

'I do have one further witness,' Peter said.

'Will it take long? I assume that will be the end of the prosecution case?'

'I don't think he will take long, and it will be my final witness.'

'Call him. I'm sure the jury won't mind sitting a little later today to get to the end of the Crown's case.' The judge turned to the jury and smiled at them. Not all of them smiled back.

'Archibald Green,' Peter said.

A few seconds later an elderly gentleman came into court. Cassie looked up at the clock below the public gallery and made a note of the time: five minutes past four.

The witness looked a little dishevelled as if he had not been given very long to prepare for his appearance in court. When the usher handed him the bible and the card with the oath on it, he blinked and searched in the pockets of his cream linen jacket. 'I haven't brought my glasses.'

‘Repeat the oath after the usher. She’ll read it out to you,’ the judge said.

After Green had taken the oath, Cassie noticed Marcus slip out of court. He had waited, as courtroom etiquette demanded, until that was over.

‘Mr Green, thank you for coming to court at such short notice. I want you to help the jury about the morning of January the fifteenth,’ Peter said.

‘I’m sorry, I don’t remember the date. The officer told me it was the fifteenth.’

‘I think your mother died recently.’

‘She did, last November.’

‘I’m sorry. Where was she living at the time of her death?’

‘In St Luke’s Road, Chelsea. She’d lived there all her married life. Myself and my sister were born there.’

‘Quite. What did you decide to do about the house?’

‘We were quite reluctant to sell it. Mother had lived there for nearly seventy years. She was ninety when she died.’

‘Did you decide to sell it?’

‘We did.’

‘And what preparations did you make for the sale?’

'It was very old fashioned and the nice young man at the estate agents suggested we might like to dispose of some of the furniture.'

'How did you intend to do that?'

'I contacted a couple of house clearance companies.'

Cassie noticed the female juror with the auburn hair start to smile and then purse her lips.

'Mr Maynard,' the judge said, 'I'm sure Miss Hardman will agree to you leading the witness about making arrangements for the Clements to visit the house.'

'As you please,' Peter said. 'Mr Green, did you contact a company called Clements and Son and arrange for them to come to your house?'

'Not my house, my mother's.'

'Of course. Did you …'

'They were due at ten in the morning, but they were very late.'

'What do you mean by very late?

'I think it was about ten thirty when they turned up.'

'Did they offer an explanation?'

'The older man, I assume they were father and son, said, he said … told me he'd had to wait for his son.'

'Did the son say anything?'

‘Something about the traffic. He mumbled and I’m a little deaf.’

‘Can you hear me now?’ Peter said.

‘Yes. That’s fine,’ the witness said.

‘Again, I think there is no dispute about this – they gave you a quote but you didn’t accept that and you’ve never seen them since.’

‘My sister decided she wanted to go and live there so she took over the disposal of the furniture.’

‘If you stay there you’ll be asked some more questions.’

Not surprisingly none of the other counsel wanted to cross-examine Green. Cassie got up and said, ‘Mr Green. How long did you spend in your mother’s house with Mr Clements and his son?’

‘Do remember to speak up, Miss Hardman,’ the judge said.

Cassie repeated the question.

‘Oh, over an hour.’

‘Can you help us as to how they were dressed?’

‘It was January and the house was cold. We’d turned the heating off when Mother had gone into hospital. I suggested they keep their jackets on.’

‘They were wearing jackets then. Do you remember anything about them?’

'Not really.'

'Can I ask you to look at Exhibit 6. It's a green bomber jacket.'

The usher searched the table on which the exhibits were laid out and pulled from a large brown paper bag a plastic bag containing Morris's light green jacket.

'Does that help you?'

'No. They were both wearing dark jackets, not so light a colour.'

Cassie breathed a sigh of relief; she had taken a risk – *never ask a question if you don't know the answer*. Neither her client nor his father could remember what clothes they were wearing, but Morris's jacket was quite distinctive and she had deduced Green would probably have remembered it.

'In your statement you said you'd sold the house and used another company?'

'We did have a buyer and that fell through. Then my sister decided to go and live there.'

'The appointment was for 10 a.m. What time did you arrive at the house?'

'I was quite early. I made a pot of tea and sat drinking that while I waited. I'd finished it by the time they turned up.'

'Do you know what time you arrived there?'

‘It could have been quarter to ten, or even nine thirty. I was there a long time.’

‘Did you wait for about half an hour in total?’

‘I waited for about half an hour. Could have been less or even longer.’

‘Mr Green, how long do you think you’ve been giving evidence?’

‘Half an hour at least.’

Cassie looked up at the clock again; it was four twenty.

Chapter 18

Alex completed some routine inquiries into a series of street robberies and returned to her desk at Notting Hill Police Station to find a note asking her to ring DS Kemp at New Scotland Yard. Alex knew him from her days at Hendon where they had dated a few times before deciding there was no future in the relationship. Then more recently he had helped her in a murder case.

'Hi, Mike,' she said when she heard his voice. 'What are you up to these days?'

'Cold cases. That's why I've called you. I've had a call from the antiques squad. I've been told you sent a photograph of a ring with a large ruby in it to them and asked if they could help you with the maker?'

'That's right. I went to see the jewellers in Hatton Garden. They reset the stone and it was assayed in 2011. They were satisfied it was legit because the owner had a receipt from Bermondsey Market when it was still a market ouvert.'

'Or at least they couldn't do anything about it. A bit laissez-faire in my book. More interested in their fees than anything else.'

'I guess so.' Alex didn't think that fitted with Abigail Vinny, and probably not her father, but she wasn't going to argue with Mike Kemp. 'What's your interest?'

'The stone was originally part of a ring stolen from a country house in Devon over twenty years ago.'

'And someone died?'

'Yes, the local bobby who went out on his own when the burglar alarm went off. Run over when he tried to stop the getaway car. He died later from the injuries he sustained.'

'And no one has been caught?'

'No one has been brought to justice for it. His widow got in touch with the local force some months ago asking for one last effort to be made to solve the case. She's not very well and wants to see those who caused her so much heartache face the full rigours of the law, hopefully before she gets much worse or passes away. So, what can you tell me about the ring?'

Alex thought for a moment. She didn't want to tell him that the original photographs had come from Cassie Hardman. 'You want to trace who's had the stone – the ring that was originally stolen – before it was sold in the market?'

'It seems reasonable to assume that whoever sold it on the market or arranged that was involved in the burglary,' Kemp said.

'Abigail Vinney – the jeweller – has the original paperwork. She didn't reset the stone. Her father did and he's dead. But the name on the receipt from the market is Poynton. Eric Poynton. He must have sold it because the ring was refashioned for a man called Henry Bolt. I've met him – Poynton.'

'You know who he is?'

'I think so. He owns an art gallery called Paint and Print in Ledbury Grove – and he's the alibi witness in a case at the Bailey. I went to interview him about it earlier this year.'

'And?'

'I'm not convinced the alibi is legit. He was very suspicious but eventually confirmed he had seen the defendant, a man called Lucas Radpole, at the relevant time.'

'We'll need to go and see him.'

'I have a better idea. He has a PA who is not over-enamoured with her boss. Let me go and talk to her. See what I can find out. I'm sure she'll have access to any records he keeps. I can try and get her to look through them and see if there's any record of this ring.'

'Ok, let me know if you get anywhere.'

'Can you let me see the files for the original enquiry?'

'I don't see why not. I'll have to get the guvnor to clear it.'

‘Who’s running the operation?’

‘DCI Colin Dean. I guess you remember him.’

Alex grunted. Of course she did. He’d been sympathetic when she’d got herself involved in the investigation of the murder of a prostitute. That had been Cassie Hardman’s fault as well.

Mike Kemp sent her copies of the files on the murder of Dennis Furnival, or at least those that were in electronic form.

Alex opened one and found a photograph of a police officer lying on the ground. His legs were twisted and one arm outstretched as if he had been pushing something away when he fell. One sleeve of his uniform was torn and his arm visible against the dark jacket. He looked like the victim of a motor accident. She searched for the summary of the incident. Dennis Furnival had been killed when he tried to stop a Jaguar motor car as it sped away from the scene of a country house burglary in Devon. The car had thrown him to the ground and despite the efforts of paramedics he died from his injuries. Further enquires revealed he had gone alone to the house when the burglar alarm had been activated. He’d told a colleague it was probably a spider getting into the sensors. It had happened on a number of previous occasions. The only occupant of the house at the time was the grandmother of the owner, who had heard a window breaking and the burglar alarm sounding a few minutes later. She'd got up and walked downstairs; it was pitch black, but she felt someone brush past her and then she had seen a man rushing away across the hallway. The bolt on the door had been pulled back; she heard it grate and then she saw the silhouette of a man as he hesitated on the threshold. She described hearing noises from the direction of the library so she retreated to her bedroom and locked the door. She tried ringing the police but the phone wasn't working. There was a statement from an officer that confirmed the cable to the house, which was above ground, had been cut; one of the consequences of living in a remote location was telephone lines that went along hedges and across fields. The grandmother had been unable to give a description of the man.

She settled down to read the rest of the files. She skimmed through the statements of the witnesses until she found the one listing the property stolen. The owner of the house described a safe concealed in the library. Someone had opened it and the contents were missing. He said he believed it had contained seven diamond rings, five or six brooches with precious stones, he couldn't remember which had sapphires and which emeralds, and two tiaras. Among the rings, the most valuable was a gold ring with diamonds and a large ruby. He had found the frames of three paintings discarded in the garden and he produced photographs of them. Alex looked through the files for the exhibits. She found copies – photographs, she assumed – of the paintings and a faded and foxed envelope in which they had been stored. In addition, she found a picture of a formidable-looking lady dressed in a brocaded gown, long silk gloves and wearing a tiara. On the third finger of her left hand she displayed a ring with a similar stone to the one reset by Abigail Vinney's father and pictured in the photographs Cassie had been sent. Alex printed a copy of the portrait and of the stolen pictures.

The lines of enquiry had been extensive. Without the help of forensic evidence, it had meant many hours spent interviewing contacts and informants. The detectives had concentrated on known safebreakers and on anyone who may have handled any of the stolen property. Among those names were two she recognised, Radpole and Clements. But these two couldn't be the same as the men currently standing trial at the Old Bailey; they would have been children at the time. Neither of the men had been interviewed.

Alex looked again at the photograph of the ring with its large and unusual ruby. She too was puzzled about where it had come from. It seemed such a coincidence that the person who had bought it on the Bermondsey Market was the alibi witness in the very case Cassie Hardman was currently defending. What was the connection, if any, between a burglary twenty years ago and one that had taken place earlier this year? Why did an art dealer buy a ruby ring?

She googled the name Harriet Wilcox, Poynton's assistant, and found her on both Linked-In and Facebook. The Facebook page was plastered with her social life. Photographs in a large garden with a white West Highland terrier apparently called Tyler. She was born in Putney and was twenty-six years of age. The Linked-In entry was more serious; she was described as an art gallery assistant specialising in twentieth-century works of art. Alex sent her a direct message asking to meet her because she wanted some advice about buying a painting for her flat. They arranged to meet at a wine bar in Ledbury Grove.

Just before six that evening Alex was sitting in the bar from where she could see the entrance to Paint and Print. She had a bottle of white wine on the table and two glasses. She sipped slowly as she watched the door of the gallery. Twenty minutes later Poynton's assistant Harriet came out carrying a jacket and a large tote. She crossed the road and came into the wine bar, looking around her. Alex waited until Harriet looked at her. 'Miss Wilcox, Harriet. I arranged to meet you here.'

Harriet scrutinised Alex. 'I don't …'

'I came to the shop the other day. DC Seymour.'

'Yes … I remember. Asking about someone who'd been to the gallery.'

'We hoped your boss might help.'

'Did he? I doubt it. He's …'

'You don't seem to think much of your boss.'

Harriet smiled. 'Is it that obvious?'

Alex filled the empty glass. 'How long have you been working in the gallery?'

'Just over a year. It's not easy getting jobs in the art world.'

'Are you an artist, a painter?'

Harriet laughed. 'I wish. No, I've no talent. I studied History of Art at college.'

'And got this job?'

'Eric's surprisingly good at selling works of art. I hoped to pick up some of his skills, but he likes to keep things to himself. I'm a bit of a dogsbody, keeping his diary up to date, making coffee, filing. Well, you saw that.'

'Do you have anything to do with his stock?'

'I do look at it and obviously we keep records of all the paintings that go through his hands. Important for provenance.'

Alex took the copies of the stolen paintings from her handbag and handed them to Harriet. 'Have you seen these in the gallery?'

Harriet shook her head. 'Eric specialises in twentieth-century painting. These are much earlier if they're genuine.' She held one up to the light. 'I can't see any signatures on them. Do you know who they're by?'

'No. You've not seen these before then? Could you find them in his records? Let's say he bought them in the nineties.'

'If Eric had them, without more information I couldn't locate them in his books. We take photographs now – online sale – but not then. I know there are no records of these in the files. Sorry I can't help.'

'Let me show you this.' Alex handed Harriet her phone with the photograph on the screen.

Harriet looked carefully at it. 'A ring. Modern setting. I've never known him to sell jewellery. Not his thing.'

'You've never seen this ring in the gallery?'

'I don't have access to the safe, so I wouldn't know if he had any rings or anything like that. Why do you think it's his?'

'The stone, the ruby, was reset in this more modern setting some years ago. I've spoken to the jeweller who did the work and your boss bought it in 1993. He must have sold it because it was reset in 2011 and the person who had that done was a man called Bolt. Do you have access to your boss's books?'

'You mean his accounts?'

Alex nodded.

'This year's are in his desk and I do some of the bookkeeping for him, so yes.'

'What about previous years?'

'There are some in the storeroom. I don't know how far back they go.'

'From the records I've seen he must have sold it at some point between 1993 and 2011, or he held on to it for eighteen years and arranged with Bolt to have it refashioned. I'm hoping he has kept the invoices or receipts. Could you find them for me?'

'Why don't you ask him about it?'

'I think someone wanted to disguise the ring. And that suggests to me it's stolen property – I want to be straight with you.' Alex wasn't sure if Harriet would cooperate with her and had decided she needed to play on her sympathy.

‘We know it came from a burglary. A police officer was killed by the getaway car. We think he knows about it, so he won’t want to talk. I think I’m more likely to trace the ring if you can find out what happened to it. Who your boss sold it to.’

Alex wrote her mobile number on a beer mat and gave it to Harriet. ‘If you find it can you give me a call?’

Chapter 19

Back in chambers, Jack asked Cassie how long the trial was going to last.

'Into next week. The prosecution has finished – depends if everyone gives evidence. Four defendants, witnesses and speeches. I'd say four, five days at best.'

'There's that drug importation waiting for an advice, and an arson as well,' Jack said.

'I know. I'll have a look at them this evening. Marcus's client is in the box tomorrow so I shouldn't have too much to do.'

Cassie loved her job, but there didn't seem enough hours in the day to get everything done, never mind have any kind of social life. She still hadn't heard from Ben and she knew that unless she spent less time working the relationship would end soon. She was sad just thinking about that happening. Why, she pondered, did she find it so difficult to make an emotional commitment? After the failure of her marriage, she had been hurt by the betrayal and doubted her judgement, but that was years ago. She hadn't thought of her ex-husband in months although there were enough reminders in her flat – the desk they'd fought over in the financial settlement and the diamond engagement ring she kept in her bedside table. Sometimes she relived the night they had quarrelled and he had forced her to have sex with him in an attempt to placate her. Did that still play on her mind? Or was it her commitment to her career that created the barrier to commitment elsewhere?

Jack broke into her thoughts. 'I've heard the results of the Silk applications are due in the next day or so.'

Cassie shook her head. That was something else she didn't want to think about at the moment. She preferred to bury herself in work than speculate about her future.

'I'd take a taxi home, if I were you,' Jack said.

'Probably a good idea.'

Cassie knew she would play very little part in the trial as Marcus and Oscar took centre stage, calling their client and his alibi witnesses. She would simply have to follow the evidence and ensure there was no reference to her client. She could devote the evening to working on the two cases Jack had mentioned. She would have supper first. She poured a glass of white wine and drank it as she put some pasta on to cook, sautéed some prawns and cut a portion of feta cheese. As she sipped her wine and stirred the prawns she continued to ruminate on her relationship with Ben. She was comfortable with things the way they were, but he wanted them to be living together. She loved her flat, but it was too small for two people. She often had two computers open at the same time as she worked on large fraud cases.

If she became Queen's Counsel, her life would alter. Eleanor, she knew, had cases in cities in the north and lived in hotels or rented flats rather than her own home for long periods of time. Would it be the same for her or did she have enough work in London? If she was working in Manchester or Liverpool, she would be tempted to spend the weekends with her family in Lancaster. Would Ben want to travel north to join her? Cassie wasn't sure Ben would be able to deal with her being away so much. She knew other women at the bar who did manage to have successful relationships and families. What she was not sure about was whether she could do that with Ben. It was a question she asked herself frequently.

She was still balancing the arguments for and against staying with Ben as she ate her meal. Just as she finished her mobile rang. The caller was Peter Maynard.

'Cassie. I was hoping to find the time during this case to talk about Richard,' he said. 'You do know about it?'

'Eleanor told me a few days ago.'

‘She doesn’t want to be head of chambers and thinks someone should be brought in from outside. I think we should wait until the list of Silks is announced at the end of the week. If you or I get it, one of us might want to take it on.’

‘Do you, Peter?’

‘I’m … I’m not sure. It would be quite a lot to do at the same time as trying to build a practice. Melissa wouldn’t be too keen.’

Cassie stopped herself from commenting. Peter’s wife was very vocal on how she thought chambers should be run.

‘And what about Jack? There will have to be changes in the way chambers is run. A new broom, you know, might be better. Anyway, neither of us may be successful,’ Cassie said.

Peter sighed. ‘We’ll have to wait and see, I guess. Could we find another Silk who might be prepared to take it on?’ He reeled off a list of names. Cassie didn’t know most of them and wasn’t prepared to commit herself to anything

‘I think we’ve got a bit of time. It’s coming up to the summer holidays and I understand Richard will stay until the autumn. We’ll talk again when the future looks more certain.’

That was something else she'd have to consider in the next few weeks. She didn't want to be head of chambers, despite or rather because she had a good relationship with their senior clerk. It would be difficult to make the kind of decisions she believed were necessary for all the members of chambers to thrive in these difficult times. Jack would expect her support in every dispute and she knew she would not be able to give it.

She pulled her computer towards her and opened up the arson case she needed to give advice about. Her client was a former soldier who was alleged to have set fire to his girlfriend's flat after a fight. He claimed he was at home about two miles away. The issues in the trial centred on the length of time it would take for him to get to his own flat before the police arrived. She began to write the advice her instructing solicitors required, but she was finding it difficult to concentrate. Something was playing on her mind about the Clements trial. She pulled the photographs of the ring up on her computer. It really was a lovely piece, but she realised she was worried by her instructions. She was breaking all the rules in asking questions she didn't know the answer to and annoying an already antagonistic judge as well. She would speak to Lee about it and get her to explain to Theo and his father it was not in Theo's best interests to pursue questions about possession of the ring.

Chapter 20

Cassie went up to the Bar Mess for her first coffee of the day. She must have been early because there were not many of her colleagues there. Among the barristers spread around the long refectory-style tables she saw Marcus deeply engrossed in a copy of *The Times*. This would be a good time to talk to him about the crisis brewing in her chambers.

'May I join you?' she said, placing her coffee on the table beside him.

'Of course, my dear.' Marcus smiled up at her as she pulled out a chair.

'Marcus,' she said, 'you remember you told me you'd heard Richard was leaving my chambers. I thought you meant he was taking a job, but he's retiring and going to live in France with a new woman.'

'Lucky man. I assume she can keep him in the style he's accustomed to.'

Cassie laughed. 'I think so. But Eleanor is very reluctant to be the next head of chambers.'

'But as things stand, she's the only Silk and the Inns do like a Silk as the tenant. What's the problem?'

'Our senior clerk. They don't get on. Daggers drawn most of the time.'

‘She gets enough work?’

‘Are you asking me or telling me?’

‘I’ve always thought Jack was a successful clerk. You’ve been well served by him.’

‘He is rather sexist, you know. I’ve been ok. I’m not sure why, maybe I’m not as posh as some of the others and he doesn’t feel inferior.’

‘The sergeant major phenomenon.’

‘What?’

‘Never mind. You’re too young.’

‘Come on, explain.’

‘Sergeant major to young officer: I’ll call you sir and you will call me sir. The difference is, you will mean it.’

Cassie was about to ask Marcus about whether he would consider a merger when Simon arrived. Instead she said she’d like to talk about it another time.

‘Of course. Always ready to give advice.’

The three of them chatted about the closure of courts and the impact low level of fees was having on the more junior members of the bar as they waited for the call over the public address system requesting their attendance in court.

When Marcus had finished his coffee, he stood up and told them he was heading downstairs to have a last-minute word with his client. Cassie picked up the newspaper he had discarded and began to read. She didn't want to engage in any further conversation with Simon; she felt nervous under his continued gaze.

She couldn't concentrate on any of the articles, so after rifling through the pages, she stood up and said, 'I think, I'll go down to court now.' As she made her way downstairs the public address system called for all parties in the case of Radpole and others to Court 9.

The session began with the judge asking Marcus if he was calling his client.

'Yes, My Lady. Mr Radpole, can you come into the witness box.'

Lucas Radpole was escorted from the dock to the witness box, where he stood and looked around him. Cassie noticed he focused on the women in the jury, his eyes lingering on the faces of the younger ones, and then he turned towards the judge. *Fancies himself as a ladies' man*, she thought.

'Mr Radpole, do you know your co-defendants in this case?'

'Thom, Mr Cravitz has worked for my father from time to time. Mr Morris I've met at the boxing club.' Radpole paused.

'And Mr Clements?' Marcus Pike said.

'We were at the same school … and, in the past, my father worked with his.'

'What about Mr Bolt and Mr Setchell?'

'We have met – or I should say, I've met Mr Bolt.'

There was an audible gasp from the jury box.

'Did I hear that correctly, Mr Radpole, you know Mr Bolt?' the judge said.

'Only a very slight acquaintance.'

'In what circumstances did you meet Mr Bolt? Can you explain?' Marcus Pike asked.

Cassie saw the man in the tweed suit lean forwards, his head on one side, and stare at Lucas Radpole.

'Over a number of years, Mr Bolt has bought antiques from my father. I became aware of that when I started working for my dad. I didn't have any contact with him myself, but I knew who he was.'

'Can you remember what he bought?'

'We do have copies of the receipts for the items.'

'Are you able to produce those?'

'I am.'

Marcus waved his fingers at Oscar who was sitting behind him. Oscar thrust a bundle of papers into Pike's hand. 'Are these they?'

Lucas Radpole took the documents and glanced at them. 'I believe so.'

'Can you look at the first one? What does that show?'

'That twenty years ago Mr Bolt bought a Georgian wine glass for seventy-five pounds.'

'My junior had prepared a list of some twenty items, mainly glass or porcelain. The first item was purchased in 1996 and there are no more after 2011,' Marcus said.

'I have seen that list and I've checked it against the receipts,' Peter Maynard said.

Marcus waved the documents around. 'Did Mr Bolt pay for everything he bought?'

'Because he was a regular customer, we or rather my father would let him take some pieces kind of on approval. If he decided to keep it, he'd pay us. My father dealt with him.'

'Did he pay for all the antiques he had from you?'

'No. The last thing he asked to have without paying was a picture. It wasn't worth much – well, a couple of hundred. But he didn't return it or bring us the money.'

'Was Mr Radpole present when his father let Mr Bolt have this picture? If not, isn't this hearsay?' Peter said as he rose from his seat. Judge Rostron-Smith said she thought it was and asked Marcus to establish Lucas Radpole's presence during the exchange between his father and Bolt.

'How do you know about the picture being taken on approval, so to speak?' Marcus said.

'I was wrapping it up while they, my dad and Henry Bolt, discussed the price, and I heard Dad agree to him taking it without paying.'

'Did you try to recover the painting?'

'We went to the address he gave, but he didn't live there anymore.'

'Did you find out where he had moved to?'

'Only recently. I saw him going into that property on the Fulham Road. I told my dad and he said he'd deal with it.'

'Did you try to recover the picture?'

'No. I never.'

'Do you know where you were on the morning of January fifteenth?'

'I went to see a Mr Poynton in Ledbury Grove.'

'Did you go alone?'

'I went with my dad. He knew Mr Poynton and he wanted to talk about this painting that Mr Bolt had hung onto.'

'What time did you get there?'

'About nine thirty. Mr Poynton had only just arrived. Dad introduced me to him and they went into the gallery. I stayed in the car – we were parked on double yellow lines.'

'How long was your father in the gallery?'

'About twenty minutes.'

'Did he tell you anything about his conversation with Mr Poynton? What he'd said about the painting?'

'No. He just said Poynton had an assistant who was a bit of alright.'

'Did your father tell you why he wanted the picture back?'

'Henry hadn't paid for it – and I'm not sure but there was some problem about its value.'

'What do you mean by that?'

'My father had told Bolt it was worth a couple of hundred pounds but then he found out it was much more valuable than that. That's why he wanted it back.'

'What had it to do with Mr Poynton?'

'I don't know.'

'Can you help us with the telephone calls between yourself and your two co-defendants on the morning of January fifteenth?'

'I think they were in connection with them helping us with a house clearance. At least the calls to Thom. Dean, well, I was hoping to arrange to meet him at the club.'

'You do a bit of boxing as well?'

'I'm not a regular but I like to do some weights.'

'Dean Morris says you all went to Bolt's address because you wanted to recover something. Did you go to Bolt's flat?'

'Not that day. I told Dean this man had something that belonged to my dad. Something the geezer hadn't paid for. We were in the Fulham Road and Dean said why don't we go and get it. I rang the doorbell but there was no answer.'

'Did you go into the flat?'

'I pushed the door, it opened. Dean and me, well, we did go upstairs. I hadn't intended to. I'd shouted. There wasn't anyone there. The picture was my dad's so I wasn't stealing. But there were a number of them on the walls and I didn't know which one was ours so we walked out again. Henry has come up with this story because he don't want to hand the painting back.'

Cassie looked at the jury to gauge their reaction to what appeared to her to be a preposterous defence. The man in the tweed jacket was scowling but the young man with a white stone earring in his left ear was scribbling on his notepad.

David Jennings told the judge he didn't have any questions for Radpole, but Simon Wade got to his feet and waited for the judge to indicate he could proceed. 'Mr Radpole, you know Dean Morris from the boxing club?'

'That's right. As I've said I'm not a regular, but I've seen him there several times. Done a bit of sparring with him.'

'You're saying you weren't there on January fifteenth but did go into the flat on another occasion?'

'I was at the art gallery on January fifteenth. So I couldn't have been in Fulham Road.'

'So when do you say you went into the flat?'

'I can't say. Don't know exactly.'

'Weeks before? Before Christmas?'

'Not sure. After the holidays. So only days before Henry says we were there.'

'Did anything get broken while you were in the flat?'

Radpole shook his head. 'I didn't touch anything. I don't think Dean did either.'

Simon sat down. Judge Rostron-Smith looked at Cassie who said she had no questions of the witness.

‘Any cross-examination, Mr Maynard?’ the judge said.

Peter stood and looked directly at Lucas Radpole before half turning towards the jury. ‘If you went into Mr Bolt’s flat before January fifteenth, can you explain why the neighbour heard a commotion and called the police on the fifteenth?’

‘No, I can’t.’

‘Or why when the police came the floor was covered in broken pottery?’

‘No. It must have been somebody else.’

‘Somebody else threatens Mr Bolt and smashes his property?’

‘Or he did it himself.’

‘You didn’t tell DS Moore this when you were interviewed, did you?’

‘He didn’t ask. All he wanted to know was where I was on the fifteenth of January. So no, I didn’t.’

‘You didn’t even say you knew Mr Bolt.’

‘I don’t think I was asked if I knew him or not.’

Cassie leaned back and scrutinised the jury; what would they make of this explanation? Some looked incredulous, but others were curious. *Glad I’m not defending him*, she thought.

Marcus then called Eric Poynton into the witness box. He was older than Cassie expected, probably nearer sixty than fifty. A large man, thin faced, with wings of white hair. He walked slowly towards the witness box. Cassie heard a noise in the public gallery. One of the attendants was speaking to a man leaning over the edge of the balcony. His similarity to Lucas Radpole was striking.

Once Poynton had taken the oath and given his full name, Marcus asked him if he was the owner of a shop in Ledbury Grove called Paint and Print. He confirmed he was.

'Can you tell us the nature of the business you conduct there?' Marcus said.

'I buy and sell paintings, mainly late nineteenth century and early twentieth century.'

'How long have you been in that trade?'

'At the shop about twenty years.'

'Do you know Lucas Radpole?'

'I've met him once. I know his father Bernard better.'

'When did you meet Lucas?'

'I have a diary entry, or rather a business card with the date of January fifteenth for an appointment with Bernard at nine thirty. We actually open the gallery at ten, but I usually get there about nine, nine fifteen, say. Normally I wouldn't make an appointment before we opened but I've known Bernard a long time. They were outside when I got there. Bernard came in. He wanted to talk about a painting. Lucas stayed in the car.'

'You're certain it was Lucas?'

'I was introduced to the young man as Lucas. Bernard told me he was his son. Actually, it was obvious they look alike.'

'What time did you get to the shop?'

'It's difficult to be sure. I would say nine fifteen at the latest. My assistant Harriet Wilcox hadn't arrived and she's frightfully punctual. Always arrives at nine thirty on the dot. Bernard and I were already in the gallery when she arrived.'

'And Lucas?'

'The car was outside and he was in the passenger seat. I could see him.'

Marcus thanked him and sat down. None of the other defence barristers had any questions for the witness, but Peter Maynard jumped to his feet immediately.

'Mr Poynton, you said you'd known Bernard Radpole a long time. Would you describe him as a friend?'

'I haven't seen Bernard for over thirty years. We'd worked together on Portobello. Buying and selling antiques.'

'Must have been quite a surprise him turning up after all that time?'

'It was, but …' Poynton tried but failed to smile. 'He wanted to talk about a painting he'd sold years before which had turned up again. He wanted to know what it was worth. As it happens, I wasn't able to help him.'

Peter handed a sheet of paper to the usher. 'I want you to look at this. I think it's a copy of a page in your diary.'

'It is and the page opposite.'

'There is nothing to indicate you had an appointment with Radpole Senior that day, is there?'

'No. I think when the officer came to interview me, we, that is Harriet, found a card. I have a card index of contacts. Bernard's card was there with the date written on it. When I saw the card I remembered him coming.'

'He's an old friend of yours. You hadn't seen him for thirty years and you didn't remember him coming to see you? Is that true?'

'I did remember him coming. I couldn't remember the date.'

'Why was the time and date on Mr Radpole's card? You wouldn't have had that?'

'I assume he'd written that on and left it behind. It's not my writing.'

'You said you didn't know Lucas Radpole?'

'I don't. I've met Bernard's son once. No, sorry, twice. The first time he was about six weeks old. I don't think that counts. The officer asked me if I knew Lucas Radpole so I said no I didn't.'

Cassie reached for her packet of mints – anything to stop from bursting out laughing. Peter wasn't getting anywhere with this witness, not that he was telling the truth. She was sure of that.

Chapter 21

Eric Poynton left the witness box and hurried from the courtroom. When the door had closed behind him, the judge asked Marcus if he was calling his client's father.

'Not today, My Lady.'

'I assume not at all then. Are you going to call your client, Mr Jennings?'

Cassie put her hand over her mouth to ensure she wasn't heard by anyone else and said to Simon Wade, 'Now the jury will wonder why the father isn't being called.'

Simon nodded in agreement.

'No, My Lady,' David Jennings said.

'Have you advised him that the stage has now been reached at which he may give evidence and, if he chooses not to do so or, having been sworn without good cause refuses to answer any question, the jury may draw such inferences as appear proper from his failure to do so?'

'I have.'

'Right.' Judge Rostron-Smith's face betrayed her incredulity at Cravitz's refusal to give evidence. Cassie had noticed Cravitz had hardly spoken to Radpole while the trial had been ongoing; was his failure to give evidence because he was frightened of his co-defendant rather than following any legal advice? She'd ask David when she got the opportunity.

'Now, Mr Wade, your client?'

'I'll call Mr Morris, My Lady.'

Dean Morris scurried into the witness box. He grabbed the bible and the card with the oath on it and then stumbled over the words.

'Take your time, Mr Morris,' Simon Wade said.

The court usher took the card from Morris and he repeated the oath after her.

'Now, Mr Morris, I'm going to be asking you questions but do give your answers to the jury, so speak up.'

Dean Morris nodded and Simon Wade began by asking him how he knew Lucas Radpole and Thom Cravitz.

'I know Lucas from down the gym. Thom is a mate of his. Seen 'em together.'

'Theo Clements, do you know him?'

'Never seen him before this case, but I was at school with Annie – his girlfriend.'

'When was that?'

'Junior school. Over fifteen years ago.'

'On fifteenth January did you go to the flat on Fulham Road?'

Morris looked towards the dock. 'Not sure of the date, but I did go to the man's flat.'

'Why did you go there?'

Dean Morris explained he had been told by Lucas that the man who lived there had property that belonged to his father.

'Did you know what he meant by property?'

'He said something hadn't been paid for. I thought he was owed money. Assumed for drugs.'

'Why drugs?'

Morris shuffled from one foot to the other. 'Lucas, sometimes, I've had … I've smoked with him.'

'Smoked drugs?'

'Cannabis, yes. Nothing else. I don't since I took up boxing.'

'Was anything said about a painting?'

Cassie noticed Morris looked towards the dock before answering. 'I don't think so … I don't remember that.'

'How many times have you been to that flat?'

'One, just the one.'

'How did you know to go there and meet the others?'

'I had a phone call from Lucas and then Thom.'

'Just the one call?'

'Several. Change of time. Where to meet. Lucas – he couldn't find somewhere to park.'

'How did you get into the property?'

'Lucas smashed the door open.'

'When you went upstairs where did you go?'

'Lucas went into the bedroom. Thom and me stayed in the TV room.'

'The living room?'

'Yes. Thom said we needed to search for money. I went into the kitchen. Opened cupboards and things.'

'What did you find?'

'Nothing. Just dishes. Plates. Pots.'

'Did you handle any of them?'

'I pulled a few bits out. Dropped them. They broke.'

'Did you take anything out of the kitchen?'

'I heard the police siren and Thom shouted we should go.'

'Where was Thom when he shouted?'

'Don't know.'

'Was he still in the living room? The room with the TV?'

'Must be. He heard the siren.'

'Was he there the whole time you were in the flat?'

'No idea. I just heard him moving around, books falling, glass breaking. That's all.'

'Did you see a wallet on a coffee table in the living room?'

'I didn't. I just ran. I wasn't staying if the police were coming.'

There was a slight chortle from the jury, which subsided as soon as Judge Rostron-Smith glared at them.

'Where was Lucas while you were in the kitchen?'

'I could hear him shouting. I think still with them geezers.'

'Did he leave at the same time as you?'

'I don't know, as I've said, I just ran for it.'

'Were you wearing a red scarf across your face?'

'Not over my face. I did have a red scarf.'

'Is Exhibit 6,' Simon pointed at the exhibit table and the usher held up the red scarf. 'Is this yours?'

'I believe so.'

'Did you throw it away?'

'I dropped it as I walked along the road.'

'At any time did you see a gun?'

'No, no, I never.'

‘Was anything said about a gun?’

‘I wouldn’t have gone if he’d said he had a gun.’

‘Did you think there was anything wrong about going to that flat?’

‘I thought Lucas was legit. Just wanting to ask for whatever it was back or get paid for it.’

Simon thanked Dean Morris and sat down with a thump. Cassie felt for him. It was a hopeless defence. She waited for the judge to invite her to question Morris.

‘You’ve said you went with Lucas and Thom to the flat. So just three of you, is that right?’ Cassie said.

‘Just three, miss. Never seen him.’ He pointed towards the dock. ‘Never seen him before we appeared in court.’

Cassie didn’t need to delve any further into Morris’s account of the burglary.

‘Now, Mr Maynard. I assume you will be some time with this defendant,’ the judge said.

‘I hope not too long.’

‘Still, I think we’ll have a short break. Twenty minutes, members of the jury.’

As soon as Cassie left the courtroom, she was accosted by Lee who asked her why she had not asked Poynton about the ring.

'You know it's not sensible to ask questions when you don't have any idea what the answer might be. Theo's case is straightforward. He wasn't there. Why start running this wild card? I've got away with it so far, but this judge is not on our side as it is, without asking what appear to her, and to me, totally irrelevant questions.'

'I instructed you to do so,' Lee said.

'I think my judgement is better than yours on this, Lee. Unless you know something I don't.'

Cassie didn't want to upset Lee; she valued the solicitor's instructions and didn't want to lose the work she got from her, but she was convinced it was not in her client's best interests and that came first. She checked her watch. There were a few minutes left before the court would reconvene. She strolled over to the window overlooking the street below. The view towards St Bride's Church she had admired in the past was obscured by a new office building. She looked up towards the sky, hoping to see a blue summer's day, but it was a light grey.

'A typical English summer.' Marcus Pike was standing next to her. 'Pity we can't see the wedding cake spire any longer.'

'I was just thinking the same.'

'How long will it be before there's no one who remembers there was a view towards Fleet Street?'

'I think I've got a few more years. You as well,' Cassie said.

'I rather envy Richard retiring to some love nest in the Dordogne.'

'You're not thinking of giving up, are you?'

'Can't afford to. It's being head of chambers. Difficult keeping our heads above water these days. The youngsters don't earn enough to keep pushing the rents up …'

'Larger sets seem to be the answer. Have you thought about a merger with another set?'

'Yours? Is that what you're getting at?'

Cassie took a deep breath. 'Eleanor doesn't want to be head. She's hoping enlarging the set will attract another Silk to take over.'

'And manage Jack?'

'And manage our clerk. Yes, that's what she wants. Would you consider it?'

At that moment the usher called them back into court.

As the jury took their places, Cassie watched them. They were more relaxed than they had been, chatting to each other, laughing together. The young woman with the auburn hair had befriended the older woman sitting next to her; she had picked up the woman's pen, which had fallen to the floor, and they exchanged a few words as they sat down.

Peter Maynard was fidgeting at the other end of counsels' bench, flipping the corners of the papers on his lectern. Cassie was sure he had bought it in anticipation of getting Silk. She wasn't so sure of herself to pre-empt the board's decision.

Dean Morris returned to the witness box from the dock and Judge Rostron-Smith reminded him he was still under oath. He said he understood. She then indicated Peter was to begin his cross-examination.

'Mr Morris, you have been to the property just once?'

'Just that one time.'

'And was that with Lucas and Thom or just Lucas?'

'The two of them.'

'So when Mr Radpole talks about going into the flat with just you to look for a painting, that isn't true?'

'I don't remember that. We went, the three of us. I know nothing about a painting. Thom said to look for money.'

'Can you look at the bundle of photographs of the flat? Photo number three, that's the living room?'

'I think so. There's a TV. That was in the main room.'

'Quite. In the centre of the photograph there is a small coffee table and on it a wallet. Do you see that?'

'Yes. I didn't stay in that room. I went to the kitchen.'

'If you were looking for money, why did you not take the wallet or at least the contents?'

'I was in the kitchen. Thom was in that room. Ask him.'

'I would if I could.' Cassie noticed Peter pause and look towards the jury as if to emphasise the absence of Cravitz from the witness box. Then he continued. 'Now, what about Lucas? Where was he?'

'He was with the two blokes in another room.'

'How do you know there were two men in the bedroom?'

'I didn't at the time.'

'A lot of things got broken, crockery in the kitchen, glasses and porcelain in the living room. Isn't that right?'

Morris shrugged his shoulders. ‘I guess so. The pictures show …’ He tapped the brown-paper-covered album.

‘Where did you meet Lucas?’

‘I’ve said, at the boxing club.’

‘I mean on that day. You said he was having difficulty finding somewhere to park and he rang your mobile a few times. Did you go to where he parked his vehicle?’

‘We met outside a shoe repair shop and walked to the flat. I don’t know where he parked the car.’

‘Where were you going to put the items you and your friends were going to steal? How were you going to transport them away?’

‘In our pockets. Money – in our pockets.’

‘So nothing about paintings?’

‘No paintings. I don’t remember paintings.’

‘Can you tell us what you were wearing that day?’

‘Jeans, bomber jacket.’

‘And the red scarf?’ Peter asked for the scarf to be handed to him and he waved it around. ‘This scarf?’

‘It looks like mine.’

‘You threw it away because you thought it might identify you?’

‘It dropped to the ground. I wasn’t going back for it. I didn’t throw it away.’

‘Why didn’t you pick it up?’

‘Thom had shouted run, so I ran.’

‘Even though you thought you weren’t doing anything wrong?’

‘I just ran.’

‘You had the scarf over your face like a mask?’

Morris shook his head. ‘Don’t think so.’

‘Did you see Lucas with a gun?’

‘Never. I’ve never seen him with a gun. Don’t think he had one. Too dangerous.’

‘You went to that flat intending to steal some of Mr Bolt’s antiques, didn’t you?’

‘No way. Those old things. Wouldn’t want them.’

‘Lucas threatened Mr Bolt with a gun …’

‘I didn’t see him do that. I wasn’t in the room with him. I was in the kitchen.’

Peter sat down shaking his head.

Chapter 22

Alex looked at the photocopy of the receipts Abigail Vinny had made for her. Eric Poynton had acquired the ring from a man called Toby Joy, if that was his real name. If she was going to find who had stolen it, she needed to find out who Joy had got it from. She couldn't find any trace of the name online that could be a market trader, but she did find a contact address and telephone number for the current manager of Bermondsey Market. She rang him but he wasn't able to give her any assistance, saying it was well before his time. He suggested she contact a man called Ted Beech who had rented a pitch for many years.

'I'm not sure if he's still at this address but you could try him.'

Alex entered the number on her mobile and as soon as she had said goodbye she pushed the call icon. The phone was answered by a woman with a strong east-London accent. 'Whatya want with him?' she said when Alex asked if Mr Beech lived at the address.

'I'm trying to trace a man who stood Bermondsey Market about twenty-five years ago. I believe Mr Beech may know him.'

'Alright, my dear, I'll get him.'

Alex heard her voice shouting, ‘Dad, it’s for you. Wanting to know something about the market.’

After a couple of minutes, a man’s voice said, ‘Ted Beech. What you after?’

‘Mr Beech, my name is Alex Seymour. I’m a police officer, and I’m making some enquires into a burglary that took place some years ago. I believe a man called Toby Joy may be able to help us. Did you know him?’

‘Toby – Toby Jug we called him. That were his thing, Toby jugs. Very popular, they were.’ He laughed. ‘Is somebody complaining he was sold a fake? Bit late. He’s been dead about five years.’

‘Did he sell anything else apart from the jugs?’

Ted Beech didn’t reply.

‘Mr Beech, are you there?’

‘I suppose there’s no harm in saying now. You can’t take a corpse to court. He had a bloke, some contact, who brought him bits and pieces to sell. Stolen, like you said.’

‘What sort of things? Paintings, jewellery?’

‘Yeah, both, and silver. Quite nice pieces. Silver was my thing. He were always a bit shy about me seeing the silver. That’s why I thought it was hot, like.’

‘Did you see who he got the stuff from?’

‘No, never. He’d just turn up with a bag with them things in. He’d put it on his stall – needed to for the law, you know. Had to be on display. He had his regulars as well, particularly for the paintings.’

‘Did he know much about art?’

‘Don’t think so. He was happy to get a tenner or so for them. Mind you, that were quite a sum twenty-five years ago.’

‘What about his regulars? Did you know any of them?’

‘It’s a long time ago. I can’t remember names. Look, miss, I don’t know what you’re after, but I can’t tell you any more than that. Burglaries happen all the time. It was a funny old system that market ouvert thing. Surprised it didn’t get abolished sooner.’

Alex knew she wasn’t going to get any further with Mr Beech so she thanked him and told him she might contact him again.

Later that evening Harriet rang her. ‘I’ve been looking through Eric’s books and I’ve found something that I think will interest you.’

Alex recognised the excitement in Harriet’s voice. ‘Tell,’ she said.

‘I found the receipt you showed me.’ She paused. ‘And there’s a record in the ledger with a price of two thousand pounds.’

'But he paid two hundred for it. Why would he want to say he paid more?'

'He sold it for two and a half thousand, so I assume he wanted to keep the profit down. Pay less tax.'

'Or disguise the transaction. Who did he sell the ring to?'

'I can't read his writing. It looks like Holt or something similar.'

'Could it be Bolt?'

'Yes. It could be.'

'When was that?'

'Looks like May 1996. I was looking to see if there was any further reference to the ring, but Eric came back as I was looking at the accounts and asked me what I was doing. I told him some research about the prices of paintings he'd sold. What sort of mark-up he was getting. He seemed to accept that so I asked him if he'd dealt with general antiques. He got quite talkative about the good old days. He'd had a pitch on Portobello and he bought all sorts of stuff to sell then. He had a friend who would tip him off about items he'd seen. Not just paintings but china, glass, ephemera and treen. He'd buy it, clean it up and then sell.'

'Did he mention buying jewellery?'

'I asked him about that. He told me he'd sold the odd piece for friends. Laughed about it.

He'd sold one guy's engagement ring when the girlfriend called it off.'

'Tomorrow can you see if there's any address for a man or woman called Bolt?'

'I'll see what I can do – 1996 is quite a long time ago.'

'Have a look for me, will you?'

'Sure. It's quite fun. Perhaps I should be a private eye?'

The next morning Alex went for breakfast in Westbourne Grove. She couldn't quite see the front door of Poynton's gallery from where she was sitting. It was a warm morning if a little overcast and she sat outside on the pavement enjoying the moment. Shortly before ten, she saw Harriet Wilcox walking along the pavement. She called out her name and when Harriet stopped, she asked her if she fancied a coffee. Harriet said she'd love one and told her she wasn't expecting Poynton until the afternoon.

'He's gone to Shaftesbury or somewhere like that to look at some paintings. I'm never sure where towns west of Winchester are – that's as far west as I'll go.'

Alex went and ordered another couple of coffees. She returned to the table and leant over towards Harriet who said, 'I stayed late last night and went through Eric's address books. I found this. Looks like Bolt is a solicitor.' She handed Alex a business card. Alex realised she'd seen it when she had gone to interview Poynton about Radpole's alibi. Poynton must have had it in his current diary.

'London Wall. Thanks for that. I've a favour to ask. I'd like to have a look at your boss's paperwork, accounts diaries, anything. Does he keep things?' Alex said.

'Obviously accounts. There's tax and stuff. He keeps records of purchases and sales, work he's had done, restoration, reframing. That kind of thing.'

'What about contacts? Does he have lists of customers?'

'Just a card index file. He's a bit cagey about who he deals with. I suggested he put them on his phone but he won't. Prefers his bits of paper.'

'I guess he knows it's harder to destroy the evidence if it's on a hard disk. Will you let me look through his papers?'

'Why not. Helping the police with their enquiries. Good excuse.'

'You are helping.'

They made their way back to the gallery and Harriet let them in. She led Alex through the room displaying a collection of paintings. Alex looked at a couple of them and checked the tiny labels showing the name of the work, the artist, and the price. She whistled and said, 'Are they really worth that much?'

'They're worth what someone is prepared to pay for them. I think this artist,' Harriet waved a hand at one that looked to Alex like a swirl of smoke, 'is talented and somebody might buy now and find it's worth a lot in a few years' time. But there again perhaps not. Fashions change.'

Alex said, 'I think I'd want something I can live with now rather than worry about what it might be worth in the future.'

Harriet pushed open the door to a dark room with a desk and two grey filing cabinets. At the back was a large safe door.

'What does he keep there?'

'Not much really. Any cash we have, some of the paperwork for paintings. Details of sales. Other odds and ends.'

'Can you open it?'

'There's a key in the desk drawer. And I know the code for the second lock.'

'What work did you have for today?'

'Not much really. Just to keep shop. Answer the phone and deal with any customers.' She flourished a magazine from her bag. 'I'd brought this to read as well.'

Alex went back into the gallery and opened the drawers of Poynton's desk. His diary was on the writing surface. She opened it and found the page for 15 January. She had been right when she thought the page opposite had been torn out.

'Harriet, have you any idea why there's a page missing from here?'

Harriet came over and looked at the diary and shook her head.

'I wonder if the missing page is here … in the desk.' Alex opened the long drawer and pushed the pens, pencils, staples and tape around. She pulled out all the pieces of paper she could find. Most of them were notes written on paper torn from a notepad, but among them was a crumpled piece whose edges suggested it had been torn from a book. She smoothed it out.

Chapter 23

The piece of paper Alex had found was covered in doodles. In addition, there was a list of names. Alex recognised a few of them: Radpole, Bolt and Clements. A couple of them had been scribbled over and there were two she didn't know. 'Harriet, do you have any idea who these people are?'

Harriet peered at the crumpled scrap of paper and pointed at one. 'Isn't that the man you were making enquiries about?'

'Yes. The others.'

'No. Don't know. We could look at the address book. They may be something there.'

While Harriet went to find Poynton's address book, Alex pored over the names she assumed he had written. When Harriet returned, she pointed out one of them. 'You know his handwriting. Could that be Vinny?'

'I guess so.'

'That's the name of the jeweller who reset the stone. Let me look at the address book.'

Alex opened the book and started with the first section – the names beginning with the letter A. Harriet leant over her. There was nothing to interest her in those first few pages. When she moved to the next section Harriet said, 'There's the man Bolt.' The name had been scrawled in the book and there was a business card like the one Harriet had shown her, with his name and the name and address of a firm of solicitors on London Wall. She went carefully through the other entries. Clements' address was in Fulham, not Lower Richmond Road. Bernie Radpole was at the top of the names beginning with R and the address was on the Clement Atlee estate in Fulham. It wasn't the same as the one he had given to her when she had interviewed him about his son's alibi. Poynton must have known both Radpole and Clements for some time. Was Bolt still working for the same company? She pulled her mobile out and tapped in the number on the card. When her call was answered she asked to speak to Henry Bolt. The receptionist said she didn't recognise the name but she would check the extension list. A couple of minutes later she told Alex that Mr Bolt had not worked for the firm for about five years.

'Do you know who he works for now?'

'Sorry, I don't. Can one of our other solicitors help? Is it a family matter?'

'No thank you. I want to speak to Mr Bolt.' She put her mobile on the desk.

'Not there?' Harriet said.

'No, and hasn't been for a while. So, your boss has known him for at least five years.'

Alex went back to the address book to compare the names in the book with the scribble on the piece of paper. Eventually she said, 'I think it could be Palmer.'

'Let me look,' Harriet said. 'Yes, it could be. Peggy Palmer.'

'You know who that is?'

'I know of her. She's quite a collector. Some paintings, but mainly curios, objets d'art. Met her once, no, twice. She came here, dressed like she'd just come from the catwalk …'

'She's a model?'

'Was. She has a flat in Monaco paid for by a lover. Or that's what Eric said. Loaded, he said.'

'Did she buy anything from him?'

'I don't know. They went across the road for lunch and were there all afternoon. I'd left before they got back. Popped my head round the door and told Eric I was off and should I lock the door.'

'There's no address.'

'I can help you there. She must have been some other time because she'd left a bag here. Eric asked me to take it to her. It's a mews house off Edwardes Square, Kensington.'

'I think I'd like to pay Miss Palmer a visit,' Alex said. 'Do you know the address?'

Harriet shook her head. 'But I can find it, I think.'

'You'd better come and show me then.'

They wandered south into Edwardes Square passing the Scarsdale Arms with its flower-filled hanging baskets on their left. In the centre of the square the trees were in full leaf and Alex had glimpses of the flowers and winding paths that only the residents of this exclusive address could enjoy. Harriet couldn't quite remember just where Peggy Palmer's mews house was, and they retraced their steps several times before they found the entrance. Alex was getting impatient when Harriet said, 'This is it,' and turned into a cobbled street. Alex followed until Harriet stopped outside a pale blue door with a dolphin-shaped knocker. There was no sign of a doorbell. Alex banged on the door and the two women waited until they heard the sound of heels tapping towards them. The door opened and Alex put one foot forward into the entrance. Framed in the doorway was a woman in her late fifties wearing a pair of sand-coloured trousers. Her dark hair was streaked with blonde highlights and held back with a black Alice band.

Alex pulled her warrant card from her pocket. 'Miss Palmer. I'm Detective Constable

Seymour from Notting Hill. I think you know Harriet Wilcox, Eric Poynton's assistant.'

'Yes. Is there a problem?' Miss Palmer said.

'There's nothing for you to worry about. I'm hoping you can help me. Can we come in?'

Peggy Palmer stepped back and indicated they were to enter. She led them into the living room of the house. It was the sort of room that looked like it was ready for a photo shoot. It assailed all Alex's senses. She was aware of a floral perfume with undertones of lemon as well as coffee. She wanted to pick up all the sculptures, the inlaid wooden boxes, the coloured glass bowls and vases displayed on a wall of shelves. The walls and floor were painted white and on one hung twenty or so photographs of a younger Peggy Palmer posed to show the beautiful clothes she was wearing. The others had paintings in bright colours, Indian wall hangings and African masks. The furniture was contemporary but there was nothing minimalist about it. Alex could see Harriet was excited by the many beautiful things.

'It's like a jewel box,' Harriet said.

'What's this about, Miss Seymour?' Miss Palmer said.

Alex pulled a photograph from her handbag. 'This,' she said, handing the picture to Peggy Palmer.

Miss Palmer studied the print and then said, 'Should I know anything about this ring? It's not mine.'

'You've never owned this ring?' Alex said.

Peggy looked at the photograph again. 'I don't believe I have.'

'What about the stone? The large ruby?'

'Tell me what is going on? Is it something to do with Eric? I thought he'd given all that up and become legitimate.'

Alex was unsure how much to tell Peggy Palmer but decided there was nothing to lose. 'Can we sit down and then I'll explain?'

Peggy Palmer lifted her hand and waved it in the direction of the sofas. Alex and Harriet sat down side by side. Miss Palmer took the Wegner chair opposite and carefully pulled the trouser legs towards her knees, straightening the knife-edge crease.

'The stone came from another ring of a more conventional design that was stolen from a house in Devon over twenty years ago. It was reset—'

'What is this to do with me?'

'Your name was among a list of people who we believe had either owned the ring or had some connection with it. So, I'll ask again. Do you recognise the ring or the stone?'

Alex waited while Peggy Palmer stared at the photographs. While she was doing that, she took her earrings off and got up to place them in a dish on a large coffee table.

'I can't be sure, but …' She sat down again. 'When I was working. I was a model, you know.' She waved her hand in the direction of the wall of photographs. 'I lived at the wrong end of the King's Road and I got to know a group of men who dealt in antiques. Eric was one of them. They sold things in the pub and quite often on Portobello Market. I couldn't afford to buy that kind of object then. Certainly not jewellery like that. Eric and his partners were fun to be with and from time to time they showed me rings, necklaces, bracelets and, on a couple of occasions, tiaras – they hinted they were stolen – they were looking to sell. As I said they wanted too much for them – too expensive for me. Anyway, I wasn't sure all of it was real. One day, I had a date with, well it doesn't matter who with, but he was taking me to a company dinner, a hotel on Park Lane, and I wanted to show off, so I asked – I think his name was Bernie – if I could borrow a few of the pieces of jewellery he had. He said I could and I arranged to meet him the next day. He lent me a necklace and I think a ring with a very similar stone to this. I remember my companion admired it. Hang on. Wait a moment.' Miss Palmer got to her feet, went over to some bookshelves and pulled out an album of photographs. She flipped through them then held the album out to Alex. 'There, that's me and, is that the ring?'

Alex peered at the photograph of Peggy Palmer wearing a long dress of dark blue chiffon, standing in front of a wall decorated with palm trees. Round her neck was a necklace of what appeared to be diamonds and rubies. She was holding her right hand in front of her waist and on the third finger was a ring whose central stone resembled the one in Alex's photograph. 'It looks the same to me. What do you think?' Alex passed the album to Harriet who agreed they did look very similar.

'Can you tell me when this was taken?' Alex said.

Miss Palmer turned the photograph over. 'It's not dated. I would have said by the style of the dress the early nineties. I was a lot younger that's for sure.' She laughed.

'What about the men from the pub? One was called Bernie. Do you know his surname and the others? What they were called?'

'Eric, you know. Then there was Bernie, not sure of his surname, and the other was called Clem or something like that.'

'Thank you, Miss Palmer. You've been very helpful. Do you mind,' Alex said; she slipped her mobile phone out to take a photograph of the picture in the album.

Chapter 24

After Morris had gone back to the dock, Judge Rostron-Smith told the jury they could go home. 'There's an issue of timing I wish to discuss with counsel.' She waited as they collected their belongings and made their way out of the courtroom. 'Now, where are we with the length of this trial? Miss Hardman, I assume you are calling your client?'

'Yes, My Lady, and two witnesses as to the alibi. My learned friend and I have also agreed that I can read two character statements.'

'How long will that take? I know it's an estimate. I have a sentence to deal with from a previous trial on Friday morning. We'll list that for ten and I hope I can deal with that before this trial is due to resume. Ideally I'd like to have speeches finished by Friday afternoon, summing-up on Monday and the jury out Tuesday. Does that sound doable?'

There was a murmur of assent from counsels' bench.

'Thank you. Tomorrow morning then.'

The judge left the courtroom and Cassie along with the others closed her computer, packed her bag and walked along the front of the benches towards the door. Marcus stopped her and asked her to wait for him at the main door.

'We can walk back to the Temple together,' he said.

Fifteen minutes later Cassie and Marcus left the court building and turned towards Ludgate Hill. Cassie looked up at the sky; it was a brilliant blue. The air conditioning in court had made the room cold but outside, despite the large office building on their right, she could feel the warmth of the sun.

'Worried about your client giving evidence?' Marcus said.

'Throwing them to the lions, isn't it? What else can you do?'

'Did you consider not calling him?'

'Not really. I think juries believe that if they were innocent, they would want to say so. It's not so easy now the directions have changed so much about not giving evidence. I thought David was quite brave not calling Cravitz.'

'Cravitz is scared of my boy. He was told not to go in the box.'

'How did you learn that?'

'Oscar overheard Radpole threatening him. He told David but Cravitz denied it. Anyway, that wasn't what I wanted to talk about. Our conversation this morning about Richard and 3 Burke Court – I've been thinking. Why don't we stop off in El Vino's and have a glass?'

'Fine. Bit early but never mind,' Cassie said. She enjoyed chatting to Marcus. He'd been at the bar for nearly forty years and as well as being a formidable advocate, he had run a successful set of chambers for the last ten years or so. In addition, he enjoyed gossiping; nothing happened in the Temple that Marcus didn't know about and had an opinion on.

When they were settled at a table in the wine bar with a bottle of rosé in front of them, Marcus said, 'I've been thinking about your chambers. Have you had any further ideas about your future? What were you thinking of doing when Richard leaves?'

'I've told you, Eleanor doesn't want to take on running chambers. Jack always rubs her up the wrong way. I have the impression she can't be bothered with his foibles. I know he enjoys a drink or two, probably too many. He says he entertains solicitors to ensure they send their work to us. I'm not convinced by that either, but as long as we continue to get instructed in some reasonable trials, I let it go.'

'It's not just that, is it?'

'The real problem is the degree of control he has over us all. He's always insisted on recruiting his own people for the clerks' room, and he pays them out of the percentage he receives.'

'They owe loyalty to him, not the tenants. Is that what you're saying?'

'Eleanor has long argued against that, and it causes a lot of friction. Jack has been very supportive to me – if I get Silk it's partly because of that. But …'

'But?'

'I do think the way we run our affairs has to change. Can we afford to wait until Jack goes to make them, or will they be forced upon us by the cuts in Legal Aid? I don't know. I think I can ride out the problems, but what's going to happen to junior members of the bar who are dependent on publicly funded fees?'

'It's a good question. Becoming a barrister is always an act of faith in one's own abilities, but it is everyone for him or herself. Do you want to stay at 3 Burke Court? If you wanted to move, I'd like you to come to my set.'

'I've thought of moving, but I've done well and it would seem an act of betrayal if I moved now. What Eleanor had in mind was a merger and she was the one who suggested I spoke to you.'

'It wouldn't work. I don't want hassle with the clerks either. I work well with Paul and we have the whole of chambers administration under control. I don't want any change. You'll have to look elsewhere. But, if you want a move, I'll ensure we take you on. Now let's finish the bottle.'

Alex's mobile rang. The screen identified the caller as Cassie. She hesitated before tapping the green icon.

'Alex,' Cassie said, 'Have you heard anything else about this ring?'

'It was stolen some years ago,' Alex said. She then went on to tell Cassie about the burglary and the death of the police officer. 'And at some time Poynton owned it.'

'The alibi witness in my case?'

'It seems so. The ring was refashioned in 2011. It looked different before. Your photos were taken after then. That ruby—'

Cassie gasped. 'The ring – is that stone real?'

'Real and very valuable.'

'Alex, I think Jeff Clements, that's my client's father, knows something about it. He gave those photos to my solicitor. Remember, you interviewed him about the alibi for his son. He wanted me to ask the complainant about them. I didn't really want to – it doesn't help my case as far as I can see.'

'Did you ask?'

'I did and he said it was subject to legal privilege.'

'He's a lawyer? The victim?' Alex said.

'Yes, a solicitor.'

'Can you talk to Clements' father? See if he'll open up to you,' Alex said. Her conversation with Peggy Palmer had led her to believe Clements Senior may well know more about the ring and who had stolen it than he was saying. She hoped Cassie could get him to talk, provide vital information.

'He's not my client. He's a witness in the case and it's better I don't discuss anything with him. Can be misinterpreted,' Cassie said.

'I can see that. I might just go back and see Poynton. There are some questions he needs to answer. It'll have to wait until tomorrow now.'

'There's one further thing. The co-defendant's father, as we left court, was arguing with Oscar. He wanted to know where I'd got the photos. Oscar's the junior for Radpole.'

It was Alex's turn to inhale sharply. Did she want to see Oscar again? Would he want to pick up their relationship again? Did she want to risk him rejecting her? Would Oscar tell her what the argument with Radpole Senior was about?

Chapter 25

The next morning Cassie woke up late; drinking with Marcus was a mistake. Attempting to have breakfast on the run she spilt coffee down the front of her jacket. She went to retrieve another one from the wardrobe and then remembered she had taken a couple of jackets to be cleaned over a week ago and had forgotten to collect them. She pulled a dark grey herringbone patterned one from its hangar and slipped it on over her black dress. She admired herself in the wardrobe mirror. Usually, she only wore this particular jacket when she went to a magistrates court; they weren't as rigorous in enforcing the dress code.

The trial had reached the point where Theo Clements would give evidence.

Simon Wade was already in court when she arrived. She took her place next to him on counsels' bench and placed her computer on the bench. 'You didn't ask Poynton about that ring?' Simon said.

'I don't want to pursue that line. It doesn't help my case and it might make the jury think my client knows something about the burglary. I'm hoping they'll have forgotten about it by the time they retire.'

'I can see that. But Bolt looked very uncomfortable when you brought it up and in effect claimed the fifth amendment.'

'Legal privilege. It does suggest he's seen it before.'

At that moment, there was a knock on the judge's door and Judge Rostron-Smith trotted into the courtroom. As Cassie rose to her feet she looked up at the public gallery. She saw Bernie Radpole and caught his eye; in response he glared at her.

'Miss Hardman. Are you calling your client?' Judge Rostron-Smith said.

'I am, My Lady. Mr Clements, please.'

Theo Clements made his way to the witness box. His blond hair fell forward as he walked and he repeatedly pushed it back. He was clearly nervous. Cassie opened her notebook and asked him to give the court his name and address. Before he could answer Judge Rostron-Smith said, 'I can't hear you, Miss Hardman.'

'I'm sorry, My Lady.'

'I can't hear you.'

Cassie could hear Marcus Pike chuckling. 'Is there something wrong?'

'Your jacket. I expect counsel to wear appropriate coloured dress in this court. I'll rise while you sort it out.' She cantered from the bench.

Marcus couldn't suppress his laughter any longer. Simon looked bewildered. 'What's going on?' he said.

'My Lady doesn't like Cassie's jacket. It's the judicial way of expressing disapproval of the way someone is dressed in court. The judge tells them they can't hear them. Personally, I thought it looked very smart. Suits you, Cassie,' Marcus said.

Cassie took off her gown and the jacket and pushed the offending garment under the bench before putting her gown back on. She was sure the judge had objected to the jacket in such a public way to humiliate her. 'You can tell Judge Rostron-Smith I've removed my very smart jacket,' she said to the usher.

Cassie began her examination in chief again. 'Mr Clements, I was asking you your full name and address before …' She was about to say before she had been so rudely interrupted but stopped herself. 'Can you help us, please?'

'My name is Theodore Clements and I live over my father's shop in Lower Richmond Road.'

'Do you live there alone?'

'With my girlfriend Annie Ellis. We met at school and we've been together since then.'

'Does Annie work?'

'At a hairdresser's in Putney.'

'Was she working on January fifteenth?'

'She was.'

'What time does she leave for work?'

'About ten to nine.'

'What were your plans for that morning?'

'I was to drive my dad to an address in Chelsea. He had an appointment about a house clearance. A Mr Green wanted someone to sort out this house, the furniture, ornaments and stuff. The appointment was at ten.'

'Did you drive your father to that meeting?'

'I did. He turned up about nine twenty, nine thirty. It's not far to Chelsea but he wasn't a hundred per cent sure of the street so we gave ourselves plenty of time.'

'Did you, between Annie going to work and your father arriving, leave the shop and go to the flat on Fulham Road?'

'No, I didn't. I wasn't sure just when my father would turn up. I waited at the flat for him to arrive. I might have done a few bits and pieces in the shop. I don't know for sure what I did while I waited for him.'

'Do you know your co-defendants?'

'Lucas was at the same school as me but he's older and I wasn't friends with him or anything. I've never met the other two until we appeared in the magistrates' court.'

'Have you ever …' As Cassie was speaking the usher placed a piece of paper on the desk in front of her. Cassie quickly read it then put it down on the desk next to her copy of Archbold. She shook her head as she worked out what was the best course to take.

'Is something wrong, Miss Hardman?' the judge said.

'Would your ladyship be prepared to rise for say half an hour? It may affect this case.'

'I really … alright. Half an hour, members of the jury.'

Cassie was at the door of the courtroom before the judge had left. Outside Lee was having an animated discussion with Jeff Clements. Cassie hurried over to them.

'Mr Clements Senior wants to know if you're going to ask him about the ring when he gives evidence.'

Jeff Clements took a deep breath. 'You didn't ask Poynton about it.'

'No, I didn't. How does it help your son's case? If I don't know what it is I'm asking about, I can't judge if it's helpful or dangerous.

Do you want to tell me where the ring fits into the case or not?'

Clements Senior shook his head. Cassie waited but it was clear to her she would get nothing else out of him. 'I'm going back into court. Theo's case will continue but I'd suggest you talk to Lee and she will advise you. What you say to her is subject to legal privilege – total confidentiality. She can't even tell me unless you agree. I do intend to call you to give evidence in support of Theo's alibi, but I'll get Annie into the witness box first. Your evidence is crucial if Theo is to be acquitted. You do understand that?'

Jeff Clements said he did and with that, Cassie went towards the door of the courtroom. Before she could open it, the usher came out and said the judge wasn't ready to start immediately.

'Lee, we've got a bit more time before we have to go back,' Cassie said. 'Time for a cup of coffee. Can you try and sort out what Jeff Clements wants and what he is on about?'

As she walked away towards the stairs leading to the robing room, she saw Bernie Radpole arguing with Marcus and Oscar. Marcus pushed past Radpole and ran up the stairs, and Oscar followed.

Bernie Radpole came towards her and shouted, 'What's that liar said to you?' Seconds later a couple of the security officers grabbed hold of him by both arms and frogmarched him down the stairs towards the main entrance.

Cassie dashed after Oscar. 'What is going on? Does he know anything about this ring?' she said.

'He said the ring was his. He thinks you have it. I've told him you only have photos. That's right, isn't it? Where did you get them?'

'I'm not saying. Confidential.'

'Really, Cassie. Come on, you can tell me.'

'Why not ask your client?'

Oscar pursed his lips and narrowed his nostrils, then turned on his heels and went down towards the cells.

Chapter 26

'Miss Hardman, I'd like an explanation for this adjournment,' Judge Rostron-Smith said when the court had reassembled.

'My solicitor is still investigating the matter, but I am in a position to proceed for the moment.'

'For the moment. I'm not having any further delay in this trial. I've given you too much leeway as it is, Miss Hardman. Now, cross-examination, Mr Pike.'

Marcus said he didn't have any questions for Theo. Nor did the other defence counsel.

'Mr Maynard, I assume you do want to cross-examine Mr Clements.'

'Yes, My Lady.' Peter half turned towards the witness box but kept his eyes on the jury. 'You've said you knew Lucas Radpole from school but the first time you met either Cravitz or Morris was at the first hearing in the magistrates' court. That's not true, is it? You know Dean Morris.'

'Annie told me she …'

'Don't tell us something someone else told you. You knew Dean Morris?'

'I didn't know him. I've never met him before this case.'

'You know Mr Bolt, don't you?'

'The first time I saw him was when he gave evidence in court.'

'What about the day you were arrested, wasn't he in the street by your shop?'

'If he was, I didn't see him.'

'He's been to your shop. Bought a few things?'

Cassie stood up. 'My Lady, I don't think Mr Bolt said he'd bought anything in the Clements' shop. Merely that he'd been in to look.'

'He did say he'd been into the shop, Miss Hardman. That's all Mr Maynard is putting to your client. I really don't want unnecessary objections. Carry on, Mr Maynard,' the judge said.

'Mr Bolt has been to your shop, hasn't he?' Peter Maynard said.

'If he has, I don't remember him. I don't know him. I've never met him.'

'Did you frequent a pub in Parson's Green, the White Horse, I think?'

'Not really. I've been in there, but we moved from Fulham about ten years ago. My girlfriend and me … Annie … we don't go to pubs very much.'

'I'd suggest you went there often enough and Mr Bolt frequented the pub as well.'

'I don't know which pub Mr Bolt goes to. I've already said I don't know him.'

'You say that between eight fifty and nine thirty you were at home alone waiting for your father to arrive?'

'That's right. I might have been in the shop rather than upstairs in our flat.'

'You have access to a car?'

'I drive the van for the business.'

'The distance between the shop on Lower Richmond Road to Flat 38 Fulham Road is what, half a mile, three quarters of a mile. How long would it take to get there?'

'Depends on time of day. Ten minutes if not much traffic but longer in the rush hour – you have to cross Putney Bridge. Often there's a tailback along our road. About twenty to thirty minutes around the morning rush hour.'

'Ten minutes, so plenty of time to get to the flat and then get back home before your dad arrived.'

'I didn't go there. I've never been there. I've no reason to go.'

'Why were you late for the appointment with Mr Green in Chelsea?'

'I don't think we were. Might have been five minutes but not half an hour.'

'You kept your father waiting at the shop before you drove him to Chelsea?'

'No. I think it was the traffic – it was quite heavy. We weren't late.'

'After Annie had gone to work you took the opportunity to meet up with your old school friend Lucas Radpole and to steal valuable antiques from Mr Bolt. Antiques you knew about because he's been in your shop.'

'No. No. I didn't.'

Cassie had just one question in re-examination. 'What is the traffic like outside your shop in the mornings?'

'Terrible. It's often queued west along the road. Sometimes I have to wait five, ten minutes to get the van into the road from where I park it.'

Judge Rostron-Smith glared at Cassie. 'Now, Miss Hardman. Have you any further witnesses?'

'The alibi witnesses, My Lady. I'll call Anne Ellis, please.'

A few seconds later a petite young woman came into court. Anne Ellis was wearing a pale grey suit and had tied her long blonde hair back from her face. She wasn't beautiful but there was something appealing, rather vulnerable about her. Hopefully she would be a good witness.

Anne Ellis stopped and looked around waiting to be told what to do and where to go.

The usher beckoned her forward to the witness box. She stepped into the box and took the card from the usher. Her voice, unlike her tentative demeanour, was steady if not loud. After she had read the oath, Judge Rostron-Smith said, 'Do speak up when you're giving your evidence. Those people,' she pointed at the jury, 'have to hear every word you say. And don't gabble. I have to write it all down as well. Miss Hardman.'

Cassie was finding it hard to keep cool. How could the woman be so rude to the witness?

'Miss Ellis, can you give us your full name, please?'

'Anne Davina Ellis.'

'How do you spell that?' the judge said.

'Which name, My Lady?' Cassie said.

'Is it Anne with an *e* or without?'

'Anne with an *e*,' Anne Ellis said.

There was no thank you; the judge asked Cassie to continue.

'Where do you live?'

'I live with Theo, above his dad's shop.'

'How long have you lived there?'

'About eighteen months now. But we've been together since we were at school. On and off.'

'Where do you work?'

'I'm a hairdresser and I work at Spinners in Putney High Street. It's only ten minutes' walk from home.'

'Can you remember the morning of January fifteenth?'

'I can't recall the specific morning, but I've looked at the appointments I had for that day and I was definitely at work. My first lady was at nine thirty and then I had a second at ten thirty. I usually go to the salon at least half an hour before the first appointment. Make sure things are clean. Combs and brushes sterilised.'

'Can you help us with what time you left your flat?'

'About ten to nine. The salon doesn't open until nine. I don't have a key so I have to wait for my boss.'

'Where was Theo when you left?'

Anne giggled. 'Probably still in bed. He's not a morning person. I get up first, take him a cuppa and leave him to it. He might get up with me if he has to drive his dad somewhere, but usually he's still in his jimjams when I go to work.'

'Jimjams?' the judge said. 'What are jimjams?'

'Pyjamas,' Anne said.

'Well say so, instead of using childish slang. This is not a nursery.'

Cassie swallowed hard and thanked Anne, asking her to stay in the witness box as other counsel may have questions for her.

'Anyone any questions, apart from Mr Maynard?' the judge said. The other defence counsel indicated they didn't wish to cross-examine Anne Ellis.

'Miss Ellis, do you know any of the other defendants? Lucas Radpole? Thom Cravitz? Dean Morris?'

'I think Dean may have been at primary school with me. That's a long time ago and I haven't seen him since then.'

'Fifteen years ago?'

'Something like that.'

'What about Mr Henry Bolt?'

'I've never heard of him before Theo told me the name when he was charged with this.'

'Do you and Mr Clements go to the White Horse public house on Parsons Green?'

'I don't drink, sir. Theo doesn't either or not regularly.'

'So, does he from time to time go out on his own to the pub?'

'Very occasionally. I don't like it. Don't have the money either.'

'Doesn't he go back to his old haunts in the Fulham area? Parsons Green? North End Road Market?'

'It's years since he left living in Fulham.'

'Didn't you both go to the Hurlingham Academy? Leaving in 2013?'

'Yes. But …'

'You had friends who live in Fulham you like to see?'

'We don't go back there very often. We've made friends in Putney. I can't see …'

'I don't see how this is relevant to the question of Mr Clements' alibi, My Lady?' Cassie said.

'Mr Maynard. It does seem a little off the beaten track. Do you really need to go this far? Isn't your best line that the witness can't be sure exactly what time she left home or even if Mr Clements was there?' Judge Rostron-Smith said.

'Miss Ellis, I'll leave matters there,' Peter said.

Cassie took a deep breath. What was Judge Rostron-Smith playing at? She wasn't exactly being impartial.

Cassie asked the usher to call Jeff Clements into court. Instead of Mr Clements entering the room, Lee came to the door and signalled she wished to speak to Cassie.

Chapter 27

Outside the courtroom, Lee was clearly agitated. 'Spit it out,' Cassie said.

'Jeff's been a bit more forthcoming. It's quite a long story. He's saying Morris is on the right track. Radpole was trying to recover something. He's not sure what to do – he's going to think about it.'

Cassie was impatient. 'I can't keep asking the judge to rise. She's not a happy bunny at the moment. Is he going to support Theo's alibi or not?'

'He says he'll give evidence, but he won't answer any questions about the ring.'

'He shouldn't be asked about it. It's irrelevant. Nothing to do with this case. Is it?'

Lee shrugged her shoulders. 'I don't know. From the little he's said, it may be. If we'd more time.'

Cassie screwed the edges of her gown's sleeves, her earlier conversation with Alex Seymour at the forefront of her mind. *It's not relevant to the trial*, she told herself, *concentrate on that, rather than getting involved in Alex's inquiry*. 'The prosecution don't know anything. The only possible source of information about the ring is Radpole's father. I don't suppose Cravitz has any idea about it.'

‘I’m sure you’re right. But what if Marcus Pike gets instructions from Radpole? What if Radpole can tell Marcus something – can identify whatever it is that’s worrying Jeff? If he starts probing?’

‘Will he though? Why would he? Does Radpole does know something about the photos?’ Cassie thought for a moment. ‘Legal privilege. Criminal proceedings. Radpole Senior has been inside for country house burglaries. Perhaps Bolt was his solicitor at the time? Though that seems unlikely. Bolt works in the City. Commercial, company law, not crime. Tim Durrant is instructing Marcus and he’s represented Radpole Senior before. I’d say Durrant was his solicitor.’

‘It does seem unlikely Bolt represented him in the past. It would be a long time ago,’ Lee said.

The court usher emerged from the swing doors of the courtroom and informed them her ladyship was getting restless.

‘We’re coming,’ Cassie said.

Back at her place on counsels’ bench, Cassie asked for Jeffrey Clements to be called to the stand. As he came into court he looked towards the dock. Cassie turned to look at her client’s reaction to his father. Theo smiled but looked anxious. Morris and Cravitz were looking straight ahead but Lucas Radpole held two fingers up in the direction of Clements Senior. The witness scowled. Once he was sworn, she asked him to give his name to the court and to confirm he was the proprietor of an antiques business in Richmond Road, Putney. He did so and Cassie said, 'Theo Clements is your son?'

'He is.'

'Before we go any further, Mr Clements, I think you have a number of previous convictions?'

'Miss Hardman, do I have a copy of them? I should have, shouldn't I?' the judge said.

Cassie handed the sheet of paper to the usher who let the judge have it.

'Mr Clements, was the most recent one over twenty-three years ago?'

'It was. I went inside just after Theo was born. I was very upset at being separated from our baby and his mother, so I vowed not to go back.'

'It was a serious offence. A robbery for which you received a sentence of six years imprisonment?'

'I served three and then was released on parole. My wife was seriously ill and died about four months later. I had to keep out of trouble for my lad and I did.'

'Alright, Miss Hardman. I don't think we need any more of the sob story,' the judge said. 'Can we get on with the relevant evidence.'

Cassie looked at the jury and noticed a few of them looking aghast at the judge. The man with the single earring pulled a face at her and the woman with the auburn hair smiled at Cassie in what she took to be sympathy. She managed to suppress her own feelings of anger. Hopefully the jury would remember this intervention and be less inclined to accept any pointers towards Theo being guilty the judge might make during her summing-up. 'Mr Clements. Can you help us with what you were doing on the morning of January fifteenth?'

Lee passed a large diary with a green Post-it sticker visible towards the front of the book to Cassie, who held it out for the witness. He turned the pages and said, 'I had an appointment in Chelsea at ten that morning. A Mr Green had asked me about a house clearance. It's something I do to provide stock for the shop.'

'Did you keep that appointment?'

'I did. I went to the shop about nine thirty, possibly earlier, to meet Theo. Then we drove to Chelsea and arrived around ten. We had a look round the house and I gave the man a quote. He said he'd have to speak to his sister, I think. That was the last I heard from him. I've written a figure of eight hundred by his name. That was to remind myself of the figure I'd given him if he rang back, but he didn't.'

'Where was Theo when you met him?'

'At the shop. I think he was up and about. He's not an early riser.'

Cassie looked at the jury; the girl with the auburn hair nodded at her.

'What you're saying is, Theo was at the shop when you arrived?'

'Definitely.'

To her relief, none of the other defendants' counsel had any questions for Jeff Clements.

Peter Maynard began. 'Of course he could have been out before you got there?'

'I don't think so. He just doesn't get up very early. Annie spoils him. Breakfast in bed.' Jeff Clements raised his eyes.

'May I see your diary?' Peter said.

The diary was handed down to him and he turned over the pages before he studied the page for 15 January. 'When did you write these entries?'

'I'm not sure when I made the appointment with Mr Green. Only a day or two before, and the figures I put in when I got back. You'll see if you look – it's what I do.'

Peter flicked through the pages of the diary again. 'How long did it take to get to the address in Chelsea?'

'At least half an hour. Morning rush hour.'

'You'd go along Fulham Road?'

'You could, but I'm sure we took New King's Road. It's the quickest. The address was up near Oakley Street.'

'Did you have to wait for your son?'

'Not that I remember. If I did it was because he wasn't dressed when I got there.'

'You had to wait for him, didn't you? And that's why you didn't arrive for your appointment with Mr Green until ten thirty?'

'I don't think we were late, or if we were it was only a few minutes at the most. It's always difficult to judge the traffic but usually we allow plenty of time. It isn't good business to keep people hanging around.'

'Do you know Henry Bolt?'

Jeff Clements didn't answer immediately. 'Not directly. I came on Wednesday with Theo, and after the trial had started I saw the officer, DS Moore is it, with this man who I thought I recognised.'

'You thought you knew him. Can you help us how?'

'Some years ago I worked on Portobello Market. Small antiques stall. This man was a regular at the time. Interested in glass and pottery. I sold him a few things. It's a long time ago.'

'So, you knew Mr Bolt would have some valuable items in his flat?'

'If I'd known where he lived, I would have assumed he had some nice glass or china. But I haven't seen him in years.'

'Did you tell your son about Mr Bolt?'

'Last week. Yes. I told him I remembered him from way back.'

'Your son knew Mr Bolt bought precious artefacts and decided to steal some?'

'It was only last week I told him. He didn't know the guy before. He was with me. Going to this Green fella's house.'

'You're lying to protect your son, aren't you?'

Jeff Clements took a deep breath. 'No, no, I'm not. There are others who know more about this than me.'

'Meaning what?'

'Ask him.' Jeff Clements nodded towards Lucas Radpole.

Chapter 28

'We'll have speeches tomorrow. I assume they'll take the day,' Judge Rostron-Smith said.

'She's determined to get through this, isn't she? Five speeches in a day,' Simon Wade said to Cassie.

'I guess so. She must have something better booked for next week.'

'Or going on holiday.'

'I wish.' Cassie hadn't had time to visit her family in Lancashire, never mind going away somewhere exotic.

'Doesn't that man of yours take you off to far-flung countries? I bet you look good in a swimsuit.'

Cassie thought about slapping his face but decided against it. 'I thought those kinds of remarks had gone out with the ark. Rather backward of you, Simon.'

'Well, I'm just some Aussie from the outback. Not used to your sophisticated ways. How about a drink and some lessons in being politically correct?'

Cassie hadn't heard from Ben all week. She had always thought that if their relationship ended it would be with a bang, not this whimper. If it was over, she might as well accept the invitation. 'Fine. Six in Daley's?'

‘Six in Daley’s. See you.’

Cassie collected her papers and was on her way out when Oscar approached her and asked if she had heard anything further about Richard retiring.

‘I’ve no idea. I assume at some time there’ll be a chambers meeting and …’

‘I guess so. Did I hear you arranging to meet our antipodean friend?’

‘Are you being a snob, Oscar?’

‘Not a bit of it. I just think you’d make rather a good pair. He’s more likely to understand your overenthusiasm for work.’

‘Oh. Stuff it, Oscar.’ She walked towards the door of the courtroom but couldn’t resist one further comment. ‘Haven’t you got another girlfriend yet?’

Oscar grimaced.

Cassie left the Old Bailey and walked back to the Temple. She was in no hurry and strolled past the branches of banks and sandwich shops on Fleet Street before turning into Middle Temple gate. She went into the clerks’ room and picked up her post, then went up to her room. She made some telephone calls and went through her letters. They were mainly circulars but there was an invitation to the Criminal Courts Solicitors Dinner from Shaw and Winter solicitors. She made a note in her diary of the date and put the invitation on the mantelpiece.

She was still a little early for her meeting with Simon Wade, but she decided to drift towards the wine bar where she had arranged to see him. In Fountain Court, the circular basin with the jet of water, which gave the cobbled square its name, cooled the still air and she sat on one of the benches overlooking it. The water sparkled in the late-afternoon sun, but the seats were shaded by mulberry trees and she breathed in the stillness before heading for Daley's, which she expected to be crowded as usual – a tribe of braying barristers boasting of their triumphs. Nobody talked of failures. Nor did they discuss their families. Cassie wasn't sure why she loved her job so much. Perhaps she too was losing her ability to feel her personal life was important. She shook the thought from her head and looked round for Simon.

When they found a table to sit at, and with glasses of white wine in front of them, she asked Simon why he had come to England.

'We need our overseas experience before settling down.'

'You're a bit old for that, aren't you? But you intend to go back home?'

'I'm not sure. My daughter …'

'I didn't realise you were married.'

'Does it make any difference? We're just colleagues, fellow lawyers working on the same case.'

'Right.' Cassie was furious with herself. She felt he'd trapped her into admitting there was something more.

'My daughter is at Oxford. I decided it was a good excuse. I planned to go home after a year or two here, but I like London more than I thought I would. There's a sense of the unexpected all the time.'

Cassie was determined not to rise to the bait and ask whether his wife was with him. 'That's how I feel about it. London is more technicolour, spicier. There's something bigger than the small town – actually it's a city '

'Where you lived. So where is home?'

'Lancaster. It's very small but has a thousand year old castle. The Crown Court sit there from time to time. We went from school and that's what made me decide to be a barrister. I thought it was so glamorous. Nobody said anything about standing outside a prison in the cold and wet waiting to be let in to have a conference in a tiny room that smelt of unwashed bodies.'

They continued to exchange anecdotes until the bottle was empty. Cassie looked at her watch. 'I think I'd better go – I need to run over my speech.'

'Really? You'll have plenty of time tomorrow. You've got to sit through four of us pontificating, although there is very little to say. They're all guilty.'

'I'm not sure Clements is. I just don't believe Bolt when he says he recognised him from some chance meeting a few years ago.'

'I'll grant you that. Morris certainly is insistent your lad wasn't there. Sure you don't want another glass?'

'I'd rather have a clear head tomorrow, but thanks.'

'Of course Morris's account is not credible, so why should anyone believe him when he says there were only three of them.'

'That's the problem.' Cassie stood up and gathered her belongings. 'Thanks again for the drink.'

'Another time then?'

She didn't reply.

Chapter 29

Cassie was pleased she would be making her speech last thing on a Friday afternoon. The jury would leave court with her words still in their minds and before the judge could make what she was sure would be unfavourable comments. She knew it was harder to change a jury's mind once they had formed a view of the evidence. Today it would be her interpretation they would have when they thought about the case over the weekend. She had prepared her speech so she could listen to those of her colleagues. She was always fascinated hearing her fellow barristers address the jury. Each one would be different, even though they had to utilise and explain the same evidence – how they approached the issues in the case, where they placed the emphasis, the evidence they skated over, how they told the story whether for the prosecution or the defence. Some found it difficult to make a coherent narrative from the facts proved in the courtroom, but she was one of those who was able to give their speech a beginning, a middle and an end. The power of storytelling was, she believed, one of the strengths of her advocacy.

Even though the trial wasn't due to resume until after Judge Rostron-Smith had finished a sentencing hearing that had been listed first, Cassie arrived well before ten. She had time for coffee and toast in the Bar Mess. She had just sat down when Peter Maynard came towards her, his face beaming. 'Have you spoken to Jack this morning?' She shook her head. 'I think you should.' He handed her his mobile.

'Mr Maynard …' Jack said.

'It's Miss Hardman. Mr Maynard says I should speak to you.'

'The results of the round of application for Silk were released this morning …'

'And …' Cassie said.

'Mr Maynard has got it.' Jack paused.

So that's why Peter was looking so pleased with himself. 'Anyone else?' Cassie held her breath.

'A Miss Cassandra Jane Hardman,' Jack said. She exhaled as he went on, 'Congratulations, really pleased for you. For both of you. It'll make a big difference to chambers. Two more Silks.'

She handed the phone back to Peter. 'Congratulations,' she said. She wanted to get up and run around the room cheering, but it wasn't quite the thing to do. She saw Marcus Pike's head as he came up the stairs into the Bar Mess. He waved and then said, 'Congratulations. I knew you were Silk material when we did that murder case. And you, Peter, as well.'

'How do these things get round so quickly?' Cassie said.

'The Temple talks and can never keep a secret,' Marcus said.

At that moment the tannoy sounded calling them into court. 'She must have finished that sentence,' Cassie said.

When they all assembled in the courtroom the usher told them the judge had requested the jury be kept out of court for a few minutes. The six barristers stood waiting for her ladyship to arrive. When she did come into court she said, 'I wanted to congratulate you, Mr Maynard and Miss Hardman, on being granted Silk. I thought it better to do that in the absence of the jury. I believe that's the best way, don't you, Mr Pike?'

'Yes, My Lady. I'm sure it is.'

'Right. I'll have the jury now. Thank you.' She nodded at the usher who dashed out of the room and reappeared seconds later followed by the members of the jury. Cassie watched them come in through the double doors. She turned slightly as they made their way round the back on the court. Marcus Pike was leaning forward and speaking to Peter but, she realised, she couldn't see Oscar. *He must be in another court*, she thought.

Peter Maynard got to his feet and waited until they were all in their places, then he looked at the judge and when she nodded he began his final speech. For once Cassie only half listened. She was still in a daze, but she caught the phrase about the number of men who had entered the flat and Peter emphasising there must have been four because of the extent of the damage. She leant forward and took a mint from the green tube in front of her. Simon Wade pushed a scribbled note onto her open notebook. *'I think you deserve champagne. This evening?'* She shook her head. This was an excuse to call Ben and patch up their relationship. Or would it be the end? Did he want a successful barrister who would spend more time travelling around the country? Did she want a family? And what about the man sitting next to her in court who she was finding increasingly attractive? She'd had to remind herself more than once he was already married. She crushed that line of thought and forced herself to listen to Peter's words as he dealt with the case against her client.

'Theo Clements was identified by Mr Bolt,' he said, 'not out of the blue, not on an identification parade with all the difficulties surrounding them, but as someone he remembered from a past visit to the Clements' family business on Lower Richmond Road. He went to confirm the shop assistant was the same person he had seen in his flat on the morning of January fifteenth and he was sure it was. It's true there are no telephone calls between Clements and the others. But the prosecution say that was because Theo Clements didn't need to be told where to go. He knew the address from his previous dealings with Henry Bolt. He says he was at home at the relevant time and has called his girlfriend Annie and his father to prove his alibi. In fact, they can only say he was in the flat above the shop,' Peter stopped to check his notes, 'when Miss Ellis left at eight fifty and when his father arrived about nine thirty. If indeed those times are accurate. Mr Green thought the father and son didn't arrive until ten thirty. He also remembers Jeff Clements saying he had to wait for his son whilst Theo Clements gave the traffic as an explanation for not being on time. If Mr Green's evidence is correct, then we say Theo Clements had ample time to get to Mr Bolt's flat and back.'

Peter didn't try to explain the discrepancies in Bolt's evidence or the lack of forensic evidence linking Theo to the damage caused at Bolt's flat. Perhaps he thought he didn't need to because of the lapse of time before Theo had been arrested, but she had expected him to say something.

Marcus began his speech with Lucas Radpole's alibi just as Oscar slipped into his seat behind him. He stressed the independence of Eric Poynton unlike the close family nature of Theo's alibi. He shrugged off the forensic evidence as just the coincidence of Radpole working in the antiques trade and emphasised the work their own forensic scientist had done in examining Radpole's other clothing for shards of glass and porcelain.

Cravitz's counsel, David Jennings, as Cassie expected, relied heavily on the burden of proof. She tried to count the number of times he said it was for the prosecution to prove Thom Cravitz had entered Henry Bolt's flat but lost count after the seventh. He told the jury to carefully analyse the evidence as to the number of men who the witnesses had actually seen.

'Henry Bolt,' Jennings said, 'was able to describe two intruders but at the same time could hear the sound of books being dropped, breaking glass and plates. He believed there were two others in the flat, but he didn't see them. Neither did Vincent Setchell. If there were only three men, one of these is innocent. If you can't decide which ones are guilty then you must acquit all of them so that an innocent man is not imprisoned for something he didn't do.'

It was an audacious approach, correct in law but unlikely to appeal, Cassie thought, to a jury. She would urge a similar one but not quite so blatantly.

Simon Wade was the next to address the jury. 'Dean Morris has admitted going into the flat with Lucas Radpole but he says he was told by Radpole that Mr Bolt had property belonging to the Radpole family and was refusing to hand it back. That's important because the charge of burglary involves theft of property belonging to someone else. If Dean Morris believed or may have believed their presence in the flat was to recover something belonging to his companion, then he would be not guilty of the burglary.' He went on to emphasise his client's good character, someone whose evidence could be relied on, and concluded by saying, 'The Crown have to prove that he intended to steal. Have they done that so that you are sure?'

Cassie wanted to be impressed by him and she was. He was eloquent and the Australian accent was hardly noticeable. It wasn't the easiest of cases but from her observations of the jury they had continued to listen.

Cassie rose to her feet and placed her notebook on top of her copy of Archbold. She had already handwritten her speech in full. It was there in case she stumbled or lost her train of thought. She really didn't need to refer to it. She rarely left anything out. She turned to the jury box and scanned the occupants. She searched their faces: the young woman with her hair pulled back in a ponytail like a dancer, the elderly man in the tweed suit, the auburn-haired woman, the man with the single earring, and for a second held their gazes. None of them looked away. She had to persuade them what she was about to say was true, or at least might be true.

She began by picking up where Simon Wade had finished. Were they sure the prosecution had proved the case against Theo Clements? 'You may like to begin,' she said, 'by asking yourselves how many men invaded the flat Mr Bolt and Mr Setchell shared? Was it two, three or four? Mr Bolt describes two men who come into the bedroom and says he heard books, plates and glasses crashing to the floor, but he never sees a third or fourth man. He describes the men he did see in different ways. He doesn't get a proper view of their faces so he relies on their clothing, in particular the colour of their scarves. First, he says the man with the gun was wearing a navy scarf then he describes it as red. It must have been a very frightening incident, confusing, and yet the prosecution asks you to rely on Mr Bolt's account as being totally accurate. The colour of the scarf is important because we know the man who discarded a red scarf was Dean Morris.

'Did Mr Bolt make assumptions about when the glass and pottery were broken? His immediate recollection when he spoke to the police who attended the scene was that there were three men. What made him decide there were four? He says it was the amount of damage he discovered afterwards. Is that a valid assumption to make?

'You may find his sudden, again unexplained, recollection that one of the men was somebody he recognised as strange. A man he either met in a pub in Parsons Green or who he had seen in a bric-a-brac shop on the Lower Richmond Road. He had described the two men he saw as having their faces hidden under baseball caps, collars turned up. The man he saw on the street was clearly Dean Morris, wearing the red scarf and a green bomber jacket. How could he remember a face he had hardly seen and recollect he had seen the same man some years before?

'Then there is the question of their respective heights. You'll remember me asking the defendants to stand up so you could see how tall they were. Theo Clements is not the same height as any of the other men. Mr Radpole and Mr Cravitz are about six foot, and Mr Morris is only slightly shorter than them. Theo Clements is five foot eight. Does that make you question Mr Bolt's identification of him as being the man with the gun? You have to be sure he is right in that identification, because there is no other evidence linking Theo Clements with the burglary that day. No forensic evidence, no links to the other defendants, certainly no telephone calls between him and them on the morning.'

She paused as one of the jurors was writing on his notepad. 'Of course, it's easy to say, as the prosecution do, that Theo's girlfriend and his father would do anything to protect him. If they are lying to provide him with an alibi, why are they not saying he was not alone at the shop at all? Are the prosecution right in claiming there was time to get to the scene of the burglary and back? It may well be a short distance between the shop and Bolt's flat, but it was rush hour and a journey that may well take ten minutes by car would take longer at that time of day. Theo Clements would have to find somewhere to park the car and if you look at the photographs, Fulham Road has double yellow lines. Would anyone park a car on such a busy road if they were about to commit a burglary? There is the evidence of Mr Green who the prosecution call to undermine the alibi evidence. What do you make of his evidence – is he reliable? Is his recollection of the conversation correct? How good is his estimate of time?' The juror who Cassie thought could be a ballerina grinned.

'If you accept the evidence of Anne Ellis and Jeff Clements, or think they may be telling the truth, then Theo was not one of the men in Bolt's flat that morning.'

She reminded the jury the prosecution had to prove the case and the defendant didn't need to prove anything. Her eyes swept along the two rows of the jury. 'Finally, you must be sure Theo Clements was one of those men before you can convict. If you think he wasn't one then your task is easy, you acquit. However, if you think he may have been, but have some doubt in your minds, then you must still acquit, and that's what I urge you to do.'

She sat down and lowered her head for a few seconds. She had done her best. Theo Clements' future was out of her hands and in those of the jury. Judge Rostron-Smith would begin her summing-up on Monday. For once she had a free weekend, an opportunity to celebrate getting Silk.

Chapter 30

Poynton, Radpole, Bolt, Clements. Alex pondered the connection between the four men, searching for whatever they had in common. Three of them had connections to the trial in which Cassie Hardman was currently defending. But Bolt – what was his connection? Peggy Palmer had hinted at Poynton being involved in some kind of illegal activity. Bolt was a solicitor; had he been Poynton's solicitor or even Radpole's? Alex rang Mike Kemp.

'Mike, the papers for the cold case you're investigating. Was anybody interviewed about the burglary?'

'Not formally. There wasn't enough evidence to pull anyone in.'

'Informally?'

'There might have been. A few names were suggested but … I think there was a bit of tension between the local boys and the Met. They didn't like the enquiry being taken over. Understandable when one of their own was dead. They were sure it was a local, but got nowhere with that.'

'Sure. Who was the OIC?'

'Don't bother. He's retired. Lives in Spain and he's made it clear he's doesn't want to know. Anyway, why are you interested?'

'That ring. Why would it turn up now? Or at least a photograph of the stone. Has something happened that's prompted it resurfacing? Any ideas?'

'Not really. Often a relationship breaks down, whether it's a domestic or mates. Could be something like that.'

'There's a list of possible suspects with the papers you sent me. Was that compiled recently? When you reopened the file?'

'You sound like you might have some ideas.'

'Maybe. I've got the names of four men. Poynton, he's an art gallery owner, Henry Bolt who's a solicitor and a man called Radpole who I think works as a market trader. And another guy called Clements. Do those names mean anything to you?'

'I don't recognise them, apart from Radpole. It's a while since I read through the files, but I think there is some reference to him. Have a look. You might find something. It might be worth looking at criminal records for the others.'

'I'll try that.'

'If you find anything let me know.'

'Will do.'

Criminal records would take time. She called Mel Haskins, who'd helped her in the past. He had been in the job for over thirty years and, although he would have been a young PC at the time, he was a great mine of information. 'Mel, it's Alex. Can you cast your mind back to 1993?'

'Long time, but I'll see what I can do.'

'Do the names Poynton, Radpole, Clements and Bolt mean anything to you?'

'They sound familiar, or at least Radpole does. Clements too. But fairly recently.'

'Aggravated burglary about six months ago. But I'm interested in the 1990s.'

'Have you checked for previous?'

'I was hoping for a shortcut.'

'I can't think of anything at the moment. Are they local?'

'Radpole lives in Fulham, but Poynton has a shop in Ledbury Grove. Not sure about Bolt, where he lives or works. Clements has a place in Putney.'

'Bit off our patch. I haven't worked out of Fulham. Avoided it – had a reputation as a bent nick. I'll ask around and see what I can find out.'

Alex thanked him. She didn't want to wait if she could help it. Until now she'd concentrated on Poynton, Radpole and Clements, but there was Henry Bolt. Did the Law Society have records about him and would they disclose them to her? She left the station and caught the Tube to Chancery Lane. From there she walked south along the lane lined with offices and coffee shops. Nearer to Fleet Street she crossed the road to look in the window of a shop selling robes and wigs. As well as the ceremonial robes for lawyers and academics the shop had a display of shirts and suits. Rather stuffy, she thought. The Law Society's Hall was on the other side of Carey Street, an imposing building with black iron railings surmounted by gold-painted lions. She walked up the steps between Corinthian columns to the black-painted double door, and through to the marble hallway. Facing her was a grand staircase leading up to the first floor. A man dressed in a uniform approached and asked if he could help. She produced her warrant card and told him she was trying to trace a solicitor. He picked up a phone and then asked her to wait.

A few minutes later Alex was sitting in the library of the Society. One of the staff had pointed out a row of books, which she told Alex were the directories of solicitors and barristers for each year. Alex searched the one for 1992 and found Henry Bolt's name. He was employed by a firm of solicitors, Doyle, Leonard and Spencer, with offices in Hammersmith. They specialised in criminal cases. Perhaps he had represented one of the three men in the past.

Alex left Law Society's Hall and walked into Fleet Street then turned right towards the front of the Royal Courts of Justice. There were a group of protesters around the main entrance and she began to weave her way through them. She hadn't got very far when somebody grabbed her arm and said, 'Alex.' She turned and looked into the dark brown eyes of Oscar Davenport. 'What are you doing here?' he said.

'I'm on my way back to the station. I've been … well, it doesn't matter. Has your trial finished – the Radpole case?'

'Not yet. I had a case in the Court of Appeal this morning and I'm on my way back to the Bailey otherwise I'd take you to lunch.'

'You haven't asked me and I haven't agreed.'

'But on a theoretical basis if I asked you to have lunch would you agree, or do you still think I'm a drug dealer?'

'I … guess I would.'

Oscar wheeled round. 'Great. I'll pick you up tomorrow, twelve noon.'

Back at the station, Alex found a handwritten note from Mel Haskins suggesting she rang a Sergeant Baker. There was a telephone number for a landline but no mobile or email address. She rang the number. The voice that answered had a Scottish accent.

'Sergeant Baker?' Alex said.

'Retired. Andy Baker. Who are you?'

'DC Alex Seymour. Mel Haskins suggested I contact you.'

'Young Mel. Thought he'd have packed it in by now. Anyway, what can I do for you?'

'I'm interested in a solicitor called Henry Bolt. At one time he worked for …'

'Doyle, Leonard and Spencer. I remember him. Clever man. Can't say he was dishonest but, well, slippery. Know what I mean?'

'Not to be trusted.'

'Ay, not to be trusted. What's he up to now?'

'Given up working the criminal courts,' Alex said. 'Commercial specialists in the City now.'

'That's not giving up crime. Just working for the buggers who get away with it. Not like the poor sods we had at West London when I was custody sergeant there. There were one or two tasty lads, mind. They probably found crime paid.'

'Such as?'

‘There was a cat burglar lived in the patch. Did the hotels in Park Lane. Can’t recall the name now. Had an Old English Sheepdog called Elvis. Funny you can remember the name of dogs but not people. And then there was another who did country houses, silver, paintings, anything he could get rid of in the markets.’

Alex was reluctant to stop the retired copper from reminiscing, but she didn’t have all day. ‘Do the names Poynton, Radpole or Clements ring any bells?’

‘Radpole. That’s the one. Getaway driver for a couple of real villains when he was younger. Got done a couple of times for driving offences. CID couldn’t pin anything more serious on him. At least not to begin with. I don’t remember Clements.’

‘Who was Radpole’s brief?’

‘There were only two who turned up regular. One was Henry Bolt. The other was called Roberts. A couple of women were regulars as well. Don’t remember their names.’

‘Did Henry Bolt represent Radpole?’

‘Can’t be sure if he did or it was the other bloke. Not the women.’

Alex thanked him and finished the call.

Where was she to go from here? She’d just have to wait until she got the result of her request to the Criminal Records Office. She closed her eyes; this wasn't her problem. She wasn't investigating the murder of a police officer. Nor was it any concern of hers why Cassie had been given the photographs. She'd go home, have a glass of whisky and a hot bath, take her mind off work. She gathered her coat and bag and walked out of the station. Her thoughts turned to the next day and the luncheon date with Oscar.

Chapter 31

What a day. Cassie was still on a high. She'd refused to join in the party atmosphere that pervaded 3 Burke Court, preferring to hug her delight to herself. She let herself into the white stuccoed house and bounded up the stairs. Once she had recovered her breath, she found Ben's contact details on her phone and tapped the little green icon. Ben answered after a couple of rings. 'Cassie, how—'

She didn't let him finish. 'I've got a bottle of champagne in the fridge. I'd like you to come and celebrate with me.'

'Won another case?'

'No, well not yet. I've been awarded Silk. I can't believe it. I thought I was a bit young but …'

'And you want me to drink to your success?'

She detected the lack of enthusiasm in his voice. 'Please. I've left a party in chambers to be with you. I know – well, things have been a little strained, but this is such an important step …'

'In your career.' There was a pause. She heard what she took to be a long sigh. 'I've got somethings to wrap up here and then I'll be with you.'

'Great. See you soon.'

Now for her parents. They at least would be thrilled for her. Her mother answered the phone.

'Mum, I've got some great news …'

'You're getting married to Ben. He's such a nice young man. That's great. Your dad will be so pleased for you. Have you decided where you'll have the …?'

'Mum. No, no. It's not Ben. I've been awarded Silk.'

'Oh, I thought …'

'Well, you shouldn't. Getting made a Queen's Counsel is absolutely great. I've wanted it for years. Such a big step forward.'

'What difference will it make?'

'I'll wear a different gown. They used to be made of silk. That's where the name comes from. Taking silk. More money, probably, but also not doing quite so many cases. Longer and more difficult. I hope I'll be able to come and see you all more often.'

'You'll be too important for us.'

'Don't say that, Mum. You're the most important people in my life, you and Dad.'

'Do you want to speak to him?'

'Please,' said Cassie.

She told her father her news and as she had anticipated he was clearly pleased for her.

'Don't take no notice of your mum. She just wants you to be happy and settled. A family of your own. More grandchildren.'

'I know, but I've worked so hard for a long time and I don't know that I can give it up. Not now. Amanda has two children – Mum sees them all the time. I won't come back north to live. My life is here … in London.'

She went on to tell him that the day she was sworn in she and Peter would be holding a party and she hoped they would come to London for that.

'I'll tell your mother. Not sure it's our kind of thing.'

'I won't take no for an answer, Dad. You have to be here. I owe you and Mum so much. I have to go. I have a friend coming over. Love you both.'

She thought about her parents sitting down to what they would call tea at the tiny table in the kitchen. The place would smell of her mother's baking, the cakes she made to supplement her dad's income as an electrician. Her mother had planned for her to go to catering college, take over the small business and expand it. They would joke about Hardman Cakes. Cassie's headteacher had suggested she might like to go to university and after a day at Lancaster Crown Court she had been obsessed by being a lawyer, defending the weak, vulnerable and inarticulate against the might of the state. Now she thought that was rather a romantic view of her work, but whoever the defendant and whatever they had done they were entitled to a fair trial.

In the kitchen she found some smoked salmon and a tin of caviar and quickly made some canapes. She went to get changed into something a little less formal than her black suit. She selected a pair of cream harem-style trousers to wear with a yellow sweater but decided against the trousers and chose to wear a pair of white chinos instead. Before she could put them on, her mobile rang. She didn't recognise the number but she did the voice, who asked her why she wasn't joining the party in Daley's. The Australian accent was unmistakable.

'I told you earlier, I have something else to do,' she said.

'Pity, I was looking forward to kissing one of Her Majesties Counsel.'

'You're drunk, Simon.'

'No, just horny.'

'Get lost.' She tapped the red button.

She finished dressing and sprayed on her favourite perfume – basil and lime. Ten minutes later her doorbell rang and she let Ben in. He was holding a beautiful posy which he handed to her.

'Congratulations. You must be thrilled.'

'Euphoric. I have to keep pinching myself. You are pleased for me, aren't you? I thought you were …'

'A little churlish. Yes, I was.' He took a deep breath. 'I don't want to spoil your day. Just. I can't help wondering where it leaves us. For the moment, let's open that bottle and drink to your success.'

Cassie took the bottle from the fridge and handed it to him.

'What does it mean for you?' he said.

'I won't get sent to Inner London Crown Court on a wet Friday to do a list of hopeless pleas in mitigation. No, seriously. I'll have more important cases and won't have to do the running around for the more trivial stuff unless it's privately paid. But …'

'But?'

'I'm more likely to have to spend time outside London at other courts. Often Silks don't get home apart from at weekends for weeks at a time.'

Ben grimaced and poured himself another glass.

Cassie's mobile rang again. She hoped it wasn't Simon propositioning her. A woman's voice said, 'Congratulations, Cassie. You're the first of my pupils to get Silk.'

Cassie sat down on the green Chesterfield. 'Thank you. I can't believe it really.'

'I checked the list in *The Times* this morning. And Peter as well. Jack will be over the moon. Four Silks and their incomes.'

'There won't be four. Richard is retiring and moving to France.'

'Nowhere near me, I hope. So, a vacancy as head of chambers.'

Cassie told her pupil mistress about Richard's holiday romance and how he decided to give up working. She went on to discuss the problems of finding a new head of chambers. As she was talking, she was watching Ben. He finished the wine in his glass, put the glass down on the table and slipped out of the door. 'Can you just hold on a minute,' she said and ran to the top of the stairs. She called out his name.

He stopped and turned to look up at her. 'Enjoy. It's your career.'

Chapter 32

Alex heard the sound of Oscar's Porsche before the doorbell rang. She pushed the button to unlock the entrance to the block of flats, opened her own door and waited for him to climb the stairs. He bounded up them, smiled at her and kissed her on both cheeks. 'We have some catching up to do,' he said as he took her hand. 'Let's go for lunch. I've booked a table at Petersham Nurseries. It's too nice a day to spend in the city. We can go for a walk along the river after we've eaten.'

'Sounds good,' Alex said.

'I see your bike's gone,' Oscar said as they walked to his car.

'I never seem to get the time to ride it. Paying for a residents' parking permit was a waste. I took it to my mother's and it's in the garage there.'

'It wasn't that you were getting too old for it?'

'Definitely not.'

Oscar opened the roof of the car and went quiet. The traffic was quite heavy for a Saturday lunchtime, the fine weather drawing people out towards the parks and gardens of West London, Alex thought. Oscar was concentrating on making his way towards

Richmond; she watched him. He wasn't particularly handsome – a straight nose, a slight upturn to his lips and dark brown eyes. His hands, clutching the steering wheel, were strong and long fingered. She shivered as she remembered him touching her.

'Cold?' he said.

'No. Not at all.' She was surprised he'd noticed. Despite her reply he slowed down to reduce the wind caused by the speed of the car.

The route to the restaurant was familiar to Alex. It was the way to her parents' home. Now only her mother lived there. She felt guilty she hadn't been to visit her for a couple of months. When her mother remarried Alex didn't feel as welcome and she had stopped going as often.

The restaurant was in the grounds of the nurseries, glass roofed with bougainvillea hanging over the tables. They sat at the end of one of the long tables. Alex studied the menu, unable to make up her mind what to order, putting off the moment she would have to talk to Oscar. He reached out a hand and touched hers. The waitress appeared and Oscar ordered a langoustine salad for them both and glasses of rosé wine. 'Now, where were we when we were so rudely interrupted.'

Alex burst out laughing as he continued, 'Do you still think I was part of the drug-dealing gang?'

'It did look a bit that way.'

'The suspicious mind of a police officer. I'll admit to having the odd wrap of coke, and I did know they were using the empty printworks. They knocked a bit off the price for me. I thought of spilling the beans, but I'd have a lot of explaining to do. I didn't want to be involved. I was stunned when they were all arrested. All you coppers racing down the street. I hadn't realised they were storing such a large quantity there. Being interviewed shocked me. I've given up being the black sheep of the family.'

Alex didn't want to talk about that incident. 'Have you brothers and sisters?' she said.

'Two brothers. Older than me. One is in the City and the other is something in property in the States. I'm the only one following in the old man's footsteps.'

'But you're not very enthusiastic about it?'

'Nepotism is rife at the bar. I chose to do criminal defence work rather than commercial law in the hope I could make my own way. At least this way I'm among the worthies, although I distrust my motives.'

'The worthies?'

'It's what barristers working in commercial fields call those of us who do Legal Aid work. You know, over the door of the Old Bailey. Defending the poor. You've not been promoted yet?'

'I'm afraid my run-in with some senior officers hasn't done me any favours.'

'Shouldn't get involved with Cassie Hardman. Dangerous woman.'

Alex looked away. 'Still not a fan of hers?'

'Has she talked to you about these photographs? It's a bit naughty being in touch with the person who interviewed the alibi witnesses.'

Alex was relieved when her mobile rang. She saw the caller was her father and decided to answer it. When he extended an invitation to supper, she asked Oscar if he would like to meet her father. He said he would, and she arranged to be at her father's flat in Embassy Gardens at six thirty.

The evening was a success. Her father was at his expansive best and Oscar responded with some style. On the way back to her flat she got a text from her father.

'Your mother would approve.'

She replied, *'The one thing that puts me off.'*

'Important?' Oscar said. 'I hope you've not been called back to work.'

'No, just from Dad. I've thanked him for supper.'

They arrived outside her apartment block at nine thirty. 'Early night?' Oscar said as he helped her out of the car.

'If you want?'

'I haven't brought a toothbrush.'

'I can find you one.'

The next morning, she made herself a cup of tea and sat at the end of her bed. Oscar was still asleep. He looked boyish, his dark hair tousled and his lips in a slight smile. She was enjoying watching him sleep when her mobile pinged. It was a text from Cassie Hardman asking her to make contact. *'I'm around all day.'*

Oscar must have heard the phone because his eyes opened. 'Was that the station wanting you back on duty?'

She shook her head. He sat up and took her arm, pulling her back down onto the bed. After they'd made love again, he said, 'I hope the call wasn't important?'

'It was Cassie Hardman,' she said.

'About those photos. No one knows what it's all about.'

'The ring …'

'She's asked you for information? I don't think Cassie knows why she's got them. My client's father was really upset when she asked Bolt about it.'

'Bolt? Who …'

'He's the occupier of the flat this little gang broke into.'

Chapter 33

Cassie walked to her Sunday luncheon engagement with Eleanor Hesketh at the Belvedere in Holland Park. In Holland Walk she paused for a moment close to the gate next to the Youth Hostel and remembered the young woman whose body had been found close by. She had been stabbed to death by the man who supplied her with drugs. An innocent man had nearly been convicted for her murder, but Cassie's persistence had led the police to the real killer. She was reminded of Alex Seymour and the call she had made to her earlier, and wondered why Alex had not yet called her back.

Inside the gate were the remains of Holland House and alongside it the white canopy covering the auditorium for the opera productions held there in the summer. Every year she promised herself she would go, but the best she had managed was to sit outside on a warm summer's evening and listen to some part of the production.

Eleanor was already at their table. Instead of the regulation black she was wearing a brightly coloured dress. She looked much less severe, particularly as her red hair wasn't pulled back from her face. She beckoned Cassie over. 'I've ordered two glasses of champagne to begin with. We should celebrate your appointment. It goes without saying I'm delighted.'

'Thank you. I can hardly believe it. It's kind of you to invite me to lunch.'

'I was surprised you were able to come. I thought you would be tied up. There was a man in your life?'

'He's not too keen on my career at the moment. Thinks I spend all my time working and not enough with him.'

'It can be difficult maintaining relationships. One has only to think of the men you know who are divorced. It is getting easier, but I don't know how it will pan out for the recently qualified if the fees get too low to afford childcare or boarding school.'

Cassie thought there was a faraway look in Eleanor's eyes.

'In addition to congratulating you, I wanted to talk about the problem Richard's leaving causes. Marcus Pike is in the same trial as you,' Eleanor said.

'I have spoken to him, as you suggested, but he doesn't want to take on Burke Court as well. He thinks if you canvassed support for a merger with the prospect of Jack being replaced there would be a split.'

Eleanor frowned. 'Have you got any ideas about where we go from here? Jack never wants to listen to me. Of course, there's no reason for him to do so. He knows Richard will back him up.'

'And others. Eleanor, what is the problem with Jack? He's a misogynist but he gives in most of the time.'

There was a pause. 'I threatened reporting him to the Legal Aid authorities for fraud,' Eleanor said. 'I'd just received payment for a long VAT fraud. The case had taken four weeks and my junior – not someone still in chambers – had appeared on the first day and then gone off to another trial in Leeds. He'd been very sure his other case would plead so he'd be back in a day or so. Or that's what he told me. I never saw him again. The client was a professional villain and the solicitors rarely sent a clerk to sit behind me. I insisted Jack get one of the pupils to take the place of the junior for the rest of the trial. When I suggested to Jack the tenant should pay the pupil the refresher, Jack said he would speak to the person concerned. I then found out he'd submitted fees not just for reading the brief and the first day but for the rest of the trial as if he'd been present. Then about two weeks later the same tenant didn't provide an advice in another case in which I was leading him. The solicitors took the case away from him and me. It left a big hole in my diary and a considerable loss of income. I tackled Jack and he made some excuse as to why the advice hadn't been forthcoming. I told him I thought the tenant was lazy as well as dishonest and Jack had been a party to a fraud on the Legal Aid fund. And, I said, if the pupil wasn't paid for her work, I would report him to the authorities. He knew I wouldn't. You wouldn't want an investigation into chambers. No one would. But I wasn't flavour of the month and we've never got on since.'

'But he's not stupid and he knows times are hard, particularly for the more junior tenants. He won't want to lose three Silks. If we can agree some sort of deal that satisfies him and us, we can put it to him. We'd have to stay united and be sure the majority of chambers backed us,' Cassie said.

'Would you go to another set? I guess Marcus would have you there. Has he offered that?'

'Yes. And not just for me. I'd prefer to stay at 3 Burke Court but …'

'It's quite reassuring to know you could go somewhere else. But it's such an upheaval.'

'Let's go through the list of tenants and work out who would side with Jack. I know Courtney will be happy when Richard goes. He thinks chambers would be more diverse,' Cassie said.

They worked their way through the thirty-three tenants from the most senior to the most recent recruit.

'It comes down to those who are afraid they'd lose too much if Jack left or became difficult with them,' Eleanor said.

'I think twenty-five would want to change the way the clerks' room operates. They'd be happy to have more tenants and probably share desks. That leaves eight who would be against any change in the current arrangements or would be reluctant. I think we need to approach each one separately and see how they might jump,' Cassie said.

'I'd start by asking them about the preparation of accounts. I was astonished by what I discovered when I was acting head,' Eleanor said.

'Such as?'

'Non-payment of rent. Behind with clerk's fees.'

'I'm surprised Jack lets anyone get away without paying him.'

'When I asked him about it, he just brushed it off. Said sometimes tenants got into difficulties, misjudged when they would get paid and had tax bills to meet. I tackled Richard and he said it was down to Jack. I don't mind the clerks' fees as much as the rent. We have to pay that every quarter and if there isn't sufficient money we have to borrow. I don't believe chambers as a whole should, in effect, be paying for an individual tenant's overdraft.'

'Has that happened?'

'Not yet. But if it isn't sorted and soon, it will. I don't want the responsibility.'

Cassie sat back in her chair. 'So, what do we do?'

'We talk to every tenant and suggest we have accounts prepared. If we split them up, we can get some feeling for who will support us and who won't. I'll deal with the problem ones and if you take the bottom half of chambers. Most of them will cotton on to what it's really about. Having proper accounts is the first step to taking more control of Jack. We don't want them talking to him, so we'd better swear them to secrecy.'

'Even if they agree to not tell anybody else, it will get out. As Marcus said there are no secrets in the Temple.'

Chapter 34

Not long after Oscar had left her flat on Sunday morning, Alex got a call from Cassie. 'I rang earlier. I was hoping you'd call me if you had any news about the photos.'

'You didn't tell me who the victim was in this trial you're doing. I understand it's Henry Bolt.

'Complainant. Is it important?' Cassie said.

'You asked him about the ring?'

'How did you know? Never mind. He wouldn't say anything. Claimed it was covered by legal privilege.'

'He had the stone reset. Originally it was in a different ring. A ring stolen in a burglary years ago. A policeman was killed by the getaway car. The case is being looked at again. Your client's father and Radpole's were in the frame but there was never sufficient evidence to arrest them and interview them.'

'No DNA?'

'There was never anything to compare any samples from the scene with.'

'But you have now,' Cassie said. 'Both Lucas Radpole and Theo Clements would have provided swabs when they were arrested for this burglary. The forensic scientists could do a comparison with those.'

Alex didn't know what to say. She didn't want to admit she hadn't realised the possibility of using the sons' DNA. 'I'll need to see if the original exhibits are still available,' she said.

'Did Oscar tell you about the party next Thursday …'

'How did you know?'

'There are no secrets in the Temple. I'll send you an invitation.'

Alex didn't have time to ask any further questions; Cassie had finished the call.

Alex wasn't sure any DNA had been found at the scene, but a call to Mike Kemp confirmed there were some small traces found on the car. Alex told him the sons of two of the original suspects were currently standing trial at the Old Bailey and suggested he arrange for the samples from Lucas Radpole and Theo Clements to be compared with those from the scene of the 1993 burglary. 'Can you let me know the result as soon as possible,' she said.

After that call Alex went over again what she knew about the ring. Peggy Palmer had spoken of three men and had included Eric

Poynton. How could she get some DNA from him? After a couple of minutes she rang Harriet.

'Harriet, can I ask you for another favour?'

'What now?' Harriet said.

Was Poynton's assistant getting a little disillusioned playing detective? 'I need to get a sample of Eric's DNA. Tomorrow morning can you get him something to eat with his coffee? Something like a croissant, so he'll need to wipe his hands after. Give him a paper napkin and when he's finished let me have it. I'll be in the coffee bar across the road. It is important and it's urgent.'

'This is ridiculous. I'm not a great fan of Eric's but—'

'Please, Harriet. I wouldn't ask you if there was any other way.'

'I'm not happy about it but – I guess helping the police and all that.'

'What time does the gallery open?'

'Nine thirty. Eric likes a coffee as soon as he gets in, so I should have your napkin around ten.'

The next day Alex hovered in Ledbury Grove. She walked slowly along one side of the road towards Westbourne Grove, peering into the shop windows. She glanced back at Paint and

Print several times and saw Eric Poynton arrive carrying a brown paper parcel that from its shape looked like a painting. He put his hand into his pocket but then withdrew it and pushed the doorbell. Harriet must have arrived, Alex thought, because Poynton went into the shop straight away. Ten minutes later Harriet came out and made her way north towards Alex. When Harriet was level with her, Alex said, 'Let's get round the corner.'

'I'm going to the coffee bar over there,' Harriet said.

They walked together to Westbourne Road and into the coffee shop. Alex offered to pay for the croissants but Harriet told her Eric had given her the money. While Harriet's order was being prepared, Alex handed her a plastic bag and told her to put the napkin into it. 'I'll stay here until you get back to me with it,' she said.

'It may be a little while before I can slip out again.'

Alex nodded, got a coffee for herself and sat at a table outside the shop. After about five minutes her mobile rang. Her screen showed the caller was Cassie Hardman. Cassie was enigmatic and wouldn't say too much but suggested Alex contact the solicitor Lee Shaw. Alex was intrigued and made the call. Lee Shaw was equally secretive but made it clear she thought Alex would learn something interesting if they were to meet. She asked if Alex could come to her office in an hour's time.

'I'm rather busy at the moment,' Alex said.

'It's rather urgent,' Lee said.

'Make it twelve then.'

'Twelve noon. Fine. I'll see you then.'

Alex continued sipping at her coffee and watching the turning from Ledbury Grove.

She waited for another three quarters of an hour before Harriet returned. The next task was to send the napkin Harriet had given her to the lab with instructions to test it against the DNA from the getaway car. As she completed the forms, she wondered why it was that any contact with Cassie Hardman always resulted in her risking her own career.

Chapter 35

The firm of Shaw and Winter was in a former shop, the name spelt out in an arc of gold letters across the large plate-glass window. Inside was an open-plan room with five desks. Alex could see the computer screen on the one to her right. There were two open windows; one was a calendar showing appointments and the other had next day's list for Southwark Crown Court. The woman sitting at the desk looked up at her and asked if she could help.

'I'm here to see Lee …' Alex said.

A tall woman in her late thirties came towards her with her hand outstretched. She was wearing a double-breasted grey jacket with jeans, fashionably torn at the knees. 'I'm Lee Shaw. Shall we go in here?' She pointed towards a door labelled Conference Room. 'Can you let me know when Mr Clements Senior arrives, please,' she said to the receptionist and then offered Alex a cup of tea or coffee.

'Cassie thought you might have some information for me.'

'It's better than that. I have a client, Jeff Clements, who wants to provide information, or at least that's what he said. He sent me the photographs of the ring. I gave Cassie copies. I think you know it was stolen, or the large stone was, in a burglary that took place some years ago.'

'Before you go any further, was he involved in the offence? And what was his role? What does he want out of this? I'm not in a position to offer anything at all. You must know that. Cassie must know that.'

'As far as I'm aware, my client wasn't a principal in the affair. He assisted in the aftermath and was told about the burglary.'

'I think I'd want to talk to a more senior officer before this goes any further.' Alex didn't want to tell Lee she had arranged for Theo's DNA to be compared with the specimens taken at the scene. She was nervous about this unusual way of getting information and if it turned out Jeff Clements was one of the burglars in 1993, this interview may prevent any prosecution of him for that offence. On the other hand, losing the opportunity to get closer to the killers of PC Dennis Furnival was something she didn't want to miss.

'Look, he wants to talk about it,' Lee said. 'I don't think he wants anything other than to help his son. The trial is coming to the end. I think the judge will start summing-up today. If you treat it as an interview, caution him, and we'll both record it on our mobiles, it'll be ok.'

'I guess so.'

The two women sat in silence for what seemed to be a long period of time while they waited for Jeff Clements to arrive. Lee broke the silence. 'How do you know Cassie Hardman?'

'I met her at a dinner party a few years ago. She lives near me and we exchanged numbers. She ran into a … well, she needed some help, and I was able to assist.'

Lee grinned. 'I've heard rumours she got arrested and you bailed her out – not in the legal sense.'

'Something like that.'

The telephone on the desk rang. Lee answered it and asked for Mr Clements to be shown into the room. A tall man with a shock of blond hair streaked with gray came through the door and Lee directed him to sit down on the remaining chair in the room. 'Now, Jeff, this is DC Alex Seymour. You've met before when she interviewed you about Theo's alibi. Miss Hardman knows her and says you can trust her.' Alex smiled at him in acknowledgement. Lee Shaw continued. 'I've told her you want to provide some information about a burglary. Is that right?'

Jeff Clements said it was.

'Right. DC Seymour is going to caution you and we'll both record the conversation.'

Alex turned on her mobile to record Jeff Clements. 'I'm Alexis Seymour and I'm at the offices of Shaw and Winter solicitors. Also present are …' Lee Shaw gave her name and indicated to Jeff Clements to do the same.

Alex cautioned Clements and then said, 'Now, Mr Clements, what is it you want to tell me.'

'It's about that ring. The ring in the photos. The stone in it came from a burglary down west somewhere. I knew, know Bernie Radpole. We lived on the same estate in Fulham. I'd been totting for a couple of years and I'd got to know a couple of blokes who had stalls on Bermondsey Market. Antiques like. Bernie came one day, all a dither. He was always a bit of a lad – middle name was trouble. Been inside a couple of times, not for long. He had this ring and he wanted me to get rid of it for him. Take it to one of your mates, he said. So I did, and he said, my mate that is, it was a fake. That big stone wasn't real. Bernie was really gutted. My mate sold it for a pony, you know, twenty quid.'

'Do you know a Peggy Palmer?' Alex said.

'Peggy … um. Friend of Eric Poynton. Glamorous. Worked as a model. I think I met her a few times.'

'She says she borrowed jewellery from Bernie Radpole and you.'

'I don't remember that. I never had no jewellery, but it's a long time ago.'

'Mr Clements, Bermondsey Market operated as a market ouvert up until 1994. Were you aware of that?'

'Of course. That's why Bernie wanted his things sold there. He'd take stuff to the market. He had a few contacts had pitches down there, and they'd get rid of it for him.'

'Why did he not use his own fence for the ring?'

'It had gone wrong. I didn't know what until I saw the papers the next day. You know this copper was killed. I think Bernie wanted to break the connection to him. You lot would come round the market looking for stolen property and then seize it before it could be sold. He didn't want that to lead straight back to him … told me I'd be looked after if I admitted buying the ring from some bloke in a pub, like.'

'Are you saying Bernie Radpole was one of the burglars?'

'I wasn't there so can't say for sure. It fits his MO.'

'What about you? Did you take any part in the burglary? Before you answer …' She cautioned him again.

‘No, I didn’t. I knew nothing about it until I saw the news.’

‘Why does telling me help your son?’

‘I think Bernie wants to get his boy out of trouble.’

‘Jeff, an eyewitness has identified Theo,’ Lee said. ‘How’s Radpole fixed that? And why single out Theo?’

‘He thinks I fiddled him about the ring.’

‘Did you cheat him? Get more than you told him?’ Alex said.

‘No way. I may have got thirty and took a fiver for my trouble. Going down the market like. But that’s it and I’d have told him.’

‘These photographs were taken after 2011. When did you get them? Who from?’

There was silence then Clements said, ‘I saw it on the internet for sale. I thought I recognised the stone, but I’m no expert. The price made me think it must be real. I downloaded the pictures. I’ve looked for the website since but can’t find it. I showed Bernie the pics. Wanted to see if he thought it was the same ring. He started swearing at me and accused me of selling it for thousands and keeping the money.’

‘Have you got a police record?’ Alex said.

'About thirty years ago. Handling stolen property. Got a bender and then a robbery a couple of years later. I served three—'

Lee butted in. 'Do you know who Bernard's solicitors were?'

'No. Somebody near West London Mags, on Hammersmith Road, you know, but can't remember the name.'

'Henry Bolt, the man who's flat was broken into, is a solicitor. Was he Bernie Radpole's …?'

Jeff Clements shook his head. 'I really don't know.'

'Do you know who bought the ring in the market?' Alex said.

'No way. Usually Eric Poynton bought the stuff Bernie had stolen. Bernie would tip him off.'

'Did Poynton buy the original ring?'

Jeff Clements shook his head. 'I don't know.'

Alex stopped recording on her mobile. 'I'll leave it there for the moment. Are you prepared to make a statement about this matter?'

'Can you get this trial stopped?'

'You know I can't.'

'I've told you what I know. That's as far as I'm prepared to go.' Jeff Clements got to his feet and left the office.

'I can't stop the trial, you know that,' Alex said.

'Yes, I do. I guess we'll just have to hope it all unravels.'

Chapter 36

The weekend had been difficult for Cassie. Ben's silence seemed to indicate their relationship was at an end. Her lunch with Eleanor had highlighted the precarious position her chambers were in and left the future looking uncertain. She felt downcast as she climbed the stairs to the Bar Mess. Across the refectory she saw Peter with a couple of the junior tenants; he was still beaming from the news of his appointment. 'You missed a good evening. Jack was paying,' he said.

'Not always a good sign,' Cassie said.

'Don't be grumpy,' Peter said.

Cassie bought a coffee and sat down on one of the two leather sofas at the library end of the refectory, picked up a newspaper from a coffee table and then put it down again. A couple of barristers she knew stopped and congratulated her. She sipped slowly at her drink; she could smell toast and bacon as colleagues had their breakfasts. The noise of their chatter was increasing – talk of clients' defences, mitigating circumstances and judges' prejudices. She didn't want to listen; she left her half-full mug and made her way down the stairs to the concourse on the third floor. As she took the final steps, she pulled her gown forward onto her shoulders and put on her wig. She didn't have any work to do on the case now, but she craved the quiet of the courtroom.

She looked across the hall and saw Theo Clements standing alone outside the doors to the court. Cassie wasn't surprised Lee wasn't with him, or his father; she hoped they were in Lee's office with Alex Seymour. She spoke briefly to Theo explaining what was going to happen during the course of the day. As she was talking the usher came out and told her two of the jurors were going to be late. Cassie asked if anyone knew why and the usher said she understood there had been a fatality on the Tube line. Cassie's heart sank as she recalled the fatal day when the complainant in a rape trial had thrown herself in front of a train at Notting Hill Tube station, just after the defendant she had been representing was acquitted. She turned to go back to the robing room and passed Oscar standing with his client and Bernie Radpole. She overheard Oscar saying something about Henry Bolt – she couldn't hear properly. Seconds later Bernie Radpole strode off towards the lifts. She heard Oscar and Lucas arguing.

Cassie didn't stay to find out what was going on. In the robing room she read some of the papers from another case until she was called back to court. She wandered over to her seat on counsels' bench and fiddled with her pens while she waited for the hearing to start. When Oscar brushed past her to get to his seat, he said, 'Stupid idiot was planning to do a runner.'

The sound of a gavel on the judge's entrance made them scramble for their seats. Cassie noticed one or two of the jury looking puzzled at the lack of order on counsels' bench. It did look as if they'd all left in a hurry on Friday evening and hadn't bothered to sort themselves out yet.

Judge Rostron-Smith trotted to her seat. She placed the papers she was carrying on the bench in front of her and swung her seat so that she was facing the jury box.

'Members of the jury,' she said. 'We have now heard all the evidence. There will be no more. You will have to consider what you have heard and decide on the facts, on what you believe to have been proved. That is your role. Once you have decided then you will apply those facts to the law on which I am going to direct you. That is my role. If I get the law wrong another higher court can correct me.

'Throughout this trial there has been much emphasis on what we lawyers call the burden of proof. It is, you have been told, and rightly so, for the prosecution to prove the case against each one of these defendants. And again, as you have been told, they must prove it to a high standard. The prosecution must make you sure that each defendant is guilty of the offence of aggravated burglary.

'So, what do they need to prove? They must prove that each defendant entered a building, in this case the flat where Henry Bolt and Vincent Setchell lived, as a trespasser. That they did so without the consent of the owner. Each one of them must have had the intention to steal – that is, to take property belonging to another with the intention of permanently depriving that other of it.

'Finally, each one of them must have known that one of their number had a firearm. Before you retire, I will set out those directions on a sheet of paper as they apply to each defendant, so you don't have to try and remember them.

'Turning to the evidence. I'm not going to repeat everything you've heard, merely to summarise the salient points. If I miss out anything you think is important or mention something you think is irrelevant then ignore my remarks. As I have told you, the facts are for you.

'If I appear to express any opinion about the facts, then if you agree, adopt them. If you don't, disregard them.'

Cassie looked at Simon who raised his eyebrows and then scribbled a note which he passed to her. *'How much on an unbiased summary?'*

Cassie wrote *'Nothing. Incapable.'* She offered him one of her mints and took one herself.

The judge didn't take long to outline the evidence of Bolt and Setchell, telling the jury there was no real dispute that a group of men had entered their flat and caused considerable damage. She told them that apart from Clements, none of the intruders had been identified by Bolt or Setchell. 'The evidence against them is in two parts. That of the scientist, Mr Nevin, and his examination of their clothing. The other is the evidence of mobile telephone calls between Radpole, Cravitz and Morris around the time and close to the flat. I should add that there is no such evidence against Clements.'

Cassie was watching the jury for any reaction to the judge's summing-up. Some were writing, their pens running across the pages of their notebooks. One or two were sitting with their arms folded; the elderly man in tweeds had his eyes closed and she thought he might be sleeping. The woman with the auburn hair was leaning on one elbow, her chin resting on her right hand; from time to time she wrote something down.

'I turn now to the defence cases and for reasons that will become apparent I'm going to begin with Dean Morris. He was the first to be arrested after being identified by a member of his boxing club who happens to be a police officer. He is the only one who has admitted going into the flat. He says he went with Lucas Radpole. Radpole says he went with Morris but not on that day. What they do both agree on is that they were looking for property Radpole claims belonged to his father. Lucas Radpole says the item was a picture, a picture Bolt had agreed to buy but then failed to pay for. He doesn't appear to have told Morris he was to look for a picture. Had Morris simply not taken on board the nature of the property they were looking for?

'Is that true or may it be true? If it is, the prosecution have failed to prove the case against those two men as they were not entering with intent to steal but to take possession of property to which they were entitled. It did not belong to either Bolt or Setchell. Of course, you might well ask yourself why one of them was armed if the property did indeed belong to Radpole Senior.

'Radpole has given and called evidence of an alibi. That is, he is saying he could not have been at the flat on Fulham Road because he was with his father at the gallery owned by a Mr Poynton in Ledbury Grove. Eric Poynton has confirmed that. The prosecution have not been able to dispute that alibi. If you think that Radpole was at the address in Ledbury Grove or may have been then he is not guilty of the offence.

'Thom Cravitz has chosen not to give evidence. It is his right to do so. As he has been told, the law is that you may draw such inferences as appear proper from his failure to do so. Failure cannot of itself prove guilt but, depending on the circumstances, you may hold his failure to do so when deciding whether he is guilty or not. Remember, he has not offered any explanation about the calls between him, Radpole and Morris or for the finding of shards of pottery on his clothing.

'Then there is Mr Clements. He too says he was elsewhere at the time of the burglary. He has called two witnesses, his girlfriend and his father. Are they truly independent?'

Cassie began writing down the judge's comments on the evidence, but out of the corner of her eye she saw Radpole lean forward and hiss at Oscar, 'Mr D, can we—'

Judge Rostron-Smith stopped mid-sentence. 'Mr Davenport, would you ask your client not to interrupt when I'm addressing the jury.'

Oscar got up and went to the back of the court. Radpole leant towards the glass front of the dock. Cassie strained to hear what was being said but their voices were so low she couldn't catch a word. After a few minutes Oscar asked the judge if she would adjourn for twenty minutes or so.

Judge Rostron-Smith smiled at him. 'I assume it's really necessary?' Oscar confirmed it was. The judge looked at her watch. 'Members of the jury, I think we'll take an early lunch break and hopefully that will give Mr Davenport the opportunity to sort out whatever problem his client has. Back here at one forty-five. Thank you.'

Once the judge and jury had left the courtroom, Cravitz, Smith and Clements asked what was going on. Oscar vanished with his client into the cells. Marcus shook his head, Stephen said he didn't know, and Cassie shrugged her shoulders.

'Perhaps our clients will have some idea,' she said. She walked towards the back of the court, but before she could speak to Theo, he and the two other remaining defendants were ushered away by the prison staff.

‘Let’s get some lunch and wait until the judge’s pin-up can tell us what my client wants,’ Marcus said.

‘She’s summing-up for Radpole to be acquitted,’ Stephen said. ‘Surely he can’t be unhappy with that, can he?’

‘He’s unhappy about something and by the look on Oscar’s face, it’s not good,’ Cassie said.

‘Lunch,’ said Marcus. ‘No good speculating. We’ll find out in good time.’

Rather than get something to eat, Cassie called Alex. ‘Have you spoken to Jeff Clements yet?’ Alex filled her in and added that it didn’t help her much. ‘In fact, it doesn’t make any sense to me. All it proves is that Radpole Senior handled stolen property. It doesn’t prove he was the person who killed this officer.’

‘Actually, it is evidence that he was one of the burglars, or it can be. If someone is in possession of recently stolen property, there’s an assumption a jury can draw that he stole the item. And as the copper was killed in the course of the burglars escaping, they’re all guilty of his murder or manslaughter. Clements’ testimony fits that – he recalls the death of the PC was in the news the next day.’

‘I’ll talk to the guys who are handling the cold case review. I’ve asked them to get the samples from the burglary and compare them with Lucas Radpole’s and your clients. And thanks for the legal advice. By the way, Henry Bolt worked for a firm called Doyle, Leonard and Spencer in Hammersmith before he went to the City. Perhaps he was Radpole’s brief,’ Alex said.

‘Interesting,’ Cassie said before finishing the call. She wasn’t going to tell Alex the same thought had crossed her mind. She hoped the results of the DNA samples wouldn’t implicate Jeff Clements in the murder of the police officer. She believed Theo would find that very difficult to handle, particularly if his father was sent to prison.

Hadn’t Marcus said he’d represented Radpole Senior in the past? Surely he would have told them if Bolt had instructed him. In the Bar Mess she joined Marcus and the rest of defence barristers after getting herself a salad. She was nervous about asking Marcus if he’d been instructed by Henry Bolt in the past, but she gritted her teeth. ‘Marcus, when you were representing your client’s dad, which firm of solicitors instructed you?’

‘Tim Durrant’s, always. I know why you’re asking. Bolt worked for a firm in

Hammersmith before moving into the City. I've never met him before this case.'

Half an hour later Oscar appeared in the Bar Mess on the top floor of the Old Bailey, got a sandwich and a cup of coffee and sat down next to his co-defending counsel.

'You're not going to believe this.' He looked round at the group. 'He wants to change his plea to guilty.'

'What?' said Cassie. 'He was thinking of jumping bail earlier. Anyway, he'll walk if our learned judge continues telling the jury he's innocent.'

'Has our toerag told you why he wants to change his plea?' Marcus said.

'I've asked him, but it doesn't make a lot of sense. He told me he expected Poynton to tell the police what was really going on. When they went to his gallery, not on the day of the offence but a couple of days before, his father went in. He stayed in the car and when Dad came back he was f'ing and blinding.'

'Did Bolt have something belonging to Dad?' Cassie said.

'Lucas said Radpole Senior was going on about having to get it back. But Lucas didn't know what it was – he assumed it was a painting that hadn't been paid for. So he decided he'd go and get the picture or the money for it.'

'The alibi is bent then?' Marcus said.

'It would appear so,' Oscar said.

'Why didn't Radpole Senior go himself?'

'Lucas has no idea. He did say his father had a funny relationship with Bolt. Seemed a bit edgy when Bolt bought things from them.'

'The gun,' Marcus said, 'does he say how they got the gun?'

'Someone in the squat had it. He thought Bolt and his boyfriend might play up. Actually, Lucas didn't think they would report the offence. He's got it into his head that Bolt is holding something over his dad's head. He told me Clements' brief knows and if he isn't acquitted Cassie'll have Bolt spill the beans. He's scared of that. Theo Clements wasn't there.'

'Is that what he's saying?' Cassie said.

'Yes. That's what he's saying.'

'An honourable thief?' Marcus said. 'Well, what a mess.'

'What do you suggest we do?' said Cassie to Marcus. 'What are we going to do at this late stage?'

Chapter 37

As they waited for Court 9 to open, Marcus and Oscar went off along the concourse outside, leaving the other barristers speechless as they tried to assess the course the trial might take. Lee had arrived at the Old Bailey over the short adjournment and joined them. Cassie was the first to move away from the group, beckoning for Lee to follow her. When they were out of earshot, she said, ‘Whatever happens now, we’re out of it.’

‘Are you sure?’

‘If he changes his plea, we are entitled to ask for a retrial. If the judge grants the application, I think both Cravitz and Morris will be pushed into a plea as well. I doubt the prosecution will proceed to a retrial for our client alone. If she refuses the application and continues with this trial and he’s convicted, we have a strong case for an appeal.’

Marcus was walking back towards the courtroom door with Peter Maynard. Cassie rushed over to them.

‘Cassie, I’ve told Peter what’s happened. Oscar has gone down to get Radpole to sign his brief confirming the change of instructions. When he gets back we’ll get her ladyship in without the jury and, well, we'll see what happens,' Marcus said.

It wasn't long before Oscar returned and held out the front page of his brief. Marcus took it and as soon as the courtroom doors were opened, he resumed his place on counsels' bench. The rest followed. He asked the usher to bring the judge into court but not the jury.

Judge Rostron-Smith plonked herself down on her chair and said, 'This is very irregular, Mr Pike. Interrupting summing-up …'

'I know, My Lady, but our client has indicated he wants to change his plea to guilty. He has confirmed that in writing.' Marcus waved the brief frontispiece towards her. 'In those circumstances we are asking for the indictment to be put again.'

'Mr Maynard, what do you have to say about this? I've never encountered such a late change of plea before.'

'Nor have I. It's difficult to think of any other course of action than to put the count again to Radpole, and if he does indeed plead guilty then …'

'Quite, Mr Maynard. What then? What will the other defendants want to do?' the judge said. 'Mr Jennings, what course of action do you want to take? Mr Wade, Miss Hardman, have you any objection to the indictment being put again to Radpole?'

Although they were all standing, no one spoke, then Cassie said, 'I'd have to take instructions from my client as to any future course he may wish to take, but my initial reaction is that the indictment should be put again and Radpole should enter a plea of guilty at the earliest opportunity. That would provide certainty on which our respective clients can be advised and consider their own positions. I also would be asking your ladyship to tell the jury of Radpole's change of plea. I do not see how they can be asked to give verdicts without knowing that. Certainly, if Radpole had entered a guilty plea at the beginning of the trial I would have applied to put that before the jury, as I suspect would the prosecution.'

'I can see that,' the judge said. 'It's such a change of tack and the jury have been told there will be no more evidence …'

David Jennings leapt to his feet. 'I too would want to take instructions from my client as to what he wanted to do in the light of that change of plea, but I would urge your ladyship to take that plea now and then allow us all time to take further instructions.'

Simon Wade said he agreed with that course and added that it might be better if the jury were sent home for the rest of the day.

Judge Rostron-Smith agreed and asked the usher to tell the jury to go home and return the next day, even though she was leaving her summing-up unfinished.

Back in chambers, Jack asked Cassie if the trial would finish the next day. She said she wasn't sure, but it might be advisable to keep her diary free for the next couple of days.

'I will anyway. Your swearing in is on Thursday. You and Mr Maynard have to be there.' As he finished speaking, Oscar came into the clerks' room and told Cassie that Marcus Pike had suggested they all meet in his chambers at five o'clock. 'Simon is already with Marcus and David is on his way. Are you coming?' Cassie nodded and they left 3 Burke Court together. She had the impression that Oscar was unperturbed by the sudden change of instructions from his client.

'Why do you think he wants to plead guilty, all of a sudden? It's not to get my boy off, is it?' Cassie said.

'No idea. Actually, I don't care. We'll get paid for the trial whatever he does. He's not worth worrying about.'

'The judge was summing-up for him to be acquitted …'

Oscar stopped at the door to Marcus's chambers. 'Look, if Radpole was acquitted, your client would be at greater risk of being convicted. You should be grateful he's playing the straight guy, if that's what it's about. Actually, I think it's more complicated than that. He's been agitated ever since you asked questions about that ring.'

'Does he know anything about it?'

'If he does he's not telling me, that's for sure.'

Paul Scanlon, the senior clerk, took them straight to Marcus's room. Cassie remembered it well: the shelves filled with books, the files and briefs tied with pink ribbon, the large leather-topped desk and the view from the windows – the silver strand of the Thames in the distance framed by the trees of Inner Temple Gardens. She had thought she would have a similar room when she took silk, but with the reduction in the Legal Aid budget she would have to go on sharing a room.

Simon Wade was lounging in one of the two easy chairs and he patted the seat of the one next to him for Cassie to sit there. A moment later David Jennings arrived and took an office chair. Oscar remained standing. Marcus came from the back of his desk and perched on the edge. Cassie had to prevent herself from laughing as his feet swung several inches from the carpet. 'This is a bit of a rum do,' he said. 'Obviously those are Radpole's instructions. We can't go behind that. What are the rest of you going to do?'

'More importantly, what line are the prosecution going to take?' Cassie said. 'I don't see how this trial can continue. The judge can't ask the jury to forget the evidence Radpole has given and now he's an admitted liar. I'll ask for this jury to be discharged and, well, I suppose the line the Crown might take will depend on what Cravitz and Morris decide to do.'

'You think they'll drop the case against your boy if the others plead as well?' David said.

Cassie confirmed she thought they might.

'Certainly the case against Cravitz is stronger if a jury know of Radpole's plea. He's admitting he was at the scene and there's the telephone calls. The obvious conclusion is that Cravitz was there as well,' David said.

'Have you taken instructions from him?' Marcus said.

'I've explained the position to him. He's thinking about it. He doesn't want another trial.

Thinks he'd be convicted. So, yes, he's considering what to do.'

'Simon, what are you thinking of doing?'

'Morris will probably plead guilty, I think, but on the basis he knew nothing about the gun and, certainly at the beginning, believed Radpole when he was told there was property that belonged to his dad.'

'Bit difficult to explain rummaging in the kitchen when you're looking for a picture – unless it was one painted on a chocolate box,' Marcus said.

'Does anybody think this trial can continue or do we all agree we should apply for the jury to be discharged?' Cassie said. She wasn't going to reveal what she knew.

Simon and David agreed. Marcus said it didn't affect them. They would ask for the indictment to be put again to Lucas Radpole.

'I'll tell Peter then?' Cassie said.

'Wait till tomorrow. Keep him on edge,' Oscar said.

'That's a bit unfair. I don't think he'll oppose an application to discharge.'

Chapter 38

Alex wondered what further steps she could take while she waited for the results of the DNA analyses to take place. She went back to the files about the murder. She put to one side those the Devon and Cornwall police had sent to the cold case reviewing team and concentrated on the information the Metropolitan Police had provided to the initial enquiry. The file of those documents was quite thin, and she soon had a list of the officers who had worked on the case. She called Mike Kemp. 'Mike, the guys who worked on the Furnival case here, do you have their contact details?'

'Are you on to something?'

'I might be. I'm interested if any of them knew a solicitor called Henry Bolt. He worked for a firm of solicitors called Doyle, Leonard and Spencer.'

Kemp said he'd see if he could get the information for her and reminded her to keep him up to date with her research.

Her next call was to the retired custody sergeant Andy Baker. She reminded him who she was and told him she was interested in a number of police officers who worked in Hammersmith in the nineties. She read out the list of six names. Baker said he knew the names but the only one he could remember was Hugh Mayer. 'He was very friendly with a couple of the lawyers. A woman he was quite keen on. She worked for the same firm as that fella Bolt you asked me about last time. Don't think Hughie got anywhere with her. They did go drinking together. The Latimer Arms I think.'

Alex thanked him and then set off for Chancery Lane. It took her some time to find the block of offices where Henry Bolt worked. It was tucked away in a newish development off Fetter Lane. A wall of glass faced onto a courtyard; the doors swung open as she approached. Inside was a row of gates manned by security guards dressed in black suits. As she crossed the marble floor of the lobby, which reminded her of an airport concourse, she noticed everyone entering had an identification card. She wasn't sure if her warrant card would be enough to gain her access, neither did she know which floor she needed to go to. She looked around; to one side of the security gates was an oak-topped counter as long as a bowling alley. The two receptionists, one blonde and one dark haired, standing behind the desk looked as if they had just come from a beauty salon. They seemed to be permanently on the phone. Alex didn't know which of them to speak to and hovered in the hope one of them would speak to her. Eventually the blonde looked up. Alex asked for Henry Bolt and showed the young woman her warrant card. The woman reached for the telephone and Alex reached forward and put her hand over the mouthpiece. 'I'd prefer he wasn't told I was here. Just tell me which floor.'

The woman handed her a pass and told her she needed the fourth floor. Alex made her way through the security and took one of a bank of lifts. There was another reception desk on the fourth floor. She asked again for Bolt. The woman at the desk said, 'He's behind you.' And then, 'Mr Bolt, this lady is here to see you.'

Henry Bolt stopped and approached Alex. 'And you are?'

Alex produced her warrant card. 'DC Alex Seymour. I wonder if I could have a word, sir.'

'Is it about this case? Have the jury reached a verdict?'

'I don't think there's a verdict. Perhaps we should talk somewhere more private.'

'Of course.' Bolt looked towards the receptionist who checked something on her desk computer and then told him which conference rooms were free. He ushered Alex to a glass-walled room that looked out across the offices in Fetter Lane. He sat down and directed Alex towards another chair. Although he gave every appearance of being calm and in control he was fidgeting with the end of his tie.

'Now, what's this about?' he said.

'I think you know. It concerns a burglary that took place in 1993. A burglary in which a police officer was killed as he tried to stop the criminals escaping.'

'Why should I know about that?'

'I'm going to caution you that you don't have to say anything but it may harm your defence if you do not mention when questioned something you later rely on in court. Anything you say may be given in evidence.' She paused. Bolt said nothing. Alex continued. 'Because in 2011 you had a ring, stolen in that burglary, reset at a jeweller's in Hatton Garden.'

'Are you suggesting I was handling stolen property? That's a very serious allegation to make, as you well know. Particularly against a solicitor.'

'Did you have this stone reset?'

'You know I did.'

'Can you explain how you came to have the ring?'

'That is subject to legal privilege.'

'I'm not sure I understand.'

'Anything received by a lawyer which is the subject of legal proceeding is subject to client confidentiality. Only my client can give me permission to answer your questions.'

'In 1993 were you Bernie Radpole's solicitor. I'm sure we can check the court records.'

Bolt pursed his lips. 'He was one of the firm's clients. I wouldn't describe myself as his solicitor. Other members of the firm represented him as well. As I recall he was frequently before the courts. I didn't work there for very long. I didn't like criminal defence work and it didn't pay enough then – heaven knows what it's like now.'

'Bernie Radpole was one of your clients. If he was arrested, did he contact you directly or did the police ring you?'

'There's a duty solicitor scheme. He'd probably be seen by whoever was on duty first and then get in touch with us later.'

'Do you remember an officer in Hammersmith CID called Hugh Meyer?'

'I do. He was always popping into the office, hoping for a cup of coffee. He was very friendly with Tricia, Tricia Doyle, the senior partner.'

'Did he talk about cases he was working on?'

'He talked like he was on the Flying Squad. Serious investigations, loads of money involved.'

'Did he mention a burglary in Devon?'

Bolt didn't reply. Alex repeated the question.

'He talked about a number of cases. My only interest was if one of our clients was in the frame.'

'Did he tell you about this burglary in Devon? A police officer was killed by the car the offenders used to leave the scene.'

'He may have done.'

'Did you tell Bernie Radpole he was suspected of that crime?'

'Conversations with my client are the subject of legal privilege. I'd need his consent.'

'I believe Mr Radpole is at the Old Bailey. A short walk down the road. Why don't we go and ask him?'

Chapter 39

As they gathered in the Bar Mess the following morning, Cassie asked Marcus if he knew who had represented Bernie Radpole in the past, whether other solicitors had been involved before Tim Durrant. He said he had assumed there must have been previous firms because the first time he was instructed to appear in court on behalf of Radpole Senior it was because he'd sacked his previous solicitors. 'I assumed he'd admitted the offence to them and then tried to run some sort of defence or something like that.'

'Could the firm have been Doyle, Leonard and Spencer?'

Marcus shook his head. 'I don't remember the name. It's a long time ago. What's this about?'

Cassie told him what she'd learnt. 'The bottom line is that Bolt and Radpole Senior have known each other for some time. Bolt was his solicitor when he was suspected of the burglary where that ring, the one I asked him about was stolen. And I'd say it was Radpole who suggested Theo Clements to him as being one of the intruders. I'd certainly like to put that to him if there was a retrial.'

'You're assuming there will be a retrial after my boy pleads guilty. You know this judge is capable of anything. And the CPS may insist on going on because of the ID. If you tell Peter what you've told me, he'd ask for further enquiries, although … did DS Crawford know Bolt had been Radpole Senior's solicitor and not disclose it? Check with Peter. We did put in our defence statement they knew each other and Bolt had a painting that belonged to the father, but being his lawyer, even if it was in the past, is rather different. If he did you could argue there has been an abuse of process and get the case dismissed on that basis.'

It didn't take long for Cassie to find Peter Maynard and ask him what the prosecution knew about Bolt's relationship with the Radpole father and son. Peter made a call to the police office and asked DS Crawford to meet him outside Court 9, then he and Cassie walked down the concourse together. While they waited for the officer, Peter said, 'I got a call from Eleanor yesterday. You know what it was about, I gather?'

'I do, and what's your view?'

'I'm in favour of getting our finances sorted out, but I'm not too keen on getting rid of Jack.'

'No one's suggesting that. At least not at the moment. If Jack finds looking at his management of the money uncomfortable it's up to him.'

'Sorry to interrupt, sir, but you wanted to speak to me?' DS Crawford said.

'Miss Hardman has queried the relationship between Bolt and the Radpoles. When you got the defence statement for Lucas Radpole, did you ask Bolt if he knew the defendant?'

'I did – and if he had property belonging to the father. He denied knowing either father or son. I didn't go any further.'

Cassie butted in. 'You didn't know if Bolt had been Radpole Senior's solicitor?'

DS Crawford's eyes widened. 'No, I did not. That was not part of the defence statement. There was no reason to suspect that, just the interest in antiques.'

'Thank you, officer. You have your answer, Cassie.'

Seconds later the usher called them into court. When the court was assembled, without the jury, Marcus applied for the count of burglary to be put again to his client.

'Isn't it better that he enters that plea in front of the jury and they can formally, on my direction, find him guilty?' Judge Rostron-Smith said.

'That's the correct procedure,' Marcus said.

'Shall we get the jury back then?'

Cassie got to her feet. 'My Lady, I wish to make an application for this jury to be discharged …'

'On what basis?'

'Had Radpole pleaded guilty in the first place the conflict between the defendants would have been minimised. I would have put Mr Clements' case differently. More importantly, I have further instructions that one of the witnesses, Henry Bolt, is not only known to Radpole's family but at one time was the father's solicitor. I know the officer in charge was not aware of that, but the police must have seen Radpole Senior's previous convictions.'

'You're suggesting there was inadequate disclosure?'

'I don't know, but possibly further enquiries should have been made.'

'Mr Jennings and Mr Wade, what do you have to say?'

Simon began. 'Morris's case is particularly affected by this plea. Once Radpole admits being in the flat, then the issue for the jury is whether Morris believed they were looking for property belonging to him. I too would ask for this jury to be discharged.'

'I would make the same application, My Lady,' David Jennings said.

Judge Rostron-Smith picked up a pen from the bench in front of her and twiddled it round for a few seconds. 'No, I'm not going to discharge this jury. I think the difficulties can be remedied in my summing-up. Now let's have the jury back.'

Once the jurors were settled in their seats the judge told them there had been a development in the case that they should hear about. She invited Marcus to make his application. Marcus asked for the indictment to be put again. Lucas Radpole was asked to stand, and the court clerk read out the charge and asked him how he pleaded.

'Guilty,' Radpole said.

The jurors shuffled in their seats. Some of them turned to their neighbour and muttered. Cassie couldn't hear but their faces expressed surprise.

'Members of the jury, Mr Radpole will be sentenced for this offence after this trial has concluded. In the meantime, Mr Pike and Mr Davenport, I assume you will be required elsewhere now your role here is over for the time being. We'll just give them five minutes to leave, members of the jury, and then I'll continue with my summing-up. Take Mr Radpole down, will you.'

Cassie watched Lucas Radpole being led from his seat in the dock to the door leading down to the cells. Suddenly he turned and shouted, 'Theo wasn't there. He wasn't there.'

Chapter 40

To Cassie's amazement, Judge Rostron-Smith continued with her summing-up as if nothing had changed. The judge emphasised they must consider the case against each defendant separately. 'Because one is guilty it doesn't mean any of the others are. It is for you to decide on the evidence and on the evidence alone. I say that because what you heard when Mr Radpole was taken into custody is not evidence.'

Cassie winced. Simon Wade reached out and picked up her packet of mints, took one and offered the tube to Cassie. As she fumbled easing one of the mints into her fingers, he squeezed them.

'I was just about to deal with the case against Theo Clements when my summing-up was interrupted. He too has said he was elsewhere. He gave evidence he was at home at the time and Miss Hardman on his behalf called his father and girlfriend in support. Annie Ellis says he was at home when she left at approximately eight fifty and his father says he arrived at the shop where Clements lived at about nine thirty to get to an appointment at ten in Chelsea. Against that you have the evidence of Mr Green who told you they were late and didn't arrive until ten thirty. You may want to consider that when you think about whether there was insufficient time for him to have gone to the flat in Fulham Road, as the defence argue. That is a matter for you. Against that you have the evidence of Henry Bolt who is sure Clements was one of the men who forced his way into his home and then ransacked it.

'You have heard that both Dean Morris and Theo Clements are men of good character. Indeed two people speak highly of Mr Clements. You should take their evidence into account and give it what weight you think appropriate. That doesn't mean they can't have committed the offence. All offenders are of good character at some stage. But it is something you can take into account when considering if they are responsible for this burglary.

'In a few moments I am going to ask the jury bailiff to take the oath and then, taking all your belongings with you, you will go to your room to consider your verdict.

'There is one final thing. You may have heard of majority verdicts. Ignore that. For the moment you must deliver a verdict on which you all agree. If that changes, I will ask you to return to court and I will give you further directions. Thank you.'

The jury bailiff stood, took the bible in her right hand and took the oath promising to keep the jury in a private place and not to speak to them without leave of the judge unless it be to ask them if they agreed upon their verdict. She waited while they collected their belongings and, holding the judge's door open, ushered them out of the courtroom. The young woman with the auburn hair turned at the door and looked directly at Cassie. Cassie hoped that was a good sign.

After they had left Cassie stood up and asked for bail for her client. The judge said, 'No, I think at this stage they should remain in custody.' She didn't wait to hear anything further.

Cassie gathered her papers and pushed them to one side then made her way out of the courtroom. Simon followed her. 'That was a bit of a stab in the back. Gives you good grounds of appeal though.'

David Jennings joined them. 'Pretty poor show in my judgement,' he said.

'I'm just hoping the jury ignore that part of her summing-up,' Cassie said. 'I'm going to see my boy.'

David and Simon walked with her and they made their way down to the basement. The door to the custody area was solid oak and had been taken from the old Newgate Prison that had stood on the site before the Central Criminal Court was built in the early part of the twentieth century. Simon pushed the bell to summon the prison staff.

Inside they each asked for their respective clients. As they waited Simon pointed to a list of barristers pegged to the wall. It was a league table of the number of acquittals various defence barristers had achieved. Cassie was at number four.

'Good record, Cassie. The only woman on the list.'

'I don't think it means that much. I've been fortunate to have a number of cases where the evidence against the defendant was poor.'

'I'm not sure that's right,' David Jennings said. 'You're really good at going the extra mile for your client. Good at finding the weak points in the evidence. You deserved to get Silk.'

'Thanks, David,' Cassie said. Barristers weren't known for being complimentary about each other's abilities.

'He's just angling for an invitation to your party,' Simon said.

'I assume you're both invited,' Cassie said. 'Do bring your wife, Simon.'

'It's a bit of a long way from Australia.'

Cassie covered her relief with a wry smile.

Further conversation was prevented by the custody officer. 'Gentlemen, and the lady, if you wouldn't mind going to an interview room while we fetch your clients.'

Sitting in the tiny cell Cassie could smell the tension mixed in with stale food. She thought about her investiture as Silk and the party afterwards. Would her parents come to London? She'd asked them and her mother had said they'd think about it. She wasn't sure they'd make the journey south. She was concerned they would feel uncomfortable in the rarefied atmosphere of Gray's Inn, among a group of self-congratulatory men and women. Then there was Ben. What would he do? She had asked Jack to make sure he was sent a formal invitation.

She was deep in thought when Lee Shaw burst into the room. 'Alex is here with Henry Bolt. He's under arrest. It looks like he was Radpole Senior's solicitor.'

Before Cassie could absorb the information, Theo Clements was escorted into the room. Cassie motioned him to sit on the chair farthest from the door – a precaution she had been taught to enable her to get out of the cell if the client became aggressive. Not that she expected Theo Clements to attack her. It was just force of habit.

Cassie wanted to hear more from Lee so she didn't linger too long with Theo. She explained there was nothing more either she or Lee could do.

'What about Lucas telling them I wasn't there? She told them to ignore that. It's not fair.'

'I know, and it will give us grounds of appeal, but he didn't say that in the witness box and she has decided to take the view that it isn't evidence,' Cassie said. 'I think it will be difficult for the jury to put it out of their minds, particularly as Morris said the same. Let's hope they don't.'

She stood up and opened the cell door. Theo followed her out into the corridor and they walked in silence to the desk. 'I'll be upstairs for the moment,' she said and patted him on the shoulder as he was led past her.

Chapter 41

Cassie and Lee left the custody area and went up the two flights of stairs to the large hall outside Number 1 Court. The light was dim here, unlike in the newer part of the building. Cassie was always impressed by the magnificence of this part of the courthouse. The floors were white marble with a geometric pattern of black. The barrelled ceiling was stone with figures carved on the upper portion of the wall and, below, brightly coloured mosaics picked out stories from the bible. Alex was sitting at a bench behind a dark oak table. Cassie went and sat at one of the matching chairs. Lee took one of the others and pulled it closer. From the other side of the hall, the blank stone eyes of Elizabeth Fry stared down at them.

'Just imagine waiting here while twelve men decided your fate,' Lee said. 'Makes me shudder.'

Cassie laughed. 'Alex, I thought Bolt was with you?'

'He's with Sergeant Crawford, who's a bit hacked off Bolt didn't tell him he'd been Bernie's solicitor. I did what you suggested, Cassie, and I'm waiting for the results of the DNA tests. In addition, I checked the court records for the West London Magistrates' Court and I found what I think was a bail application made by Henry Bolt on behalf of Radpole.'

'When was that?'

Alex took a piece of paper from her pocket. 'The writing is bad but I think it's fourteenth June 1992. I know it's 1992 because the records are for a calendar year. It's a guess but I think Bolt discovered Bernie was a suspect for the murder and tipped him off. Presumably Bernie confessed and showed Bolt the ring. I assume Radpole's confession to him is confidential?'

'It's flying a bit close to the wind, in my view. But he probably wouldn't want to go to the police. No client would ever trust him again,' Cassie said.

'It may have been the reason he left Doyle's. Didn't want to have anything more to do with Radpole,' Lee said.

'That's quite a gap of time. Nearly thirty years since. I'm not sure I'd remember a case I did five years ago, never mind after half a lifetime,' Cassie said. 'Would it make a difference to our case? I'm not sure. Unless there was an ongoing contact it's just a coincidence isn't it? Marcus told me he'd represented Radpole Senior on a couple of serious burglaries, but I know he wouldn't have represented the son if Bolt had been the father's solicitor.'

'Tim Durrant is Lucas's solicitor,' Lee said.

'And from what Marcus said, he's been the father's for some time. Look, I've asked Marcus about which other solicitors might have represented Bernie Radpole and he doesn't know. I could ask Tim as well,' Cassie said.

Her next enquires didn't take long. Tim Durrant, although he knew the firm of solicitors Doyle, Leonard and Spencer, had no recollection of Henry Bolt. 'The firm was run by Tricia Doyle. I'm surprised you don't remember her,' he said. 'A tall blonde-haired woman, rather large. Had a bit of a run-in with the local CID when a crate of whisky was stolen from her office just before Christmas one year. The other partners did conveyancing and a bit of personal injuries. If he worked there it wasn't for long.'

'What about acting for Bernie Radpole? Marcus told me he'd been instructed by you to represent him previously?'

'Cassie, I suppose it's a matter of public record. I have been instructed by him on a number of occasions, but I'm not saying any more. Legal privilege. You might like to think about that.'

Cassie knew Tim was giving her a clue. When Bolt had claimed legal privilege, she thought, he must have been instructed in a case involving the ring or the ruby. It made sense to Cassie that the case was the ill-fated country house burglary in Devon. Bolt, she surmised, had been consulted by Bernie Radpole about the disposal of the items stolen during that burglary. If they had hoped the ruby had vanished for good, its reappearance, even if it was just in a photograph, must have frightened them both.

Waiting for the jury was always tense. Cassie had brought work with her; she knew it wasn't a good idea – she rarely managed to get anything done. Her discussion with Alex and Lee and then the telephone call to Tim had filled some of the time. She didn't want to continue sitting with Lee so she made her excuses and retreated to the Bar Mess where her co-defending counsel were chatting at one of the long tables. Oscar was with them. She joined them.

'Peter's told me Jack has organised your bash on Thursday evening,' Oscar said.

'Is it only in two days' time?' Cassie said.

'You can't have forgotten. Your big day,' he said.

'No, it all seems a bit unreal.'

‘Then we’ve got this problem of chambers hanging over us. I wish somebody would tell us what’s going on.’ Oscar pointed at Peter. ‘Is he going to take on being head?’

Peter leant forward and in a conspiratorial whisper said, ‘Eleanor will do it, if there’s no alternative. And there isn’t at the moment, is there?’

‘She doesn’t want to deal with Jack,’ Cassie said.

‘Pity you’re not more senior, Cassie. He likes you,’ Peter said.

‘Well, I’m not. I’m not ready to take on chambers.’

‘No commitment, Cassie,’ Oscar said, ‘of any kind. Apart from your own career.’

Chapter 42

By four o'clock there was still no word from the jury. In the Bar Mess, Simon Wade was playing a game of Sudoku on his phone, David was reading a copy of the *Shooting Times* and Cassie was sitting with her computer open staring at the screen. 'Do you go shooting, David?' she said.

'No way. I just like to know how the other half lives.'

'Let's go and see if her ladyship is ready to send the jury home for the night,' Simon said.

'Where's Peter?' Cassie said.

'He went off with DS Moore.'

The three of them went down to the concourse on the third floor and walked to the doors of Court 9. Cassie went to open one, but they were locked. She moved back into the hall. 'Do we go back upstairs or wait here?'

'Wait here,' said David and went to sit down on one of the marble-faced benches. Cassie sat next to him; Simon wandered over to the windows. There was nobody else about and it looked as if all the other courts had risen for the day.

'Too quiet,' Simon said. 'Are we the only ones here?'

'No,' said Cassie, 'I think there is life in the Bailey.' She had seen a court clerk walking the length of the concourse. Outside Court 12, he took down the court list pinned to a noticeboard to the right of the door and replaced it with the one for the next day. Cassie got up and approached him. 'Do you know where the usher for Court 9 is?'

The clerk told her he didn't but as soon as he'd finished, he would go and find out. Cassie thanked him and returned to her seat. He went to the noticeboards for the other two courts and then pinned up the next day's list of cases. After he replaced the sheet outside Court 9 she went to look at which cases had been allocated the next day. 'We are listed for tomorrow as well as some plea and directions hearings,' Cassie said. She went and stood by Simon. 'It won't be long before the judge sends us away.'

'I hope not,' he said.

In the silence that followed Cassie heard the sound of the doors to the court being opened. Peter was loping along the concourse towards them, a sheaf of paper in his hand.

Peter took his place on counsels' bench as Cassie and Simon walked round the back of the courtroom. David pushed his way past Peter. The judge strode in, followed by the jury. Judge Rostron-Smith waited until the court clerk had scurried to her desk before directing her to ask the jury if they had reached a verdict. The jury foreman stood and said they were not all agreed. The judge said she was sending them home and then reminded them not to do any research on the internet and not to talk to anybody about the case. 'We'll start at ten tomorrow. I hope that's convenient for everybody.'

A couple of the jury put their hands up and one said she may be late as she had a child to take to school.

'Do try and be here for ten. We'll start again as soon as everybody is here.'

After the jurors had left the court, she said, 'Bail as before,' as she scampered off the bench.

Cassie started to pile up her papers, as did the others. Peter Maynard walked along the front of counsels' bench and handed her a few sheets of paper. 'You need to read this and decide what you want to do.' He gave similar documents to Simon and David. Cassie recognised it as a further statement. It was handwritten by one person and signed at the bottom of each page by someone different. Cassie looked at the signature. It was that of Henry Bolt.

I am a qualified solicitor and in the early nineties I worked for a firm called Doyle, Leonard and Spencer in Hammersmith, West

London. It was a busy Legal Aid practice. I was employed as one of two advocates; the other was the senior partner, Tricia Doyle. One of the firm's clients was Bernie Radpole. I have been shown a copy of the court records for 24 January 1992, which shows I appeared for Mr Radpole on a charge of driving without insurance and again twelve months later for driving without due care and attention. I have no recollection of either case.

In late 1993 I became aware that Radpole was suspected of being involved in a burglary in Devon. I have been asked if I knew a police officer called Hugh Mayer. I do remember Hughie. He was a bit of an old-fashioned copper. He enjoyed a drink and after a few pints was inclined to let things slip. Usually I ignored them – it was better that way. If he told me Radpole was wanted for a serious offence, I probably didn't take any notice. I don't remember it. I had only represented Radpole for very minor driving offences.

I did not tell Radpole he was under suspicion. I would not have risked my career.

I left Tricia Doyle's firm in late 1995. I had decided I wanted to do commercial litigation rather than be in a Legal Aid practice.

Some years later, I think in about 1999/2000 I met Radpole again with Eric Poynton. I have an interest in antiques and paintings. Radpole had a stall on Portobello Market and Poynton a shop on Ledbury Grove. I had no reason to suspect either of them was involved in any illegal activity. From time to time I bought various things from them. I did have some items on approval. Usually paintings. I always paid for anything I wanted to keep.

I have been shown a picture of a ring with a large ruby. In early 2010 I was asked by Radpole to do him a favour. He showed me a ring, which had this stone in a more traditional setting. He said it was his wife's and he wanted to sell it, but it needed a more modern setting. He asked if I could arrange this for him. He knew my office was on London Wall at the time and he said it would be easier for me to get to Hatton Garden than it was for him. He went on to say he admired my taste and I would be better at choosing an appropriate design.

I asked him if the ring was stolen and he told me it wasn't. He showed me the receipt from Bermondsey Market showing Poynton had bought it from there. I assumed the stone was a spinel, not a ruby, and that was the reason for the low price. I did know the law on market ouvert and that meant Eric had good title to the ring. I also knew Bermondsey Market was used for the sale of stolen goods.

At first, I was reluctant to do as he asked as I was not convinced by his account. It was then he suggested that some of the paintings I had bought were stolen. He implied that if I didn't do as he asked, he would inform on me. He had friends in the police force, he said. I didn't want that so I had the stone reset. I was shocked when I was told the stone was a ruby and it did make me suspicious, but Bernie assured me it was legitimate. I returned the ring to him and assumed that would be the last I heard about it.

I did continue to buy antiques from Radpole and occasionally from Poynton but by then he specialised in twentieth-century paintings and they were too expensive. I didn't always pay for things I took from them. Radpole didn't seem to mind and I thought he knew I'd done him a favour.

When the police arrived after the burglary I was concerned about the provenance of some of the paintings I had bought from Radpole and Poynton.

I was surprised when I was told a Lucas Radpole had been arrested for the burglary. I had never met him but I assumed he was Bernie's son. I knew Bernie would be very angry. He rang me and told me to withdraw the complaint. I'd got his boy into trouble. He threatened me with informing the police I'd bought property knowing it was stolen. He mentioned some items I'd bought from Eric. I now believe they were things Bernie had stolen and they'd been laundered if you like through Bermondsey Market. I have a good job in the City and if I was arrested and charged, I would lose that and my ability to practice.

I did consider telling the police I didn't want to proceed with the allegation. I made a tentative approach to DS Moore but he went on about Lucas Radpole having a gun and I realised the case would have to proceed.

I contacted Bernie and told him the police would not drop the prosecution and his son had been very foolish to bring a gun. Bernie was still very angry. I calmed him down and we talked about the case; I told him the evidence against his son appeared weak and he'd probably be acquitted. He wasn't convinced. Told me I'd been a crap advocate. He told me who the others were and said Clements' son was involved. Shouldn't be allowed to get away with it, he said.

I knew Jeff Clements when he had a stall on Portobello. But that's years ago as well. Anyway, Bernie told me about the shop in Putney so I went to have a look and I thought the young man could have been one of the burglars. I called the police.

I would like to add that, on reflection, I'm not sure there were four men.

'Does Moore agree Bolt spoke about not proceeding,' Cassie said.

'He says something was said, but he explained because Lucas Radpole had taken a gun to the scene, the police would want to continue. Bolt didn't mention it again.'

'Shouldn't we have been told that?'

'Moore has only just told me. He says he didn't take it seriously. But, yes, you should have been told.'

Cassie shook her head in disbelief. She looked at her three colleagues and saw they were as stunned as she was. She waved the statement at Peter Maynard. ‘What are you going to do about this?’

‘I don’t know. I need to think about it and take instructions.’

Chapter 43

Cassie met Lee the next morning on the concourse outside Court 9. She had sent a text asking Lee to be there by nine thirty.

'What's this about?' said Lee.

'I tried ringing you last night but you weren't answering your phone. Peter gave me this yesterday.' Cassie handed Lee the copy of the statement from Henry Bolt. It didn't take her long to read it.

'Well,' Lee said, 'that lets us out, doesn't it?'

'Peter is taking instructions from the CPS. If they abandon this trial, how would they proceed? There is clear evidence that an offence took place and with a gun. Radpole has pleaded guilty to that. On the basis of that statement from Bolt there were two other men there. Morris agrees he went into the flat. That leaves one other. Is that Theo or Cravitz? There is an argument for letting this trial come to a conclusion and letting the Court of Appeal sort it out.'

They were soon joined by David Jennings and Simon Wade.

'This statement from Bolt,' Cassie said.

'Any idea what the prosecution will do?' Simon said.

'It's a tricky situation, isn't it? Cassie and I have been here before. Last-minute revelations that should have been given in evidence, the jury already deliberating,' David said.

'What happened?'

'The jury returned a not-guilty verdict and that was the end of it. There wasn't a ruling we could point to that could help us in this case,' Cassie said. 'How can any court say justice has been done when the jury is unaware of such important evidence? Anyway, we'll have to see what our learned prosecutor is going to do.'

While they waited for Peter Maynard to turn up, Cassie paced the concourse weighing up the effect of Bolt's statement on the evidence. She wasn't convinced the new information deviated enough from his original statement to justify the trial being aborted. As the time for them to go into court approached Peter still hadn't appeared, but the usher emerged from the entrance and told them she was going to bring the jury down.

'Mr Maynard isn't here yet,' Cassie said.

The usher shrugged her shoulders and went towards the lifts at the far end of the hall. Seconds later Peter marched towards Cassie. 'I've taken instructions from the CPS. They want to leave it to the judge. I'll tell her what's happened and say we don't think it makes any substantive difference to the evidence. I assume you'll all make applications for the jury to be discharged. Let's go in. I'll speak to the clerk and give her a copy of Bolt's statement for the judge.'

When Judge Rostron-Smith was on the bench, she waved the document at Peter and said, 'I've just been given this. Before I hear what any of you have to say, I'm going to have the jury in and ask them to continue deliberating.'

The jurors filed into the jury box. The judge reminded them they needed to reach a verdict on which they were all agreed and then the usher asked them to follow her to their room. They picked up their bags and whatever other items they had brought with them and disappeared. Cassie caught the eye of the young woman whose hair made her think of a ballerina. The young woman smiled.

Peter got to his feet. 'My Lady. As a result of enquires into a burglary and murder that took place over twenty-five years ago, Mr Bolt was interviewed about the ring. Your ladyship may remember …'

'Yes, I do remember. Continue.'

'Bolt explained his involvement with this ring and with the defendant, Lucas Radpole's father. I do accept on behalf of the prosecution the two men were better acquainted than he led us to believe. However, he does not retract any of the evidence he gave in this court and therefore this trial is not affected in any substantial way.'

As he was speaking, Simon handed Cassie a note from David Jennings. *'Cassie. Why don't you make the application for the jury to be discharged? We can then agree.'* Simon let her read it then leant towards her and nodded his agreement.

Cassie didn't have time to argue. The minute Peter sat down David had bobbed up and told the judge Miss Hardman would make an agreed application on behalf of all counsel.

'At least it might save some time,' Judge Rostron-Smith said.

'My learned friend's assertion that this evidence doesn't deviate substantially from his original evidence is, I would submit, erroneous. From this latest statement, Mr Bolt knew Bernie Radpole, the father, well, even if he had not met the defendant, Lucas Radpole. In evidence to this court when Mr Wade asked him if he knew Lucas, he was careful to say to his recollection he had not met him before. It may have been an honest answer in as far as it went, but it wasn't the whole truth.

'Similarly, in his reply about the purchase of medals from Mr Poynton, Bolt replied he couldn't remember who he bought them from. He may not have recollected who he bought them from, but he did know Eric Poynton. He now says he did have items from Radpole Senior and Poynton, some he hadn't paid for, something he had denied in evidence. It is Dean Morris's case that Radpole told him the person who lived in the flat had property belonging to his father. It appears that is true.

'Bolt did not answer when I asked him the name of the person with whom he had been talking when he remembered where he had seen the fourth man. I think your ladyship thought it was irrelevant, but it now appears that Bernie Radpole told him Clements was one of the intruders – a man who had a motive for trying to involve a fourth person.

'Then there is the ring. Bolt claimed legal privilege when I asked him about the ring. Yet his handling of the ring was not in the course of litigation so could not have been subject to client confidentiality. He was hiding his relationship with the father of one of the defendants as well as protecting his own career.

'Finally, he now says he is not sure there were four men in contrast to his assertion during the trial.

'It must be in the interests of justice that this trial is abandoned and a retrial ordered.'

As David and Simon told the judge they adopted her submissions, Cassie sat down and took a deep breath.

Chapter 44

Alex checked her phone almost every minute, willing the results from the forensic scientist to appear on her screen. She jumped when her mobile rang but didn't want to answer and delay any call about the DNA screening; however, the call was from Harriet.

'Alex,' Harriet said, 'Eric's at the gallery. He's told me he's going away for a few weeks and he wants me to run the shop in the meantime. His car is outside and it's loaded up. I think he's planning to be away for quite a while. He's taken his passport from the safe.'

'I'll be there. Can you keep him talking or something?' Alex said. She ran out of the door, wishing her Ducati bike was still outside. It wasn't a great distance to Ledbury Grove but without a car it would take her ten minutes. She broke into a trot, not sure if she could keep the pace up.

As she turned into Chepstow Villas she saw Poynton's Volvo cross from Ledbury Grove into Chepstow Crescent. As Harriet had said, it looked like he was going on a long trip.

Alex pulled out her mobile and called Mike Kemp. After telling him Poynton was fleeing the country, she suggested he arranged for someone to stop the vehicle. 'On what grounds?' Kemp said.

'Come on. Make something up. I assume he's heading for one of the Channel ports. We should have the results of the DNA tests soon. We need to delay him.'

'Alex, what if nothing comes of it? What if his DNA doesn't match? I can't have other officers making an illegal stop.'

Alex cut him off. She knew he was right, but they were so near knowing who had killed PC Dennis Furnival. She walked on towards the gallery. Harriet was standing in the centre of the shop staring at blank spaces on the walls. 'He's taken the more expensive paintings – at least the ones he could get in his car. I got here about a quarter of an hour ago and he had shredded a load of paperwork.' She pointed to strips of paper on the floor in the office next to the box for the shredder. 'And he's left the safe open. He's taken his passport and whatever else was in it.'

Alex stepped into the rear of the gallery. The first time she had been there it had been an oasis of calm. Now it looked like a whirlwind had blown through.

For a moment she stood and surveyed the scene, then her mobile sprang into life. She read the text that had arrived. 'Yes,' she said and grabbed hold of Harriet by both shoulders. 'Yes.'

'Good news?' said Harriet.

'For some, but very bad news for your boss and his co-conspirator. Harriet, don't touch anything. Lock up and go home. I'll be in touch.' Her phone rang again.

'I'm coming to pick you up,' Mike Kemp said. 'Stay where you are.'

'What's going on?' Harriet said.

'We're going to arrest Eric Poynton for the murder of a police officer in 1993.'

'I'm going to be without a job,' Harriet said.

When the police car arrived, Alex jumped into the rear seat. Mike Kemp was driving and DCI Colin Dean was in the front passenger seat. Immediately they were driving back towards Kensington Park Road and heading towards Fulham.

'Where are we going?' Alex said.

'To arrest Bernie Radpole,' Dean said.

'What about Poynton?'

'I've put out a general alert for him, concentrating on the routes to the Channel ports and the Tunnel. He can't have got very far.'

He was right. Before they reached North End Road, the radio in the car crackled into life with the message that Poynton had been stopped and was on his way back to Kensington.

'The address is on the Clem Attlee estate, sir?' Kemp said.

'Margaret Herbison House,' Dean said.

Alex was keeping quiet; she wasn't sure he would remember her from her encounter with his boss when he was still a detective sergeant.

'Alex, how's that pesky lawyer friend of yours? I understand she gave you a tip-off about the stolen ring?'

'Yes, sir. And reminded me that any DNA found at the scene of the murder could be matched against the sons'.'

'Makes a change. Usually she's just trouble for us.'

'She's a good advocate and …'

'And what?'

'Believes in justice.'

Colin Dean chuckled. 'Glad to hear it.'

Mike Kemp brought the car to a halt. Alex and the two men got out of the car. Someone on one of the balconies shouted, 'Rozzers are here.'

As they crossed the green sward in the centre of the estate, a woman appeared at the bottom of the stairs. 'If you're looking for Bernie Radpole, he's not here.'

'We'll just check, love,' DCI Dean said. He ran up the flight of stairs with Alex not far behind. The door to the flat was open. It didn't take long to search and confirm there was no one in the premises.

Kemp was still talking to the woman who'd told them Radpole wasn't there. 'She thinks he's gone to see his son in the Scrubs.'

'Did you see him leave?' DCI Dean said.

'He was loading stuff into his van this morning. Suitcases. I asked him what he was up to and he said he was taking some stuff to his son,' the woman said.

The three officers raced back to the car and retraced their route towards Hammersmith Broadway. The traffic was heavy round the Broadway but they weaved their way through and into Shepherds Bush Road. They continued to head north on the western side of Shepherds Bush Green and into Wood Lane. To their right was the monolith of the Westfield Shopping Centre and on their left the building that had been the headquarters of the BBC and was now a fancy block of flats. They tore under the West Way and turned left into Scrubs Lane.

'Slow down,' DCI Dean said, 'we don't want to alert Radpole.'

Mike Kemp hit the brakes and seconds later they had stopped adjacent to the prison. The yard in front of the visitors' entrance had a snake of people queuing from the gates. Near the front Alex saw the tall figure of Bernie Radpole. She was the first out of the car, followed by Kemp and Dean. She crossed the stone-paved yard and approached Radpole from behind. Alex looked round to make sure the two other officers were still close enough to help her and pulled out her warrant card. She put a hand on his shoulder and he spun round.

'What the devil,' Radpole said.

'Bernard Radpole, I'm arresting you for the murder of Dennis Furnival.' She cautioned him but he made no reply. As Alex and Kemp escorted him back to the car, Radpole said, 'I was hoping to see Lucas and warn him.'

Chapter 45

Judge Rostron-Smith didn't say anything in response to Cassie's submission at first and then said, 'I'm going to retire for a few minutes before I make my ruling.' She was standing up to leave the bench when the jury bailiff opened the door from the judges' corridor. She was waving a piece of paper in her hand, which she gave to the judge. There was silence as Judge Rostron-Smith read the contents. 'A note from the jury,' she said. 'I'm not going to tell you what it says except that it is not a verdict. I'm going to give a majority direction and then retire.'

As they waited for the jury to come from their room and take their seats, Simon said to Cassie, 'Why aren't we allowed to see what they've said?'

'My guess is they've given figures as to how many are for a guilty verdict and how many are not.'

'Thank you for your note,' the judge said when the jury were seated. 'The court clerk will now ask you if you have come to any verdicts.'

A young man wearing a gown but no wig hurried into his seat below the judge. He asked the defendants to stand and then looked at the jury. 'Can the foreman please stand.'

The young man who had an earring in one ear stood up.

'Members of the jury,' the court clerk said, 'have you reached any verdicts on which you are all agreed?'

'We have not,' said the foreman.

'Thank you, members of the jury,' the judge said. 'The time has now come when I can give you the direction about taking a majority verdict. I want you to go back to your room and see if you can reach a unanimous verdict, but if you can't I can accept a verdict on which at least ten of you are agreed. Can you go with the jury bailiff and continue with your deliberations.'

Cassie watched the jurors as they stood up. The young woman who looked like a ballerina was looking at an older woman, her shoulders slumped and her eyes widening. The elderly man in the tweed suit who had been called to serve on the jury in place of the woman who had a holiday booked scratched at his jaw.

Seconds later Judge Rostron-Smith followed them out of the courtroom.

'It looks like they're well and truly hung,' Cassie said. 'And I guess her ladyship has run off to find another judge for a second opinion on our submission. What do you think, Peter?'

'I'm surprised they haven't reached any verdicts,' Peter said and marched off.

Cassie picked up her tube of mints and offered them to Simon and David. 'Well, a bit of a shock, that. I didn't think that juror would be foreman. I so wish I was a fly on the wall.'

The court clerk was still holding the note the jury bailiff had handed to the judge. He pinned it to the indictment. 'I wouldn't stray too far,' he said.

'Is there time for a cup of coffee?' Simon said.

There wasn't. No sooner had Cassie sat down with her mug than they were called back into court.

‘Has the judge made up her mind what to do?’ Cassie asked the clerk as she took her place. ‘Or do we have verdicts?’

He shrugged his shoulders.

When Judge Rostron-Smith was back on the bench, she said, ‘I think the jury have solved our dilemma for us. They have indicated they cannot agree on any verdicts against any of these three defendants. I’ll have them back and discharge them.’

The judge did as she had said she would and thanked them for their service as jurors. She waited whilst they made their way past the dock where the three defendants were sitting with blank features. ‘Now, Mr Maynard, are you going to seek a retrial?’

‘I need to take instructions.’

‘Right, I’ll grant bail to the remaining defendants. Miss Hardman, I think Mr Davenport is in your chambers. Can you tell him that I’ll sentence his client when the Crown have come to a decision.’

Later that evening Cassie got a call from Simon Wade. ‘I thought I’d let you know Morris will plead guilty. I’ve agreed a basis of plea with Peter. Entering as a trespasser and committing criminal damage. No intention to steal as believed recovering property for Radpole and no knowledge of the gun,' he said.

'You'll get away with a suspended, I would think. Do you know what Cravitz will do?'

'I think the same. Now if you've nothing planned for the rest of the evening, how about having supper with me?'

'I'll see you on Thursday,' Cassie said and finished the call. She found Lee's mobile number and called her. She told Lee Cravitz and Morris were pleading guilty and she thought the prosecution would not proceed against Theo.

'Have you spoken to Peter Maynard?'

'Not yet, but it would be very difficult for them to call Bolt and say he's a truthful witness. Don't say anything to Theo yet. I'll speak to Peter and confirm it and ring you back.'

Cassie did as she had promised and then, satisfied with the outcome of the trial, she prepared her evening meal. She deserved a glass of wine so she opened a bottle of Fleurie, then she fried some asparagus, added balsamic vinegar and topped it with an egg and parmesan. After she'd eaten, she sat down and turned on her TV. The news was on – the usual squabbles between politicians and then a shot showing the police with two men who had been arrested for the murder of a police officer nearly thirty years ago. The men's heads were covered with raincoats but one of the police officers was Alex.

Cassie smiled and held her glass up towards the TV screen. 'Congratulations,' she said and took a good mouthful.

Chapter 46

It had been a long day – the swearing-in ceremony in Westminster Hall and then the presentation in the Royal Courts of Justice. The hired full-bottomed wig was more uncomfortable than her own; it didn't fit so well and she was afraid it would slip down over her eyes. The patent-leather shoes with the silver buckles were a little tight. She had to stop herself from laughing at the sight of the men in their breeches and borrowed black tights – not all of them had elegant calves. She kept thinking of Malvolio and how he was made to look a fool. However, the party in Gray's Inn was a different matter.

The medieval hall was already quite crowded when Cassie arrived with her parents. Jack pushed his way towards them, introduced himself and led them away to show them the splendours of the room. Cassie looked round hoping to see Peter – it was their joint party. She couldn't find him in the swirling crowd. Nearly all her colleagues from chambers were there, always ready for a free drink, particularly champagne. Soon she was surrounded by many of them ready with their congratulations, some sincere, some not so. Many barristers would have been invited not only to this party but to some of the others being held in and around the Inns of Court and they would float between them.

Cassie caught the eye of David Jennings who was chatting amicably with Judge Rostron-Smith. He waved at her and beckoned her to join them. She wasn't ready to forgive the judge yet for her behaviour during the Clements trial even if he was. Eleanor came over to offer her congratulations again. The room began to fill up and she moved towards the Benchers' dais at the far end of the room. The notes of one of her favourite pieces of jazz music came from a grand piano being played by one of the pupils, Spencer Watson. She thought of the day she'd teased him about not disturbing her papers; she didn't know he was such a talented pianist. She caught his eye and put her thumbs up, then felt an arm snake round her waist and James Callan pecked her on the check.

'I could do better,' he said and pulled her towards him.

She pushed him away. 'Stop it. I've told you, you're far too young for me. But … I do hope I'll get the opportunity to lead you in another case soon.'

'Thanks.'

Apart from her parents, the only non-lawyers Cassie had invited were Ben and Alex.

She wasn't sure they would come, but she continually glanced towards the oak screen said to come from a Spanish ship sunk during the Armada, and through which all the guests would come. Jack was pointing out the heraldic shields that lined the walls of the hall; he moved to the portraits including the one of Elizabeth I. Cassie had a fancy the portrait of the queen in all her finery winked at her.

Two of the other women in her chambers gathered round her. 'I'm so pleased for you,' one of them said. 'It's very encouraging for us when another woman makes it to the top.' She thanked them.

She wasn't surprised to see Peter Maynard chatting to Judge Rostron-Smith. He did like associating with the high and mighty.

'I thought I'd never get away,' David Jennings said. 'She's such a hypocrite. She went on about what a superb advocate you were.'

'It'll take some time for me to forgive her,' Cassie said. She heard her mobile ping. 'I should have turned the thing off.' She couldn't resist looking at the screen. There was a text message from Ben. *'I've decided not to come to your do. Have a good time.'*

'Bad news,' David said.

'Not really. Or at least not unexpected. And not serious.' She switched the phone off.

Although there was no point in looking for Ben she continued glancing at the entrance to the hall. A few minutes later she saw Oscar Davenport coming towards her with an older man who she assumed was his father, Mr Justice Davenport, and, with her arm tucked firmly into the judge's, Alex. They pushed their way towards her. 'Congratulations, my dear,' the judge said. 'My son tells me you're a very talented advocate. I hope to see you in my court before too long.'

Not if I can help it, Cassie thought. She wasn't too keen on being kicked around the Court of Appeal.

Alex added her best wishes as well.

Cassie thanked them and raised her eyebrows at Alex who just smiled back at her.

Before she could say anything, Peter was next to the High Court Judge. 'So glad you could come, judge. We're delighted, aren't we, Cassie? Do let me introduce you to my wife. She's just over here.' The judge followed Peter.

'You don't appear to have a drink,' Cassie said. She waved at one of the waiters who was ferrying trays of wine round the room. Oscar and Alex picked up a glass each and raised them in a toast. 'Santé,' said Cassie. They drifted off, more interested in each other than her.

Marcus came and stood next to her. 'Congratulations. It's well deserved in your case. I expect you to go on to greater things.'

'I'm not sure I want to. I'm an advocate. Sitting in judgement on others is just not my thing.'

'You may change your mind. The profession is not what it was.'

'But defendants can't go unrepresented in anything that calls itself a civilised democracy.'

'Who says this is a civilised democracy?'

'What's that about being civilised, Marcus?' Richard Jago said as he sidled through the crowd.

'Just saying things have moved on since you and I took silk.'

Richard took Cassie's arm. 'Just want a quiet word with my chambers' new Queen's Counsel.' He manoeuvred Cassie to one side of the room. 'Cassie, I plan to retire at the end of the year. I think you know that. I would like to think I will be leaving chambers in good hands.'

'I'm sure …'

'Cassie, that means you. Eleanor doesn't want to be head of chambers. Peter is willing but not as astute as you. I believe you'll make the best head. I'm well aware that Jack can be difficult to manage but you can and do. Think about it. The future is yours.' He slipped away leaving Cassie rather stunned.

The party was really getting going now and wherever Cassie turned there were smiling faces, everyone giving her their best wishes. Simon Wade came to her side and put an arm round her shoulder. 'A brilliant result in court and congratulations on the Silk gown.'

'Thanks. I'll think of you if I need a junior.'

'I'd prefer you thought of me when you need a new man in your life. Is he here by any chance? I'd like to see my rival.'

'It's none of your business.'

'I think it is. I'm being serious, Cassie.' He drifted away. She realised her glass was empty and went in search of another one.

A Final Note

My aim in writing these books about Cassie Hardman was to present a portrait of life as a criminal defence barrister as well as tell interesting stories. I wanted to describe the conflicting emotions felt by every advocate who appears in the criminal courts, and I was determined to get the law right. Since I wrote the first of these books the life and work of a barrister has changed beyond recognition. It is still a difficult profession for women although better than when I qualified many years ago. The use of technology has changed dramatically the way lawyers work and, while it may be more efficient, the camaraderie and mutual support has diminished. The reduction in fees for Legal Aid work has led many talented advocates to choose other areas of law or to combine appearing in the criminal courts with regulatory work. If this state of affairs continues there will be a diminution in the quality of lawyers who are competent to either prosecute or defend. These changes have convinced me I can no longer write about the criminal justice system with any authority and so I leave Cassie Hardman's future to your imagination.

Margaret Barnes

London and Devon 2020

Printed in Great Britain
by Amazon

66697121R00234